WARRIOR ON THE WESTERN WATERS

Praise for Warrior on the Western Waters

***Warrior on the Western Waters* is...an emotional roller-coaster of a story** and the author effortlessly captures the intense emotions that each character is feeling, which reminds me of the emotional rumination of Suzanne Collins' *The Hunger Games*. Still's writing has a simple eloquence to it. It has a way of leading you through a story with simple language, which leaves your mind free to imagine the intriguing world that she is creating in her book. —Literary Titan

I review very few American writers, but this is a particularly good historical fiction series that all can enjoy...*Warrior on the Western Waters* is a Miramichi Reader "Pick"! —Miramichi Reader

***Warrior on the Western Waters* is even better than the first two books.** It is as fast-paced as the first two books with unexpected twists and turns that prevented me from putting the book down. But what made *Warrior on the Western Waters* even better is giving the perspective of the Indians in the region. The detail of life with Indians is so good. I want to go back and read it again to soak it all in. —Homeschool Teacher

Warrior on the Western Waters

Dangerous Loyalties, Book Three

Phyllis A. Still

Climbing Tree Publications

To the descendants of the brave men, women, and children mentioned in this historical fictional account. Be strong!

BOOKS BY PHYLLIS A. STILL

Dangerous Loyalties Series

Defiance on Indian Creek, Book One

Fleeing the Shadows, Book Two

Warrior on the Western Waters, Book Three

Palisades of the Heart, Book Four

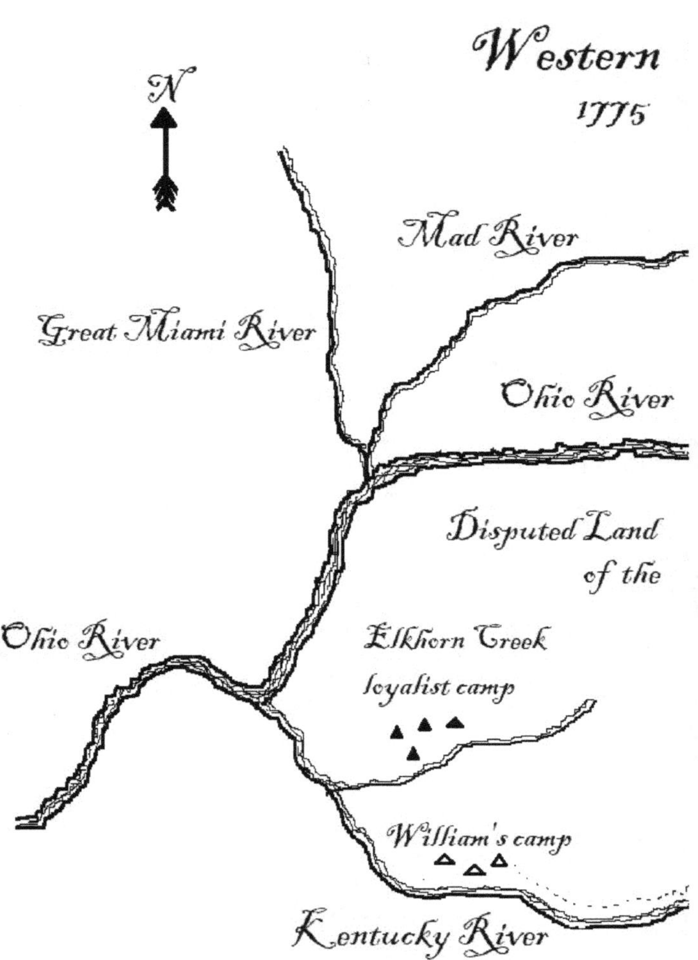

Western
1775
N
Mad River
Great Miami River
Ohio River
Disputed Land
of the
Ohio River
Elkhorn Creek
loyalist camp
William's camp
Kentucky River

Waters
1776
Piqua Village
Lodge
Chief
Dance Circle
Whisper
Corn Flower

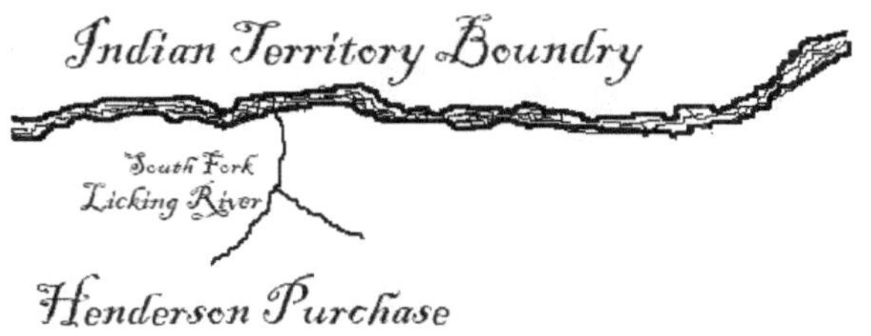
Indian Territory Boundry
South Fork
Licking River
Henderson Purchase

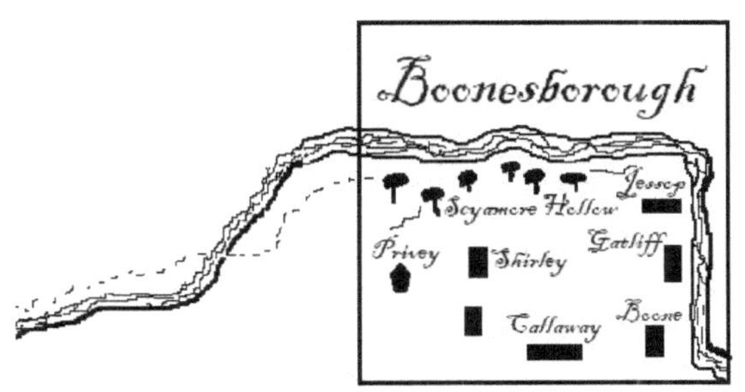
Boonesborough
Jessop
Scyamore Hollow
Privey
Shirley
Gatliff
Callaway
Boone

Chapter One

My head throbbed more than my bandaged foot, as the Gatliffs' unrestrained three-year-old son, Reese, jumped and squealed on the hard-packed dirt floor beside me, the morning of September thirteenth. I sighed and raised the shredded hem of my brown petticoat. *Momma said she'd come this morning. Has Papa's wound worsened?* I stretched out my bandaged foot along the log bench, growing more fidgety and annoyed. *I want to go see about my family. I want to see this new settlement called Boonesborough.*

Hazy beams of light from the shuttered window danced on the table where I sat. With another sip of warm willow bark tea from a clay mug, my headache eased, and I wiped a fallen tear from my cheek. *She said Papa would recover.* I shook the thought from my head. *My faith isn't as strong as Momma's.*

The burly Charles Gatliff clomped to the door, adjusting his tan linen shirt before shouldering his pack and rifle. He topped his bushy red head with a round-brimmed hat. "I'll take Reese to dig fishing worms."

"Yippee." The rambunctious copper-headed boy in a fringed buckskin shirt and breeches bounced toward him.

When the door closed, my nerves settled. I smiled with gratitude at the pretty dark-haired Mrs. Gatliff, still in her chemise, rocking in a creaking chair while humming to her suckling infant, James. I'd learned of him when his cries woke me from reliving the nightmare of Shawnee warriors leaping from bushes with raised tomahawks three days ago.

I'd guessed her to be in her twenties, but I didn't dare ask. She insisted on being called Letitia instead of her name, Christina.

She detached the infant from her nipple and eased to her feet, carrying the babe to a cradle in the back corner, whispering in an Irish accent, "There now, wee one. You're a good lad, so you are."

Letitia tucked an escaped wisp of black hair behind her ear and moved to the hearth, tying the drawstring of her chemise. She lifted a steaming kettle to a trivet. "Charles said you've come from Indian Creek, near Fort Culbertson."

"Yes." I refrained from adding *ma'am* as she requested when meeting yesterday.

She turned toward me with a pleasant grin. "My da is Cornelius McGuire. Have you heard of him or my ornery brothers, Thomas and William?"

My mind reeled. *How much do I say?* "My papa has surveyed for them—and bartered horses from William. But I haven't heard of Thomas."

"Thomas is the eldest." Letitia pulled a folded paper from her apron and held it up. "This is from William himself. He and Thomas plan to visit in November." She returned the letter to her pocket and sighed. "If they stay alive."

My breath caught. "What do you mean?"

She frowned and poured hot water into a clay mug. The aroma of sage tickled my nose.

"They delight too much in foilin' loyalists' plans for the thrill of avoidin' capture."

My throat tightened before I could confess babbling William's name to loyalists. *He's in danger because of me.*

A loud knock launched me from the bench to my feet. *Land sakes.* I clutched my chest and stared at the silhouette in the doorway.

"Good morning, Mary." My nine-year-old sister, Lizzy, beamed and bounced through the doorjamb. "Momma sent me to fetch you. We've moved into our own cabin."

Her abrupt entrance made me dizzy. I bent forward to keep from fainting and blew out a breath. *Calm down.*

My sister caressed my back. "I'm sorry. Didn't mean to scare you."

I straightened with another deep breath and shook my head. "I'll be all right in a moment. Still jumpy's all." My heart beat like a drum.

Letitia stepped toward Lizzy. "Good mornin', lass."

"Morning, ma'am." Lizzy smiled and curtsied.

Letitia handed me a cloth containing one of her delicious hoecakes from breakfast. "Come callin' when you can."

I reached my arm around Letitia's waist and laid my head on her shoulder. "I will. Thank you for everything." I moved back and peeked inside the cloth. *Still fluffy.* "How do you make them rise like this?"

"'Tis a secret I'll be keepin', so it is." She grinned. "Now, off with you." She moved toward the hearth.

I giggled and slid the hoecake into my apron pocket and clasped Lizzy's arm. "I'm ready." She held my elbow as I hobbled beside her into the gray morning. I didn't recognize the dingy brown petticoat and the pale-yellow blouse she wore. "That shade of yellow is pretty on you, but where did the clothes come from?"

She grinned. "From the Boones. Momma is bartering with Mrs. Boone for borrowed clothes until we can make our own."

"Oh no. Remember Eliza from Moore's Fort? She told me how Jemima and her friends had snubbed her for having a half-Cherokee mother. She'll probably look down on us for being destitute—just like what happened to the Wakefields in the book we read on the trail."

Lizzy stopped and peered at me wide-eyed. "They're a generous family. I don't think Jemima's mean at all."

My face burned with shame as we moved ahead. "I'm sorry. It's wrong of me to judge before meeting her for myself." *Thank you for the Boones, God.*

"You're a silly goose." Lizzy shook her head and pulled me forward.

The new settlement consisted of maybe a dozen scattered cabins that still smelled like oak sap. A few children played chase nearby, including my young sisters, Susie and Nancy. They grinned and waved as we passed.

"Slow down a minute. I want to see if I recognize the scout who found me. I want to thank him."

Lizzy slowed as I scanned the faces of two dozen men scattered around the settlement. They were hammering, chopping, raising cabin walls, and hoisting beams for roofs, but none matched the image in my mind.

Tiny hairs on the back of my neck prickled. I stopped and glanced around the settlement twice. *Something's missing.* I gazed past a large elm tree in the western meadow. Four black men drove mules that dragged logs toward the central yard, where a group of tan-skinned young men chopped notches. I peered back at the looming eastern ridge across the north-flowing Kentucky River and then at the ridges above a grove of large sycamore trees to the north. I remembered the words a soldier at Martin's Fort said. "All the Injuns have to do is stand on the ridges around Boonesborough and pick 'um off."

Movement in the grove caught my eye. A man dressed in a tan shirt, dark-blue woolen britches, and a beaver-skin hat sneered at me before stepping into the shadows. My gut knotted. *Why did he glare at me?* My throat tightened. *Where are the stockade walls?*

Lizzy pointed beyond a few scattered cabins. "We'll be fetching water from the spring near that big rock. What's wrong? You dizzy?" She peered into my eyes, sounding worried. "Do you need to sit down?"

"No." I gulped and stepped forward on wobbly legs. "Get me to Momma."

Lizzy and I hobbled toward a long clothesline where Momma and twelve-year-old Katie hung bedsheets. They were also dressed in borrowed petticoats and blouses.

My eyes watered as we neared.

Momma came around the kettle, smiling and drying her hands on her apron. A rosy glow tinted her cheeks, and strands of auburn hairs flitted in the breeze from the bun she always wore. I limped into her outstretched arms and sobbed.

"You're trembling." She pulled me back and felt my forehead. "No fever. What's wrong?"

"I'm scared." I sniffled. "There are no walls being built for protection, and a man just gave me an evil stare."

She stroked the side of my head and nodded. "Papa will speak to Daniel Boone about the security today. Now, let's get you inside. Papa's eager to see you."

Momma held my arm as I teetered forward and struggled to breathe.

"Where's George?" I glanced among my gathering siblings for my eight-year-old brother.

"Helping the men outside make shingles in exchange for meat and supplies."

I shook my head. "But it's not safe."

Momma laid her hand on my shoulder. "Trust in God's protection. He'll provide all of our needs, and the neighbors are generous."

Her strong faith didn't calm my fears. *Where was his protection when we were ambushed by Indians—when my beloved dog, Drummer, was killed?*

I dried my cheeks and entered the small, oak-scented cabin.

Papa pushed to his feet from a log chair in front of the window and fumbled with his crutch. "Mary."

His gaunt face brightened as he hobbled toward me through the only beam of light in the room, and his long black braid bounced behind him. I rushed into his arms, snuggling against his tobacco-scented chest as if I were still a little girl. My worries faded. "Oh, Papa. I'm glad you didn't die."

"Thanks to my brave girl." He eased back, peering with glistening eyes. "Please forgive me for being so foolish. I should have heeded the warnings to travel with others. Thanks be to God, we are all safe now."

I blinked away tears and stepped back, shaking my head. "But we're not safe, Papa." I pointed out the window and frowned. "Have you seen the high ridges? Not even pickets will protect us if Indians shoot from there. We should go back to Indian Creek as soon as we can travel again." Frustration rose in my tone as my eyes watered. "We've already lost everything—including Drummer."

He frowned at the dirt floor.

Before I could apologize, Papa topped his head with his round-brimmed hat and toddled out the door on his crutches. I sniffed back tears.

Momma raised her eyebrows and held a finger to her mouth while pointing to Charlie and Sally, who napped on straw pallets.

"Make peace with Papa. He's guilt-ridden and anxious enough. He rose before dawn, wanting to provide fish for breakfast. I had to put my foot down. You both need to rest a few more days and let everything come out in the wash."

"Yes, ma'am." I sighed with renewed shame for sassing Papa.

"I need to take Mrs. Boone her laundry and help her prepare supper for a share of milled corn and potatoes. I should be back before Charlie and Sally wake."

She went to the table and held up a clean white chemise, dark-blue petticoat, and tan blouse. "Change into these and take care not to rip or stain them. They're borrowed. We're fortunate the Boones have extra and a daughter your size."

"Yes ma'am. Thank you." I fake-smiled and took the garments.

"Pile your soiled clothes in the corner." Momma pointed to a bundle to the right of the small, opened window, where a corner-shelf held wooden cups, plates, and a basket of utensils. When she lifted a folded stack of garments from the table, a large rectangular sheet of parchment paper coiled. She kissed my forehead. "There's rabbit stew in the kettle outside. Eat some meat. You're looking a little pale."

"Yes ma'am." Curious, I draped the clothes on a chair back and unrolled what was a map of the settlement and the surrounding area. I traced the Kentucky River with my finger to its mouth at the Ohio River. I shuddered at the words *Indian Territory* in the north where a river marked Great Miami flowed south into the Ohio. Three rectangles marking Indian villages were shown on squiggly lines I assumed were unnamed rivers. I stared a moment more. *We're this close to hornets without protection?* I huffed and let the map recoil.

I placed the hoecake on the table and then slipped on the clean chemise, noticing my breasts protruding more than when we left Indian Creek almost two months ago. Momma had said my menses should start within the year. *As if I need something else to fret about.* Some days I wanted to stay a little girl, but then I'd miss being courted and having a family of my own. *Will being naked in front of my husband someday be as awkward as my sisters noticing and giggling? Not as awkward as someone coming in with me standing here.* I shook my head and dressed.

Jemima's clothes fit as if they were mine. I hobbled to the corner, dropped my garments, and then reached a cup and spoon from the shelf. After a deep breath, I slipped the hoecake into my clean pocket and limped out the door to face Papa.

He glanced at me from a stump where he sat carving something from a block of wood. I swallowed the lump in my throat and concentrated on ladling stew into my cup. I inched toward a separate stump beside Papa and sat without spilling a drop on Jemima's petticoat. I peered at him. "I'm sorry for sassing, but I'm terrified of this place."

He nodded. "Soon as I can get around, I'll find men to help build picketed walls. The scouts say there are fewer Indian signs now that more settlers are coming."

"I hope so." The gnawing feeling remained.

I pulled Letitia's hoecake from my pocket, dipped it in the stew, and savored the bite before handing the rest to him.

"Thank you." He grinned. "I also need to locate a claim soon. Land is going quick. I'll find a safer location and build our own blockhouse to live in."

His enthusiasm drew a slight smile to my lips. "I'll pray your leg heals quickly. I don't like it here. Are we safe from the loyalists who want to hang you? A man glared at me from that grove of trees earlier as if I'd crossed him in some way."

"Try not to worry so much. Maybe he thought you were staring at him. I don't think any loyalist would last long around here." He grinned and dipped his bread in my cup. My palm caught the drips as he withdrew his bite.

"Mighty tasty." He licked his lips.

A twig snapped behind us. We leapt to our feet at the same time.

My cup landed on the ground, spattering stew on the skirt up to my knees. *Tarnation.*

I turned toward a rugged man who looked a foot taller than Papa. His black hair was pulled back in a tight knot under his round brimmed hat. Papa extended his hand. "Hello, Daniel."

"Good to hear you're on the mend, Michael. Sorry for your trouble." He shook Papa's hand and then smiled at me, tipping his hat. "And you must be Mary?"

I beamed. "Yes sir. Mr.—"

"Boone." He nodded and looked back to Papa. "Scouts have gone to escort the Callaway party. They should arrive in a few days with supplies. You folks'll get first pickin's from the cloth goods and whatnot. Work out barters as you can."

Papa adjusted his crutch. "We're sure thankful for everyone's generosity."

"Mr. Boone. Sir." I curtsied. *Be strong.* "Why haven't men set stockade walls?"

Papa frowned at me, but Mr. Boone's face remained pleasant.

"Can't convince them of the need. Everyone's clearin' land and stakin' claims as fast as they can. Most of the Indians have accepted Judge Henderson's purchase and are settlin' in for the winter." He removed his hat, swiped his hand across his forehead, and turned toward Papa. "It's that rogue band of Cherokee, led by Dragging Canoe, that's worrisome."

My heart sped. *I've heard his name...from the men of Martin's Fort.*

"It was probably some of his scouts that waylaid you."

Mr. Boone's voice faded as my ears rang. I leaned closer to hear. "Soon as Judge Henderson gets here, he'll take charge. And not a day too soon. I got a lot of folks clamorin' for surveys." He glanced beyond me and tipped his hat.

I turned around as Momma approached with a dark-haired, plump woman and a girl about my age.

"Here is our daughter, Mary." Momma motioned me forward. "Say hello to Mrs. Boone and her daughter Jemima."

I swallowed, then drew a deep breath, and smoothed my hair. *My appearance must be horrid. She'll notice the spill.*

I forced a smile and limped toward them, stopping in a half curtsy. I addressed Mrs. Boone first. "Pleased to meet you, ma'am." My heart pounded as I peered at Jemima, who had the pretty features of her momma but the tall lankiness of her papa. I moved closer. "And you, Jemima."

"Pleased to meet you, too." Her smile dropped to a frown as she gazed upon the soiled petticoat.

Our mommas went back to chatting. I waited for Jemima's focus to return to my face. "I'm sorry about the spill." I forced a smile. "I'll wash it out soon, so it won't stain."

She smirked, then glanced up, and turned toward our mommas.

I glared and pressed my lips to keep from confronting her about passing judgement. *Conceited like Eliza said.* I took a deep breath and moved closer to Momma. *Can't smack someone I just met. Best to avoid her.*

"I'll be over in the morning as soon as I can." Momma stepped back.

"Thank you, Mrs. Shirley. I'll be spry again in a few days." Mrs. Boone's tone was pleasant, but her eyes drooped as she looked at Mr. Boone with the same kind of impatient stare Momma sometimes gave Papa. "Daniel, I need help lifting the laundry kettle."

"I'd better get then." Mr. Boone's weathered face beamed a smile and a twinkle from his eyes as he extended his hand toward Papa. "Look forward to workin' with you when you're able."

Papa shook his hand again. "Hope it won't be too long. I'm ready to stake out my own claim."

He nodded. "Just say when."

I enjoyed Mr. Boone's pleasant manner and humor.

Jemima strode in front of me, peering with kinder eyes. Her lips parted as if to speak, and then she stared at her feet and hurried away with her momma.

Did she want to apologize for her aloof manner? Was she expecting me to grovel? I shrugged. Then a pang of conviction came. *Momma would expect me to be cordial, even if Jemima wasn't.*

I shouted, "I'll come visit soon." *There—I said it. I'll try to be friends.*

Jemima stopped and turned, wearing a real smile. "Yes. Please do."

I waved, and she waved back.

"Hi, Mary."

I turned to George, who wrapped his arms around me for a quick hug before stepping back. "Glad you recovered. Thank you for going for help. Were you scared?"

"Terrified. Thank you for telling me to be strong."

He grinned and held out his arm. "I'll help you inside."

Upon entering, Charlie and Sally came for hugs, and then we all sat at our borrowed table. Papa gave thanks for our donated foods and kind neighbors.

George cleared his throat. "How soon before we have a claim?"

Papa leaned forward and smiled. "As soon as I can help survey and see what sections are available. We'll plant corn this spring and build a proper cabin. I think we need a two-story one like the Muellers. What do you think?"

"Yes." Lizzy beamed. "With whitewashed walls inside."

Momma shook her head. "I believe we have a greater need of leather and fur if we are to survive our first winter in Kentucky. The Boones need their clothes back."

"I'm sorry, I was just hoping." Lizzy hung her head.

I reached for her hand and squeezed. "Me too." I pictured the Mueller's beautiful home on the Bluestone River.

Momma looked at Papa. "We'll need a spinning wheel and loom by spring."

He nodded. "Supplies will be here soon, but I'll barter for deerskins—better than going naked." He grinned.

We all laughed, and then Papa's mouth drooped. "Boonesborough is mighty disappointing so far."

I straightened my back, surprised by his admittance.

"But remember, it's a new settlement. Replacing what we've lost will take time." He scanned us. "Our first winter will be hard, but by spring, life will be good again. The field is bountiful with seed corn. Soon this will be a thriving community, and Sunday, we'll have a divine service under that large elm tree in the hollow."

"Pickets need to be a priority." Momma used her firm voice. "I'm not happy about the lack of security. Trusting God includes heeding his warnings." She turned from Papa and gazed at each of us. "None of you may go into the wooded areas without an armed escort until they erect pickets—that includes the sycamore hollow beyond the freshwater spring."

We all responded, "Yes, ma'am."

Peace settled in my spirit, knowing Momma's relationship with God gave her quick understanding. *Do I hear him too, but fail to trust?*

My siblings took turns telling about their favorite part of the day. I waited for an opening. "Mrs. Gatliff is the daughter of Mr. Cornelius McGuire. Isn't that interesting?"

Papa's eyebrows rose. "It is."

I smiled. "Her brothers, Thomas and William, might come visit in November."

When Katie peered at me and snickered, my face flushed. *She knows I wanted to meet William the day he came to visit Papa. She always knows too much.*

Chapter Two

Within two weeks, Papa felt strong enough to go hunting with other men, and I could help forage. I also kept my promise to visit with Jemima, but discovered our manners clashed. She wanted to dominate, and I wanted to be independent. But I enjoyed stopping in to visit Letitia. She wouldn't let me help make hoecakes, but I enjoyed the stories passed down in her family, especially the one about a Scottish warrior named William Wallace. I couldn't help comparing his bravery to that of the Shawnee leader, Cornstalk, who shouted, "Be strong," to his braves at Point Pleasant. But I didn't dare say so.

The afternoon of the twenty-sixth, as I left Letitia's, several mules burdened with more supplies than I could have imagined arrived with a large party of people. Among them were two girls who looked about my age, but they appeared exhausted and haggard from the trip. I smiled and waved to them before going to help my family select provisions. As I walked, I scanned the crowd for the man who had rescued me, but the constant movement of people made it impossible.

I saw Momma carrying a twenty-yard bolt of linen and a bundle of flax stalks toward our cabin and hurried to help.

She handed me the flax and hugged the bolt of cloth, smiling. "Papa wants us girls to use the cloth. He and your brothers will wear buckskins a while longer."

My heart melted. "Oh, Momma. I hope there will be enough for them too. Maybe more supplies will come in soon."

Katie and Lizzy rushed into the cabin.

"It's beautiful. Is there enough for everyone?" Lizzy ran her hand over the unbleached linen.

"We'll need measurements." Momma handed us the tape measure.

For the next hour, we took turns measuring one another for new clothes. I recorded the numbers on a square of my old apron. Momma smiled and handed me a slate and a piece of chalk. "Deduce what we can make from our bolt. I need to go to the Boones. The rest of you may go meet the new children so Mary can think in peace."

My sisters tumbled out the door with Charlie and Sally in tow. The breeze carried their shouts and laughter through the open doorway. A pang of jealousy rose, but

I laughed. *Getting my own clothes made so Jemima can have hers back is worth giving up pleasure.*

I went to work estimating the yardage needed for everyone's chemise, bodice, petticoat, and apron. It became clear there wouldn't be enough material for all of us. *Maybe my figures are wrong. Why have I neglected arithmetic?* I shook my head and plopped down on the bench at the table. I reviewed my figures and shrugged. *Momma needs to decide what to make.*

Momma returned with Katie, Lizzy, and new scissors. "What did your estimate reveal?"

"Only enough material for one complete outfit or several smaller items." I flicked a visiting leaf from the bench.

Momma nodded. "Well, then. We'll decide by greatest need."

"You deserve the first set of clothes." I put my elbows on the table and cupped my chin.

"I agree." Katie plopped on the bench beside me. "We need our momma to look as fine as Mrs. Boone and Mrs. Callaway."

Momma's hands went to her reddening face.

Lizzy laid her hand on Momma's shoulder. "Yes, and you'd be beautiful in a dark pink bodice to go with your brown petticoat."

Momma smiled and patted Lizzy's hand. "Thank you, Daughters. I'm touched by your sweetness. I'll look over everyone's needs before deciding. However, I'm partial to light sage with brown."

I grinned. *Good. Because I want a dark pink or red bodice.* "I'll collect Lady's Bedstraw for making red dye, the way Whispering Leaf instructed."

Momma stared at me a moment. "Red? I think a dark pink would be more appropriate for your age."

"Yes ma'am." I lowered my eyes, remembering the day I met the half-Shawnee woman at the Crab Orchard settlement. And what she said the men of the fort called her. "I guess red would be too bold."

All I knew for sure was I wanted to feel pretty for the harvest dance.

In the morning, a crisp breeze shook acorns from the oak trees overhead—one bounced off my bonnet; the others pelted the ground around me as I finished hanging my wet dishrag on a bush. *Perfect day for foraging.* I turned to Momma and waited until she stepped back from kissing Papa's cheek.

"May we forage for plants and roots to make dye?"

Momma dried her hands on her apron and smiled. "You may all go. I will call you back for lunch."

Papa shouldered his pack and rifle. "Remember to find a guard to escort you first. There have been no sightings, but don't go out alone." He shook a leaf from his hat.

George bounded from the bench and shouldered his rifle. "I can guard you. Come find me helping Caleb and Flanders Callaway when you're ready."

"Thank you." I smiled and donned my bonnet. "I want to find plants for dyes."

Nancy's hand went to her hip. "I want to go play with my new friends."

"Me too." Susie pounced forward, frowning.

Katie turned her head toward me and huffed. "Lizzy and I promised to play stickball, and we have to take Charlie. Can we help gather nuts and plants later?"

I smiled. "I'll ask the new girls if they'd like to go with me."

Momma chuckled. "Sounds like you girls are becoming independent. Come back for lunch later if you don't hear my call."

We nodded and spread out in different directions.

I tucked loose strands of hair under my bonnet and headed toward the large cabin in the central yard. *Maybe I can meet the Callaway girls before Jemima butts in.* I tried to like her and be friends, but each time she visited, I ended up annoyed by her belittling air.

"Hello." A husky voice boomed in front of me.

I jumped and clutched my throat.

The man removed his hat and took a step back. "Sorry to scare you, miss. I'm Sam Henderson. The one who found you."

I released a breath and moved closer. My stomach fluttered. He was tall with chestnut hair and deep brown eyes. The moment of rescue flashed through my mind. *He lifted me onto his horse, cradled me in his arms, and I asked, "Are you taking me to heaven?"* I hid my flushing cheeks with my hands. *Maybe he doesn't remember.*

He cocked his head and then grinned down at me. "Glad to see you've recovered. Didn't think you'd make it, to tell the truth."

I swallowed the lump in my throat and curtsied. "Thank you for saving me, Mr. Henderson. I'm pleased to meet you."

His chin jutted when he smiled. "I was in the right place is all. Pleasure to meet the daughter of Cage."

My breath caught. *He knows Papa's secret name.* Sweat dripped from my temples and slithered down my neck. *Does he know about me too?* I couldn't speak.

Mr. Henderson eased forward. "You're quite a brave girl, Mary Shirley. I heard about you dressing like your brother to deliver that dispatch a while back."

What do I say? "Who told you?"

"Well, now. I can't divulge my source." He chuckled. "Just wanted to let you know how impressed I am. Few girls have that kind of fortitude. And how in the...well, how did you get thirteen miles alone in the dark?"

"My papa was dying—I had to."

He smiled and nodded. "Well, I wanted to check on you."

My face burned. "Th-thank you."

He tipped his hat and made a quick retreat.

I took a deep breath. Momma's "guard your heart" warning flashed through my mind, but I laughed. *He's too old.*

As I passed the children playing stickball with a blown-up pig's bladder, Katie and the new girls ran over. "This is our sister, Mary," she said, half out of breath, and then ran back into the game.

The girls stepped closer, beaming smiles. They had fair complexions, red hair platted with blue ribbons, and fine-weaved clothes with flower designs.

Another family of means, and here I am in borrowed clothes. Better than wearing my rags.

"Hello." I straighten my back and gave a weak wave. *Will they like me?*

The eldest held out her hand and curtsied. "I'm Elizabeth Callaway, and she's my sister, Frances."

"Stop trying to be so uppity." The younger girl sneered at her. "I'm Fanny, and she's Betsy."

I chuckled. "Pleased to meet you."

"How is your foot?" Betsy stared at my tattered moccasins. "We heard about your infection from Jemima."

Why am I not surprised? She's had a whole day to tell all. "Healed nicely. Thank you."

"That's good. You wouldn't want to miss the harvest dance in November. We expect it to be great fun. More families will arrive by then, but I hope Sam Henderson asks me to dance."

My mouth flew open.

Fanny huffed. "Stop daydreaming, Betsy. Sam looked my way yesterday." She stretched her chin up as she tossed her head back.

"Humph. No, he didn't." Betsy shook her head and scowled at her sister.

I glanced from one to the other, not sure what to think. "He saved my life two weeks ago. I met him a few minutes ago. He seems nice."

Betsy's eyes widened, but her mouth turned down. "Oh...yes. I heard he rescued someone."

"And he's so handsome." Fanny sighed as she tilted her head back and raised her hand to her forehead as if to swoon.

I couldn't help but chuckle.

Betsy growled and pranced away, shaking her head.

"Don't mind her." Fanny giggled. "She's been pining for Sam ever since she met him on the trip here. I'm not interested in him, but it's fun to annoy her. He's too old."

I nodded. "How old is he?"

She shrugged. "Up near thirty, but I'm not forward enough to ask."

I shook my head.

Fanny shooed a fly from her face. "How old are you?"

"Thirteen until February." I smiled and tried to catch the fly but missed.

"Good. I'm thirteen too. Betsy is fifteen but tries to act older." She glanced behind me.

Fanny and I will get along fine. My eye caught Betsy waving goodbye. I waved back. *Betsy's practically grown.*

"I need to forage for good supplies to make dye. Would you like to get permission to go with me? My brother George will be our guard."

"Yes, thank you. I'll be back in a moment."

She returned five minutes later with Betsy and Jemima.

Jemima sauntered in front of me. "I asked Flanders Callaway to be our guard while we forage. He's older."

I refrained from tripping Jemima as she walked past.

We went to the stockyard, where George helped two young men hitch up a team of oxen.

"This is my sister Mary." He pointed. "I'm supposed to be her guard so she can go foraging."

They tipped their hats. The tall, sandy-haired one stepped in front. "I'll be going, if you please, George. You'll enjoy helping Caleb finish the cabin."

George glanced at me. I shrugged and tilted my head toward Jemima. He nodded.

"I'm Flanders." He tipped his hat again as an acorn hit his arm.

Jemima giggled.

He responded to her flirtations by beaming with glowing blue eyes. Jemima latched onto his arm, and the two strolled toward the grove of sycamore trees. Betsy followed behind them, and Fanny and I shook our heads at the same time before following.

As expected, Jemima kept Flanders distracted. Betsy and Fanny stayed near, gathering hickory nuts for their momma, but I moved several yards away from the annoying scene. I needed more colorful foliage for cloth dye. So far, my basket contained only oak bark and acorns for brown shades. I turned to Flanders. "I want to go beyond this hollow."

He nodded, but kept his attention on Jemima.

"Flanders." I glared. "You can't keep watch from there."

He held his elbow out to Jemima, and the two came toward me, arm in arm. I shook my head and whacked a clump of vines from the path. As I eased into a small clearing, short stalks of greenery caught my eye. The saw-toothed leaves grew in clusters of five, like the ones used for rope making and fiber for cloth. These were smaller and withering. *Should make a green or yellow. Hopefully not brown.* After snipping off several with my knife, I spied what used to be a bright yellow cluster of Lady's Bedstraw a few yards away, near a grove of shrubs. I stood still and scanned my location. *Where is Flanders?*

I huffed, moved to the roots, and squatted. After digging up several and placing them in my basket, leaves rustled a short distance in front of me. My head jerked, and then I stilled and shallowed my breaths while waiting for discernment.

Muffled voices drew closer, but they weren't Flanders or my friends. With a pounding chest, I parted the skinny branches of the shrubs.

My breath caught. Two men dressed in buckskins stood a few feet from me with their backs turned. Black-spiked hair topped their red-painted heads. *Indians!* A white man stood in front of them with his pulled-back chestnut hair showing under his round-brimmed brown hat. He was dressed like the other men in the fort, with a tan linen shirt and dark-blue woolen britches.

My breaths shallowed as my chest thumped.

The Indian men spoke in guttural sounds I didn't understand.

The white man turned his face enough for me to see. My hand stifled a gasp. *The man who glared at me two weeks ago.*

He responded in their language and then said, "The plan is working. Gunpowder and lead are running low. Men will have to go far to bring back more. The salt is also running low. Tell Blue Jacket and Dragging Canoe now is a good time to attack."

My stomach knotted.

"No. Not good now. But soon." One of the Indians handed the man a small pouch.

The white man fingered inside, then growled. "This isn't the price agreed on. I won't give any more information until I get what he promised. Tell Dr. Smith he'd better make good. I need to clear out soon—can't risk being caught."

My heartbeat thumped in my ears, and everything went dark for a second. My arms and legs tingled as I forced a breath.

"Mary, where are you?" Fanny shouted from the trees behind me.

The men dashed back the way they came, shuffling leaves in their haste.

I leapt up. The trees swayed. *No, can't faint. God, make Fanny go back.* I rushed toward Fanny with my basket.

She gasped and jumped back, flushing birds from the bushes.

I grabbed her hand and yelled, "Run."

"What is it?" Flanders met us, aiming his rifle toward the woods.

I flew past him. "Just run."

Chapter Three

We stopped in the meadow, out of breath. My friends stared with frowns.

"I heard a man talking to Indians about attacking the fort."

Flanders shook his head. "Pshaw. Just one of our scouts getting information from a friendly is all. I thought you saw a bear or something. Don't do that."

"No, he—" I watched the wooded area to the left. "There he is." I pointed.

The man strolled out of the woods. He glanced our way but headed toward Squire Boone's blacksmith shop in the central yard.

Flanders laughed. "That's Alex Jessop. He's a surveyor and trusted scout."

"Then why was he telling them—?" I glanced at the others. *They're already frightened.*

"How should I know?" He frowned and turned to Jemima. "I'll walk you home now."

She placed her hand on her hip. "You shouldn't be so jumpy, Mary. You scared everyone."

As the two strolled away, gazing at each other, I fumed. *How dare they brush off my concerns?*

Betsy curtsied. "Well, I'm going to tend to these nuts once my heart settles down. Good day, Mary." She walked on.

Fanny laid her hand on my arm. "I would have been scared too. I know you and your family were ambushed by Indians on the way here."

Her carefree manner didn't untangle the knots in my stomach. "Thank you." I forced a smile. *Wish I could tell you all my fears.*

She sighed. "I promised to hem Betsy's new petticoat if she cracked the nuts." She hugged me and moved back. "My father will make the men begin on picketed walls in the morning. Then we won't worry so much about Indians attacking. See you later." Fanny waved and strode toward her cabin.

I waved and sighed. *I know what I heard.*

I kicked through the leaves as I stormed into the settlement to find Papa.

A man stepped in front of me.

Dazed, I stumbled backward.

"Sorry, miss. Clumsy of me. Must be too much 'shine." He tipped his hat. "I'm Alexander Jessop. Aren't you Michael Shirley's daughter? Been surveying with him. Don't believe I know your name?"

My heart raced as coherency returned. He didn't smell of liquor. His eyes focused on me, and he didn't slur. "Excuse me." I sprinted from him, scanning the yard.

I spotted Papa speaking to a couple of men and rushed toward him, breathless and trembling.

The men stared as Papa hurried to my side. "What's happened?"

"I'm sorry, Michael." Mr. Jessop interrupted and rushed around me. "I'm afraid I startled your daughter. Didn't mean to. I was headed to the privy when our paths met."

Papa nodded and moved in front of me, but I held on to his arm. "She'll be all right in a few minutes. Been through a lot this year."

I glared at the man and swallowed.

"Sorry, miss." Mr. Jessop tipped his hat and continued toward the privy.

I didn't care if he was still in earshot. "He's lying, Papa. Mr. Jessop deliberately stepped in front of me, wanting to know if I'm your daughter and my name. He knows I overheard him a moment ago, speaking to Indians in the small clearing beyond the hollow. They're going to attack the fort soon."

Papa's eyes narrowed, but I finished reporting everything I'd seen and heard. "He's a turncoat."

Papa pulled me to his chest and wrapped his arms around me. "Shh, try to calm down. I hope you're wrong, but I've known good men to turn." He moved away. "Come with me. This warrants a hearing."

"No, Papa." Tears welled in my eyes as I gulped down the lump in my throat. "I can't give public testimony. I'll throw up."

He took my hand. "Be strong, Mary. This is important. The accused has a right to face his accuser, and the leaders must decide."

Papa motioned for Mr. Boone and several of the men to come as we walked to the western blockhouse. When we entered the dim oak-scented room, a shiver of fear rushed through me. Men piled inside. I drew in deep breaths while Papa relayed my account. Some shook their heads and glanced at me. One left to fetch Mr. Jessop.

When the door opened, I saw a crowd gathering outside. My cheeks burned with embarrassment.

In a few minutes, the accused entered, removing his hat. My stomach churned. Judge Callaway spoke to him. "Miss Shirley witnessed and heard a meeting between yourself and two Indians this morning."

Mr. Jessop nodded.

The judge went on. "She said money was exchanged for information about our supply status, and you've encouraged the Indians to raid. These charges can be construed as traitorous. Explain your actions, sir."

The traitor smirked and then cleared his throat. "As you know, gentlemen, the British are paying for information. I've been spreading misinformation among them through these associates of mine." He glanced at me and then back to the judge. "This girl has given a true account of what she heard, but my statement to the Indian scouts was for the Shawnee and Cherokee to raid Harrod's fort—not this one."

I gasped and blurted out, "That's a lie. He told them he had to leave before he's found out."

The judged glowered at me, and Papa placed a hand on my shoulder. "Shh, let him finish."

Men murmured behind me as Mr. Jessop smirked and continued. "I need them to continue to believe I'm a loyalist." He jutted his chin, grinning while pointing at me. "Pshaw. She's a better spy than the rest of us."

Laughter erupted in the room. My face burned. I slipped beside Papa for solace.

Judge Callaway stepped forward. "You're dismissed, Alex. And as for you, young lady." His stern eyes pierced like daggers. "You're forbidden from concerning yourself with the actions or whereabouts of Mr. Jessop." He looked from me to Papa. "Mr. Shirley, I recommend a firm hand if she doesn't comply. Furthermore, Mr. Jessop deserves an apology for being publicly shamed before this community."

I gasped at the judge's reprimand. *How can he be so callous? Why does everyone trust Mr. Jessop without question?*

"I'll see to it, sir." Papa took my sweaty hand, and we headed out the door.

Angry tears streamed down my cheeks as I stared at the ground, avoiding onlookers.

"I'm sorry, Mary. You did the right thing reporting what you heard." Papa slowed our pace. "There are many things going on in these parts that even I don't understand. Don't be afraid to tell me what you hear. I'll pass information on to my sources so they can investigate."

"Thank you, Pa—" To my horror, we arrived in front of Mr. Jessop.

"You must apologize." Papa's voice was firm but soft.

Breathe. My gut churned as I stood before Mr. Jessop, wanting to spit in his haughty face.

Helpless, trapped, frantic, I whispered, "I'm sorry, sir."

He snarled like a panther ready to pounce. "No one heard you, girl—speak up."

Quick breaths didn't keep the foul contents of my stomach from exploding all over Mr. Jessop's chest.

Gasps and laughter from the crowd followed. I ran a few steps away before falling to my knees and heaving again. Papa squatted next to me, rubbing my back. "Come now. I'll take you to Momma."

My legs teetered as we left the crowd.

When he handed me off to Momma, she escorted me to the spring. "Try to calm down now. 'All things work together for good…'"

The Bible verse didn't bring comfort. I scoffed. *Work together for good? I'll never live this humiliation down.* I splashed cold water on my face and sniffled.

She helped me up. "I'll walk you back to the cabin. You missed lunch."

"No, Momma." I released her arm. "I'm not hungry. Please. I just want to be alone now."

She nodded and kissed my cheek. "It will come out in the wash."

I sighed and turned toward home. *Not this one. It's an eternal stain on my reputation.*

I entered the solitude and warmth of our cabin and cuddled a blanket around my shoulders. Then I sat cross-legged on the dirt floor in front of the hearth and spoke to the flames. "Best to stay out of sight for a while."

For the first week of October, men chopped sharp points on about ten logs but never raised them. I stayed out of sight, helping Momma near the cabin, experimenting with strips of cloth in dye baths, and learning to extract the best colors from the substances I'd found. I used a copper pot for the Lady's Bedstraw and clay pots for the bark, acorns, and leaves.

A nice tan developed from the bark and nuts, but I squealed at the sight of the beautiful raspberry-red that emerged from the Lady's Bedstraw. *Now, if I only had a new bodice to dye.*

The hemp fronds produced a wonderful sun-kissed green, which would have been perfect for a new neckerchief. But when I went back to rake out the handful of dried leaves that had fallen onto the coals, a skunky rope-smelling smoke blew into my face. I coughed, and then giggled for no reason and became lightheaded.

Momma led me out of the smoke. "You found the type of hemp used by the Indians for medicine and rituals. It made a pretty color, but don't use it again."

I chuckled and sat on the bench at the table. "I suppose I'd better stick to Black-Eyed Susans in the cast-iron pot."

Momma smiled. "Yes. Breathe fresh air for a while and then finish cleaning up."

Lizzy grinned at me. "Guess what? More supplies came in. Now, we'll all have new outfits for the harvest dance."

I beamed and drew a deep breath. *Powerful little leaves. I don't feel worried anymore, but I don't like being dizzy.*

I smiled at Fanny, who was marching toward me.

She offered me a piece of candied maple syrup. "When are you coming out of hiding?"

"Thank you." I popped the soft sweetness in my mouth.

Her hands went to her hips. "You might as well laugh with the rest of us. After all, it was funny. You can't help your nervous condition. Besides, most people say Mr. Jessop deserved what happened because he didn't accept your first apology."

I half-smiled and sighed at the ground.

"Flanders saw the whole thing. He said Mr. Jessop's reaction was something like this—" Fanny leaned back, raising her hands to ear-height while baring teeth and widening her eyes.

I spit the candy into my hand as I leaned forward, laughing.

"Let's go annoy Jemima and Betsy." Fanny held her elbow out to me. "You'll feel better."

"Help me clean up, then I can go." I didn't tell her about the leaves.

Chapter Four

October's harvesting and preserving ended, and work on our new dresses commenced. As the chilly late-morning winds of November fifth blew outside, I finished hemming the edge of my new neckerchief and grinned. *Two days to spare before the dance.* I glanced at the sunbeams dancing through the shuttered window. Katie squatted at the hearth, frying hoecakes for lunch, while Lizzy, Susie, and Nancy finished chopping onions for the pot of pungent turnip stew. Momma sat in the corner quizzing Charlie's arithmetic, while Sally practiced writing numbers on a slate.

I stood from the log bench, stretching. "I'm going out for fresh air. I'll bring back water."

Momma nodded as I wrapped a shawl around my head. I lifted the bucket from the peg in the wall and opened the door, welcoming the cold blast.

Before I reached the freshwater spring behind our cabin, Mr. Jessop crossed my path, glaring. I averted my eyes, but my gut knotted. *You venomous, slithering snake.*

My moccasins squished in mud as I neared the bank. I found firm footing and knelt before a clear spot in the water before dipping the bucket. A few feet away, a group of men stood, grumbling about the scarcity of supplies. A gray-haired man's voice boomed. "Now that Hamilton has command of Fort Detroit, we'll see no more provisions from there."

Why do I overhear these things? I set the filled bucket down and stood. "Excuse me, sirs. Where is Fort Detroit, and who is Hamilton?"

They all turned my way, wide-eyed and frowning. I curtsied.

The elderly man drew closer. His face looked as weathered as his buckskin shirt, and his smile beamed with a missing tooth. "About six hundred miles up Canada way, miss. 'Twas the quickest supply route because of the rivers."

I eased back from his rank breath.

"Henry Hamilton's the British devil in charge. Been payin' Indians for settlers' scalps—women and infants too. And now he's made tradin' with rebel strongholds on the western waters punishable by death." He tipped his hat and motioned the others to follow. "Good day, miss."

Does Papa know about this? I carried my sloshing bucket back to the cabin, ready to beg Papa to take us back to Indian Creek with the next group of disgruntled settlers. A large party left this morning as soon as they transferred newly arrived supplies to their mules. I didn't blame them. Disputes broke out daily over surveys and deteriorating order. Many times, it reminded me of the lawlessness of Fort Blackmore, where men were shooting each other over thefts.

When I entered our home, Papa stood beside Momma, fuming. "I lost my claim on a nice track of land because some fool chopped down my initialed boundary trees. Either they didn't check or didn't care. This is why so many surveys are becoming shingled. If there wasn't a shortage of gunpowder—" He shook his head.

Anger rose in me, too. Papa had been surveying for others every day and sometimes overnight. His face revealed exhaustion and puffy skin under reddened eyes. *Now, a greedy man has dishonored him.*

I joined my siblings around the table. Papa sighed and plopped down. "Mr. Floyd said Virginia legislators will most likely win their claim against Colonel Henderson. At least everything will be resurveyed. Bad news is many will lose their claims."

His voice calmed as he asked God's blessing over our meal. After the *amen,* he crumbled hoecake into his bowl of stew. I was in the middle of slurping the broth from my spoon when he said, "Oh, I forgot to mention those McGuire boys sneaked in here during the night as smooth as butter."

I held the hot liquid in my mouth until I could swallow. *William's here?*

Papa continued. "William said the guard on duty looked straight at him—oblivious."

"Well, that guard should be punished." Momma huffed. "What if those men had been Indians? We could've been killed in our sleep."

"Now, Katherine, it's not the guard's fault. Even if we had stockade walls, William would have gotten through. He's just that good. That's why he's still alive with all he does. His brother is good to boot."

The skin on my arms prickled with the memory of William sneaking up on me, shoving me to the ground in the dark—the sound of his voice in my ear asking who I was. *I'm not ready to face him. His life's in danger because of me.*

"Mary?" Momma's soft touch made me jump.

I stared at her. "Yes ma'am?"

"Please help Katie bring in the dry linens when you finish."

Katie bumped my arm with her elbow. "May we go meet Letitia's brothers first? We won't stay long."

My mouth dropped open.

Momma shook her head. "No, you may not."

Papa frowned at us but continued his report. "They brought gunpowder, lead, salt, bear jerky, and news." When he stroked his chin, I stood from the table.

"May I be excused? I want to get started. You ready, Katie?" I waited for Momma's and Papa's nods and then rushed outside.

I fled to the fresh-smelling sheets that flapped in the breeze.

Katie caught up with me, out of breath and glaring. "What's your problem?"

"I don't want to meet the McGuires yet." I removed a wooden clothespin from one corner. "And I can't handle Papa stroking his chin. It's always bad news."

Katie tilted her head and frowned as she took the bottom corners of the sheet in hand and brought them together. "I thought you'd want to meet William. Let him see you as you and not dressed like George."

I folded the sheet I held. "No, and I don't want to talk about it anymore."

"Oh, all right, but calm down." Katie moved to the next sheet.

As we completed our job, the rest of the family went to the blockhouse, where a crowd had gathered to distribute the goods. Katie and I carried the laundry inside.

After putting away the linens, I glanced out the window toward Letitia's cabin. *She'll be expecting me.*

Momma entered, holding Sally's hand and a bag of ground corn. She peered at me. "Letitia wants you to come visit. You may go, but don't overstay your welcome."

My stomach did a flip. "May Katie come? I don't want to go by myself."

Katie beamed and came toward me. "We'll behave." She slipped her arm in mine. "I promise."

Momma shook her head. "Not this time. One of you is enough."

Katie kissed my cheek and whispered, "You must tell me everything." She backed away, watching.

I gave her a nod, then stood in the doorway, staring at the Gatliff cabin a moment before stepping into the yard. *Now or never.* I blew out a breath and walked down the hill on shaky legs.

When I arrived, the door was ajar. I gulped and knocked before easing inside the too-quiet cabin. Letitia was alone and squatting at the hearth, stirring a pot. The extended table held dishes for two extra people.

"You're about to eat. I can visit later." I backed away.

"No, no." Letitia stood and waved me inside. "I want you to meet my brothers. They'll be in soon." She placed a pot on the table and smiled at me. "Please fetch the hoecakes."

I grabbed a dishtowel and lifted the pan from the coals. As I approached the table, Mr. Gatliff bounded through the door, followed by two younger men and Reese. My stomach fluttered. Suddenly, I felt small and awkward.

The men hung hats and rifles on pegs and then turned toward me. They were both handsome, tanned, and muscular, and wore their coal-black hair tied back. My limbs went numb.

"Aye, and here's Thomas and William." Letitia pointed to each one and then turned to me. "And here is Mary Shirley, the brave girl I've written of."

My face grew hot.

William moved closer, beaming. "Pleased to meet you at last, Mary."

The voice. I wanted to flee but couldn't stop staring into the shades of rawhide in his eyes. I couldn't answer—couldn't breathe.

He chuckled. "You're punier than I remember. Perhaps the dark night and your brother's clothes made you appear older."

Puny! He thinks I'm a puny little girl? Hurt added to the awkwardness. I placed the pan of hoecakes on the table and moved toward the door. *How can he be so rude?*

"Hush." Letitia fussed. "She's not used to your teasin'."

"Aye, and don't be scarin' her off." Thomas whacked the back of William's head with his hand.

I couldn't help grinning, but irritation remained.

"And you're both heathens. You are." Letitia touched my arm. "I'm sorry my brothers' are lackin' good manners. Please stay."

Thomas scooted the bench out and patted it. "Come sit by me, lass. You'll get used to us."

William bowed. "Please accept my apology."

I returned to the table wondering why William's brogue wasn't as strong as Letitia's and Thomas's. "I'll stay for a few minutes, but I've already eaten."

As I lowered onto the bench, William plopped down beside me before Thomas could. *Like unruly children.*

Letitia sighed. Thomas shook his head and sat next to Reese.

Still seething, I glared at William. "I might be puny, sir, but I'm not weak."

His head jerked back, his gaze and tone turned serious. "This I know, lass. Isaiah Brown still curses the daughter of Cage for shooting him in the knee and leaving him for dead."

Isaiah's alive. Panic rose in my gut as his image flashed through my mind. *What if Isaiah comes after me?*

William bumped my arm with his elbow. "I never want to be on your bad side, Miss Shirley. Please forgive me and pass the hoecakes."

I lifted the platter but held it still, staring until I felt a hand brush mine.

William took the hoecakes and chuckled. "Thank you. Glad your family survived the Indian attack and festering wounds. Sorry about the lost horses. I'll keep a lookout for Rebel."

"Welcome." I placed my hands in my lap. A lump rose in my throat at the memory of Indians leading my horse away. My eyes watered.

"He was my favorite of the bunch I sold to your da. I wanted to buy him back on my way to Fort Cook the day I visited."

Beaming an ornery grin, he bumped my arm again. "Then your da said he'd been tamed by a girl."

I peered at William as he watched my eyes and finished chewing.

His words replayed in my mind. I smiled and nodded. "Unruly males need taming, Mr. McGuire. Some in this room could use a good switching."

He chortled and nodded. "So, we do. So, we do."

Laughter erupted from everyone, but William's made my stomach flutter.

I took a deep breath. "I need to get home and help Momma now."

"I'll walk with you a bit. Headed that way." William gulped down his last bite and scooted from the bench. He retrieved his hat and rifle, then stood at the door waiting.

Thomas stood and bowed. "Good day, lass."

"Good day." I curtsied and walked past William.

He waited a moment and then fell in step beside me, clearing his throat. "You've fire in your eyes when you're riled, Miss Shirley."

My face burned. I stopped walking and faced him. "I'm sorry for my childishness, Mr. McGuire. I know now you were teasing before. Please forgive me."

His eyes widened and held me captive. "Aye, and I don't think you're childish at all. You're as docile as a honeybee." He snickered. "Until provoked."

I giggled and felt my face burning despite the cold wind. "I meant to thank you for helping Papa find me on the bank of Indian Creek. That day you brought my horse Rebel home."

His lips pressed as he shook his head. "'Twas the day I learned I'd shoved a lass to the ground. Disturbs me still, and I hope you forgive me."

"Forgiven." I gazed at his watery eyes and warm prickly tingles made me shiver.

He blinked and glanced away a moment before sighing. "Sorry about the teasing. I can't help myself. I'm easily humored. It's in my raising. We're all like that." He glanced at the ground and then back, without smiling.

"You seem like family 'cause I know so much about you. Sis raves about your strength and spunk in her letters." A wry grin rose on his face. "I'd like to be your friend. And please call me William."

The care in his voice and playful manner equaled Papa's. I smiled and nodded. "I accept. But I'm not as brave and strong as people think. I worry too much—about everything. You mentioned Isaiah Brown being alive, and now I'm sick with fear. Will he come after me?"

He stepped back, his eyebrows raising. "I'm sorry to worry you. Honestly, I don't know. He lost the lower part of the leg you shot. Last I heard, he was headed toward Fort Pitt. I don't think he'd be foolish enough to risk coming into rebel territory just for revenge, but I'll get word to your da if he does."

I sighed. "Thank you for telling me. I'd rather expect trouble and plan for it than be surprised. I just have this constant need to know."

He nodded. "Then you should know the dispatch you delivered in August made it to scouts on the Greenbrier River. They alerted settlers this side of the Ohio River. Scouts are scrambling to counter British alliances with chiefs from the Six Nation Tribes. The loyalists in West Augusta County are fuming. Most of them have gone into hiding—so they think." William grinned.

His news made my head spin. I took a deep breath. "I'm sorry I gave them your name."

William smiled down at me. "Don't worry, lass. They won't find me." He tipped his hat and winked.

"You don't drop the *G* in your speech the way most Irish do. Why?"

He chuckled. "You noticed that? Well, when I was a lad, I heard a man speaking the way you do. He sounded more sophisticated. That's when I decided to distinguish myself a bit from my kin. Well, I'm off to...hunt with Jeb Turner. Have a good day, Mary."

I smiled. "Thank you. I enjoyed meeting you. Stay safe."

He nodded, adjusted his pack, and walked toward the corral.

My heart danced. I couldn't look away from his stride and didn't want to. *Finally met the mysterious William McGuire.* Infatuation and worry for him latched on to my soul. "What's wrong with me?" I asked aloud.

Papa came up behind me with furrowed brows and pressed lips. "Too much excitement for one day, I suppose."

I held my chest. My cheeks burned. "Mr. McGuire reported that our dispatch made it to the intended parties. Maybe it's safe to return to Indian Creek?" I rubbed my chin, and my stomach knotted. I knew it wasn't. Not with all that William reported.

"Not yet." He held out his elbow. "Going my way?"

I threaded my arm through his and cuddled next to him as we walked.

Did I just rub my chin?

Chapter Five

As Papa and I neared the cabin, Katie and Lizzy peered up from the outside table under the oak tree. They watched me with wide eyes. Each held an unpeeled potato suspended in one hand and a paring knife in the other.

They're waiting on my report. I chuckled and released Papa's arm. "I'll go help my sisters with supper preparations."

He nodded and continued inside.

"You look bewitched, standing there like that." I pointed to their hands.

Lizzy grinned at her spud and then swiped the knife down one side.

Katie laid hers down with a loud sigh. "Well?"

I waited for Lizzy's attention again. "Tantalizing brown eyes. Well-groomed and fine-featured from face to feet." I giggled and felt the flush on my cheeks. "They're ornery and untamed, though. Took me a bit to get used to their teasing manner. I wanted to punch William more than once until we had a chance to talk alone."

My sisters' mouths dropped open. I chuckled. "We spoke on his way to meet someone for hunting. Papa came upon us as William departed, but he didn't scold me."

"Maybe we can meet them tomorrow." Katie smiled and whittled the skins off her potato.

"I want to meet Thomas." Lizzy giggled. "He tipped his hat to me a little while ago as I returned from the spring with water. He's handsome." She resumed peeling.

I gaped before chuckling. "You're not even ten yet, and he's over twenty. Don't let Papa know you're sweet on men. Trust me. He doesn't do well." I grinned at Katie. "I forgot to ask how long they're staying. Maybe Momma will allow us to go visit together."

George jutted his chin and laughed as he and Charlie passed us carrying kindling. "I heard Mr. McGuire tell a group of men, 'That Shirley girl is . . .' Well, I better not say." He wrinkled his nose and continued to the cabin.

"What?" I rushed to catch him. "Wait. You can't say things like that and leave."

He shook his head and continued walking. "Can't make me say." He and Charlie giggled into the cabin.

An hour later, two gunshots echoed from the high ridge north of the river. I smiled. *That was a quick hunt.* But a shrill whistle in the distance turned my stomach.

Men shouted, "Indians. Women and children to the blockhouse."

I froze and clutched my chest. *Oh, God. No.*

Papa rushed out draped with his powder horn, a pack, and his rifle shouldered. His wild eyes scanned ahead as he hurried toward the gathering men.

George appeared in the doorway donned like Papa, but holding his rifle by butt and barrel, as if ready to defend us.

I gulped and ran into the cabin, expecting to help calm my younger siblings. Everyone stood still and quiet, watching Momma hoist Sally to her hip.

Charlie frowned and grabbed my hand. "No scared."

"Let's go." Momma hurried outside.

Katie held Nancy's hand. Susie ran to catch up with Lizzy. George flanked us through the yard, holding his gun level but not cocked.

My gut wrenched with worry for William in the woods somewhere and now for Papa, who knelt behind a log where the fort wall should be.

Women and children swarmed from every direction and converged in front of the narrow-doored blockhouse. We squeezed single file into the middle of the dimly lit room and the door closed. Betsy and Fanny were smashed together in the corner, and Jemima stood calm-faced beside her mother. I glanced around for Letitia and her boys, but she hadn't come. My throat tightened with worry. *How is she not afraid?*

No more shots were fired, but someone began whispering the Lord's Prayer. Sniffles and whimpers prevailed a few minutes more, then a hymn began in soft, shaky voices. Within seconds, Mrs. Boone's strong voice rallied the rest into a boisterous battle hymn that ended with a resounding "amen."

I wiped tears from my cheeks and added, *please, let us live.*

At least two hours passed before a double knock came, giving the all clear. The door opened to fresh air, and bodies surged forward.

A man stood before us, holding his hat. "Someone's been killed."

George rushed toward the group of men, lifting a body from a canoe.

I tighten my grip on Charlie, who tried to pull free and follow him.

Momma sighed. "Take everyone inside." She handed Sally to Katie.

Tears slid from my eyes as Momma headed toward the other women. I sent Charlie to Lizzy. "I'm going to stay and help."

When a woman screamed and wept, I clutched my throat. It didn't sound like Letitia, but I couldn't move. A crowd huddled around the weeping woman, who had fallen to her knees on the ground. Momma helped coax her up as two men carried a blood-soaked corpse toward a cabin near the spring. *Not Letitia. But where is William? What if he's met the same fate?*

"It's Mr. Turner." George staggered toward me with an ashen face and sat on the ground, holding his belly. "Feel sick. Never saw a man skinned and gutted. His wife identified his shredded shirt."

Choking back tears, I took a deep breath. "Any word about Will—Mr. McGuire?"

George shook his head and held his knees, sucking in deep breaths before looking up. "Sorry for teasing you about him earlier. He told the men you're feisty."

Tears welled in my eyes, but I spotted Letitia stepping away from the crowd, zigzagging and teetering. I rushed toward her, but Thomas arrived first. Once she was steady, he peered into her eyes. "Charles and I will find him, Sis." He handed Letitia to me and bolted away with his rifle.

Her breaths were shallow as we entered the cabin.

Reese pointed to the hearth, whining, "Eat."

Baby James babbled from his highchair and gummed a wooden block.

Letitia's eyes darted from them to me, then to the door.

I nodded and fought tears as she fled from the cabin. She stumbled a few feet away and slumped to the ground, sobbing and throwing up.

I sighed and pushed the door closed with my foot before Reese could escape. "Momma needs to rest. I'll make your supper. Play with your soldiers."

He remained near the door, pouting.

Still shaken, I went to the hearth, assessing at what stage Letitia had left supper. Wrapped hoecakes were staying warm in the Dutch oven to the side of the hearth. Sliced salt pork lay on the chopping block. A frying pan was heating on a trivet. I sucked in a deep breath. *Must focus now.* I placed the strips in the hot pan.

As they sizzled, I used the cast-iron lifter to raise the lid from a small cast-iron pot that hung low from a chain. With a quick stir, I saved the diced turnips from scorching and raised the chain three links.

The door latch jiggled behind me. Startled, I glanced back at Reese, who stretched up to finger the latch. I cleared my throat and pointed to the bench at the table. He crossed his arms and stomped his foot. I glanced at Letitia's switch. Reese huffed and marched to the table.

"Thank you." I nodded and prepared his plate.

When I placed the food and a cup of milk before Reese, James tossed his block to the floor and patted his wooden tray.

I smiled. "I'll be back with yours."

I dipped the last of the milk from a bucket into a bowl and crumbled in half a hoecake. I placed the bowl before James and went to the small window. *Where are you,*

William? I pushed one shutter back and peered into the yard. *Please be alive.*

A moment later, a plop turned my attention back to the table. James's discarded wooden bowl lay upside down on the hard-packed dirt floor. "No, no." I shook my head and lifted him from the chair to his bed. Then I grabbed a towel to sop up the gooey mess. The baby cuddled his blanket and lay down.

A second later, the door flew open.

I dropped to the ground, unable to breathe, and squinted at the entering figures of Thomas helping William inside. I sprang to my feet, clasping my mouth as Reese slid from the bench and stood beside me, whimpering.

"Unk Will hurt."

"Yes." I swallowed and held the boy's hand, wanting to rush to William's aid as he moaned and plopped down on the bench, shivering. My heart sank at the sight of blood dripping from the scrapes on his face and oozing from a wound on his shoulder. His shirt was torn and mud caked.

"Augh." William grimaced as Thomas removed his shirt.

I dropped Reese's hand. "Stay here while I help your uncles."

I rushed to Letitia's basket of bandages, flung a handful into the water bucket, and placed it and the basket on the table beside Thomas.

"Needs stitchin'. Where's Sis?" Thomas held a wad of cloth tight against William's shoulder.

"I'll find her." I sprinted outside, scanning until I found her sitting on a secluded stump near the blockhouse. I shouted, "William's alive but wounded."

Letitia leapt to her feet and ran ahead of me. She entered the cabin and peered back, shaking her head as she closed the door.

Leaving me out? A lump caught in my throat. *I want to help.* Tears welled in my eyes. *Why did you shut me out?* I waited a minute more in case she would change her mind. Then I trudged home, pleading for William's recovery.

A small group of people stood crying with Mrs. Turner at a fresh grave. *How horrible to be widowed in a place like this.*

I wiped my face before going inside our cabin.

Momma turned to me. "Where were...what's wrong? Sit down and put your feet up. You're pale and trembling."

"William's alive but injured. I don't know how badly." My eyes watered.

Momma placed a damp cloth on my neck. "Breathe."

My siblings sat huddled together on the ground near the hearth.

Papa entered with a sigh and hung his hat and rifle on the peg. "Charles has headed out with a group of men to find the raiders. Mrs. Turner is among the twenty families determined to head back east in the morning."

"We need to go with them." I stood up, fuming with my heart racing.

Papa's head jerked back.

I continued. "Why must we stay here and die in this cursed place? At least we'd have a chance back on Indian Creek, or we could move to Fort Cook."

"Yes, please," my sister Nancy whispered behind me.

I sat back down on the bench, looking up at Momma and my sisters. They stared at Papa with glistening eyes. George nodded at me. Charlie climbed onto my lap, frowning and spouting, "Home."

Papa stroked his chin. "I've made a commitment for a year. I'm needed here, as militia. We can't let this area fall into British hands." He focused on Momma. "You and the children may leave in the morning with the other families. But move into Fort Cook until I can come."

I gasped and watched Momma. Her head shook with narrowed eyes. "We'll do no such thing. We'll fight and live or die together. Maybe now you'll head the building of stockade walls?"

She sighed and stepped into his arms, sniffling. He cuddled her. "I'm sorry, liebchen. I'm must leave in an hour to survey. I'll be gone overnight."

Tears welled, my throat tightened, and hope dropped to the floor with my heart.

Charlie climbed down and joined our parents in the hug, followed by my sisters.

George stared out the window, shouldered his rifle, and shrugged. "I'll go help tend to the horses." He went outside, easing the door closed.

I swallowed hard and stood from the table as a firm but gentle voice in my head whispered, *Be strong.*

Chapter Six

After breakfast the next morning, I lifted the bucket of dirty dishwater and followed George into the yard. Twenty families, suddenly gone, caused a noticeable void. The few people moving about were quiet, with solemn faces. George continued to a group of young men standing around the stack of sharpened logs, talking, but not working. I huffed my disgust and glanced toward the Gatliffs' cabin. Letitia stood in front of someone seated on a log chair. All I could see were a man's legs as she moved about his head, dabbing it with a cloth. *Has to be William.*

I marched across the fresh-tilled ground of the communal garden in the central yard, dodging chickens as they scurried about feasting on upturned grubs. After dumping my bucket, I glanced back at our cabin. *Maybe Momma won't mind if I'm gone a bit longer.* My desire to know his condition overpowered the need to ask permission. I stamped dirt from my moccasins and headed to the Gatliffs'.

Jemima, Betsy, and Fanny waved for me to come to the Boones' cabin. I smiled but shook my head and continued my pace, leaving them to wonder. *They'll pepper me with questions later.*

Dust in the air tickled my nose as I approached Letitia, but the glare from the sun made me sneeze.

Letitia frowned and raised her hand for me to stop. "God be with us."

I stood still. "I'm not sick. Promise."

"Come, then." She waved me forward. "Gave me a startle, ya did. Sneezes can bring curses to our home."

"I'm sorry. It's the dust. My family says *gesundheit*—be in good health."

William chuckled. "Hi there, puny girl."

I pressed my lips to prevent a smile and feigned a scowl.

Letitia whopped his shoulder. "Stop tormenting her."

"Ow, that's my bruise." He grinned as he rubbed the spot.

"Well, behave." Letitia smirked, then glanced at me. "I'll leave him with you. I need to tend to Reese and James." She wiped her hands and went inside.

Alone with William? I scanned the yard for Papa in case he'd returned earlier than expected from surveying. Not seeing him, I inched closer, staring at William's bandaged shoulder, concerned. "How badly are you hurt?"

He eased to his feet. "Sore and bruised a bit, but I've been worse." He backed away from the chair. "Would you like to sit?"

"Yes, please." I set the bucket down and smoothed my petticoat before sitting. "What happened yesterday?"

He leaned against the cabin wall. "Sure you want to hear?"

I nodded. "Except the details of poor Mr. Turner."

William stared at the ground and then at me. "We were trackin' a couple of Shawnee scouts seen in the area the night before."

"Wait." I frowned and held up my hand. "You said you were going hunting after lunch. So, you didn't mean game?"

William nodded. "Would have brought in game too, if I could have. I didn't want to worry you."

"Now see here." I stood, placing my hands on my hips. "If we're to be friends, I need truth, not coddling."

He stared a moment, smiled, and then nodded. "All right. The truth."

He lifted a milking stool from a peg on the cabin wall and tilted his head at my chair before easing down upon the stool. I plopped down again and waited.

"The Shawnee and five other tribes are considering an alliance against us. They're negotiating with the British through an informer in this area, but I can't prove it."

I gasped. "I know who it is—but no one believes me."

His eyes widened. "Tell me."

"Alexander Jessop." My heart raced as I gave William every detail of what Mr. Jessop had said to the Indians and his slanted explanations at the hearing.

William's eyebrows rose more than once during my discourse.

"Aye. This fits with what I've been hearing. And if he continues supplying information to the Shawnee war chief, Blue Jacket, families aren't safe here—especially without walls."

His serious tone made my skin prickle. "Papa gave Momma permission to move us back to Indian Creek. But she won't go without him."

William sighed and shook his head. "I wish she'd reconsider. Conditions may be worse by summer. Raids will make receiving supplies impossible, and soldiers can't be spared for defense. And the Shawnee know it."

Images of the Cherokee men who attacked my family made me gasp.

He touched my arm. "Sorry to frighten you."

After a deep sigh, I nodded and stared at my moccasins. "Maybe God will spare our lives again."

"That he must." William's hand reached toward mine, but then withdrew as he cleared his throat. "Thomas and I are leaving within the hour. Do you still want to know what happened yesterday?"

My breath caught. "Why are you leaving so soon? The harvest dance is tomorrow night." My cheeks grew hot. "I...know you can't dance, but—" I wiggled into a more comfortable position.

He nodded and smiled. "We're escorting the Simmons party back to Cook's Fort before the weather turns. If we make it in three weeks, they'll pay with Spanish silver dollars." His grin widened. "So, you'd be wanting to dance with me, eh?"

I gulped and stared at my folded hands.

He chuckled. "Well, maybe your da will change his mind about coming to Cook's Fort."

"Uh," I moaned. "Not likely."

"Hello, lass. Is William annoyin' you?" Thomas came out from behind the cabin with a string of salted trout.

"Not at the moment." I grinned and stood, fluffing my skirt.

"Did he tell ya we're leavin'?" He stopped beside his brother and hooked the string between the porch posts to dry.

I nodded and gazed at William. "I hope you'll come back again soon."

William's cheeks flushed to raspberry, and he stared at his moccasins.

I chuckled, enjoying the moment. *He's embarrassed for once.*

Thomas shook his head. "Afraid not. The militia is callin' for volunteers. We may be enlisting by spring. Courtin' must wait."

I flinched. *Enlisted? Courting?*

William shoved Thomas away. "Go. Saddle the horses."

Does William want to court me?

Thomas tipped his hat and headed to the stockyard.

William's brown eyes held my attention. "I'm not joining the Continentals. I'll be scouting for Cook's Fort. But I'll come back this way about mid-August."

I cleared my throat. "Please finish your story."

He nodded and looked out at the forest a moment, then sighed. "The two braves we were tracking must have doubled back. When we reached the top of the eastern ridge, Jeb clutched his chest and fell to the sound of gunshots. Then a bullet ripped through my shoulder."

William rubbed his wound. "I dashed into the brush, scrambled to the edge of a sloping cliff, and held my breath as I slid down jagged rocks into the icy river." He sucked in air while I smoothed the prickly sensation from my arms.

"The shock took my breath. I struggled to stay alert. Then the swift current smashed me into a boulder. Somehow, I shoved off and then swam several feet before grabbing tree roots. I clawed my way up the bank and lay still. That's when I heard Jeb's screams." William turned his head away and wiped sweat from his forehead.

I sniffled and rubbed burning tears from my cheeks. Silence hung between us like fog until he cleared his throat.

"When my senses returned, I soldier-crawled through vines and briars until too weak. 'Twas Thomas's whistle that revived me enough to pull to my feet using a large grapevine. I managed a shout and hobbled toward him."

I peered at William. "Why are Indian scouts staying so close instead of clearing out before winter?"

"Most likely they were expecting news from Mr. Jessop." He moaned and eased from the stool onto his good leg. "Time to go confront the man."

I held my chest and gasped. "Not alone. What are you going to do?"

"First, I'll walk you to your da."

"He's gone, surveying." I lifted my bucket.

He grinned and tilted his head toward the yard. "He came in a bit ago. Been watching us ever since."

My jaw dropped. Sure enough, Papa was leaning against the wall of the blacksmith shop. He pushed his hat back and stood up straight as William and I approached.

I faced William. "Please stay safe. I want to see you again."

Papa raised his eyebrows at me and then reached for William's hand. I sighed and continued several steps toward our cabin. My chest hurt. My eyes watered. *No, don't cry.* I turned around and stopped to watch.

They walked toward Mr. Jessop's cabin, motioning for Sam Henderson, who had been standing in the Callaway's yard visiting with Betsy. William talked to him for a moment and then Mr. Henderson dashed off to the Boones' place. My heart pounded as William and Papa hurried to Alexander Jessop's cabin among the sycamore trees. They knocked and stepped inside.

I held my breath. Seconds later, they emerged without Mr. Jessop. Papa's face was drawn up somewhere between worry and anger as Sam Henderson and Daniel Boone arrived.

Has Mr. Jessop lied his way out of a beating again? My head pounded.

A few minutes more, the men shook hands and went separate ways in a rush. Papa came toward me and stopped.

I clutched my throat with my free hand. "What happened?"

"Well, polliwog. Seems you've been exonerated. Mr. Jessop has cleared out unseen. He acted pensive the other day when I told him the McGuire boys were here. No one saw him around yesterday when Mr. Turner was brought in."

My heart raced in my chest. *Was he one of the men that waylaid William and Mr. Turner? What if he's still out there?* I glimpsed William marching straight to the stockyard. I wanted to run after him.

I startled at Papa's touch on my arm.

"Try not to worry. John Connolly will be captured before he can take command of Fort Detroit. Perhaps the Indian tribes will be more agreeable to dissolve their alliances with the British, and life can settle down. I've marked a new claim for us that needs plowed and planted with a good crop of corn in the spring." He smiled and held out his elbow.

I frowned. "Mr. McGuire says things will get worse." I switched the bucket to my other arm and slipped my free one through Papa's. His eyebrows rose, but he didn't refute me.

As we headed toward our cabin, Papa cleared his throat. His face seemed to pale.

"William asked to write to you."

I gulped and stood still, searching Papa's face. "He did? Why?"

He sighed and shook his head. "Seems you've made an impression on the young man."

My belly fluttered at the thought.

"I told him no. You're too young. Besides, you're already in danger for helping us deliver the documents that exposed John Connolly's planned invasion from Fort Detroit. If William's letters were apprehended, loyalists would have an additional reason to capture you to get to me."

A shudder rushed through me as we resumed our walk in silence, but irritation rose. *Damn the loyalists for ruining my chances of courtship with William.*

Momma met me at the door with raised eyebrows and cut-through-you eyes. *The look.* I mustered my most contrite voice. "I'm sorry. I just meant to check on William and come back."

She nodded. "You may go help stitch our new dresses at the Boones' cabin. Katie and Lizzy are already there."

While I gaped, Momma grinned and turned back inside.

She must know that spending the rest of the day enduring Jemima's nosy questions is punishment enough.

Chapter Seven

On the evening of November seventh, Papa and my brothers waited outside while we dressed in our new outfits. I smoothed my tan petticoat and straightened my pink-raspberry bodice one more time, beaming. *I'm going to forget all the bad things that have happened and have fun.* I wrapped my sun-kissed-green neckerchief around my shoulders and tied the strings of my new white bonnet under my chin. Then I smiled at my sisters and Momma. "We look beautiful. Won't everyone be surprised?"

Momma chuckled and nodded. "Yes. Now, carry the food we prepared to the tables. Walk slowly. Don't spill anything on your new clothes. Is everyone ready?"

"Yes, ma'am," we answered in unison.

Sally opened the door to a light crisp breeze that wafted with savory hickory-smoked meats and foods that had roasted and simmered all day. I let the others go out first. My stomach fluttered with one part excitement and one-part nerves as I balanced my sloshing bowl of stew in the dark. *Where is the full moon?* I looked up. Slow-moving clouds blocked it.

Papa grinned. "Are these my daughters? What a beautiful sight. I see I'll be on guard duty all evening against hooligan young men." He chuckled and then glanced between Katie and me. "You may dance with me, your female friends, or George."

Momma shook her head. "No sir. You're my dance partner. Your daughters know how to behave like proper young ladies." She gave Katie and me her, *don't you,* look.

Papa smiled and tipped his hat. "Yes, ma'am."

George slapped his leg. "Can we go now? I'm starving."

Katie and I smirked at each other as we strolled like princesses across the lantern-lighted yard toward the tables.

After we placed our dishes on the long table under the canopy, I whispered in Katie's ear, "Don't act like Sophia in *The Vicar of Wakefield.*"

She bumped me with her elbow. "Pshaw. You either."

We giggled and parted ways, she to her friends and me to find Fanny and Betsy.

A group of men blew harmonicas, and their spirited tune added bounce to my steps. Other men patted pots, slapped metal spoons, and rubbed washboards with wooden blocks. When a black man joined in with a fiddle, whoops rang out from the crowd.

Sam shouted, "Play it, Uncle Zeke," and leapt into a high-stepping jig.

I gasped. *How can that man be Sam's uncle?*

Zeke's smile beamed as he worked the bow and jigged in place. He reminded me of Big Jim, the slave Papa had borrowed back in the spring. I glanced to the side of the tables where other slaves were doing various tasks. They worked while keeping time with the music. An elderly woman smiled up at me, then went back to carving meat as her hips swayed.

I approached her. "Excuse me, ma'am."

The woman startled. "Yes, child?"

"Is the man, Zeke, Sam Henderson's uncle?"

She chuckled. "Why, lordy no, miss. His name be Uncle Zeke. The Hendersons are his owners."

"Oh, I see. Thank you." I curtsied and slunk away, embarrassed by my lack of understanding in these matters. *Surely his momma didn't name him Uncle. Maybe it's a nickname, like Papa calls me polliwog.* I shrugged and weaved through the crowd in search of my friends.

Once in the clear, I stopped and scanned. A sudden touch on my shoulder made me jump.

Fanny stepped in front of me, giggling. "Sorry to startle you. I love that shade of pink. And the bright-green neckerchief is pretty." She leaned to my ear. "Is that the color from those hemp leaves Katie told me about?"

That Katie. "No. I didn't make enough to use and can't make anymore. I cooked Black-Eyed Susan in a cast-iron pot."

Betsy approached, pointing and whispering, "There's Sam. How can I get his attention?"

He had moved to a nearby tree where a group of men stood talking in the candlelight of a hanging lantern. He never looked our way.

"Well, move closer to him, silly." Fanny nudged Betsy. "Maybe he'll ask you to dance."

I giggled.

Betsy's eyes widened. "I don't want to be obvious."

Fanny shook her head and grabbed my hand. "Let's dance, Mary. I don't want to wait to be asked. I've been itching to dance forever."

We skipped into the dancing crowd in time to do-si-do around each other twice, and then held hands, side-hopping through the line of other dancers.

Sam came along beside us, holding his hand out to me. "May I cut in?"

I stepped back, gaping, and then glimpsed at Betsy. She stood nearby pouting with folded arms. Papa's instructions came to mind with relief.

"No. I'm sorry, Sam. My papa won't let me." I curtsied and smiled. "But Betsy is free."

Fanny giggled and took my arm. We promenaded back into the crowd of dancers and watched Sam take Betsy's hand. She grinned at me. Soon, the couple were smiling into each other's eyes. I sighed, remembering William's eyes when he smiled at me. *I wish he was here.*

When a faster-paced fiddling began, someone threw a handful of sand onto a platform made from planed boards and then shuffled around on it while tapping their heels to the music. Others watched and clapped. Soon, people were taking turns and cheering for the best back-stepping moves.

"I want to give it a try, but I better visit the privy first. Do you need to go?"

Fanny shook her head. "Mr. Holder is about to dance. I want to watch him." She grinned.

"I'll be back in a minute." I laughed and headed down the flickering golden path lit by several lanterns that hung from tree branches. My stomach growled. *Time to eat.*

A guard leaned against a nearby tree. He turned his head my direction, smiled, and tipped his hat.

I went inside the smelly, dark privy and latched the door.

A loud moan preceded leaves shuffling outside. Then someone tried to open the door.

Poor soul. "I'm almost finished."

I straightened my petticoat, opened the door, and returned to the fresh air. No one was waiting. *Guess they went to the woods.*

The back of my neck prickled as I stepped forward, then a wide hand clasped my mouth. I couldn't scream—couldn't breathe. I swung my elbow back, but an arm reached around from behind and bound me. I yanked my head sideways toward my captor's fingers, which released my nose. I gagged from the stench of his body odor. I squirmed and tried to stomp on his foot, but the grasp tightened, and I was dragged backward. *Am I to be raped? God, help me. What's happening? Where's the guard?*

I struggled to wriggle free as flickering shadows danced in the settlement to the fading sound of fiddles playing the frog courting song. *Papa, come for me. Is this a nightmare?*

Tears and snot flowed onto my captor's hand as the forest thickened around me and smothered all hope of breaking free. *Why, God?*

We stopped moving. The hand over my mouth lifted, lowered, and fumbled behind my rear. "No!" I sobbed and writhed. "Let me go." Something whisked as if from a sheath. The hand raised with a sharp object against my throat.

Foul breath accompanied a gruff whisper in my ear. "Scream again and I'll kill you." His grip released. "Start walking, daughter of Cage."

Mr. Jessop. I gulped and moved forward. "Why are you doing this? Where are you taking me?"

"I've fetched a good price from the loyalists for your capture. It's your treacherous father they want to hang at Fort Detroit. He is your ransom price. Too bad those rebel dogs didn't believe you. Now no talking." He shoved me into the darkness.

I tripped over a tree root but fell to my belly on purpose and rolled under a bush. *He can't find me in the dark.*

His hand grabbed my braid and pulled.

I screamed and scrambled to my feet, crying.

A sharp blade poked my back. "Try to get away again and I'll cut you."

My eyes and scalp burned, but the desperation to escape intensified. But how? *Time is short. Leave signs.* I untied my neckerchief, eased it off, and pretended to trip while leaving the garment on the ground beside me. A few more steps without Jessop reacting emboldened me to stumble again for good measure. I recovered my balance and continued walking. *Which direction is this?* I pictured the layout of the settlement and remembered what I saw at the moment of ambush. *We're headed northwest.*

The ground sloped downward. I heard sloshing water and muffled voices. Moonlight peeked from the clouds enough for me to see the silhouetted canoe and a horse. Then my blood ran cold at the sight of two men with Mohawked hair and what looked like feathers sticking straight up. *Indians.*

I froze, sucking in deep breaths to keep from blacking out.

Mr. Jessop lifted me off my feet, carried me forward, and swung my body into the canoe with the Indians. "Tell Smith this concludes our deal."

I tried to stand, but he shoved me on my rear. "Behave yourself, Miss Shirley. These Cherokee men won't receive payment if you're harmed."

My stomach churned as I stood and yelled in a raspy voice, "Don't leave me with these Indians." Without looking back, he led a horse away from the riverbank.

The canoe quaked, forcing me to squat and grip the sides. A musty-smelling man held a hunter's knife before my eyes and grunted. "Scream—you die."

My stomach knotted. I gulped and sat, but deep breaths didn't prevent me from heaving bile over the side for several minutes. As the craft sloshed and jostled into a swift current of the Kentucky River, my faith waned. *Where are you, God? How will I get away?* My teeth chattered, and my body trembled from the cold. *Can't go into shock.* I hugged my legs to my chest and lowered my head to cry into my new petticoat.

The Indians paddled with rapid, near-silent swipes that sliced through the water with barely a ripple.

I straightened my back, reminding myself to pay attention so I could find my way back. I stared into the dark sky. Clouds hid the stars. Then I remembered the current behind the Gatliff cabin flowed north to northwest.

I shook away fear and cleared my throat. "Where...are...you...taking me?"

Only crickets answered.

I closed my eyes, picturing the layout of the Boonesborough settlement and the map Papa had left on the table. *I was put in the canoe facing...west. If the current changes to northerly, we'll flow into the Ohio River.* Tears flowed again. I sniffled and took a deep breath. *Does Papa know I'm missing yet? My neckerchief won't be found until morning. Searchers will come. I must be strong.*

I rocked forward and back to relieve the aching in my rear and spine. Grabbing the sides of the canoe, I twisted to the right and then left. Next, I stretched my arms up straight. *They don't seem to mind my movements.* My stomach fluttered as I rolled to my feet in a squat and glanced to the right, watching for an opportunity to leap from the canoe and swim for the bank. The craft tilted left and threw me to my rear. I grabbed the dugout's sides to stop wobbling.

The men paddled harder, and the direction changed. I peered past the man in front of me as a sliver of light revealed a narrow creek. *We're headed east, upstream from the Kentucky.* I concentrated on breathing so I wouldn't bawl. *Can't jump now.* I untied my bonnet and flung it from my head toward what appeared to be a bush on the bank. *Maybe rescuers will see where we left the river.*

The sky disappeared above a thick canopy of tree limbs that creaked and snapped. The shivering stopped and my mind numbed. Night creatures howled and squalled around us, then something large growled from the bank, so near it could have taken a swipe at my arm. I squealed and squeezed my eyes closed.

For hours I fought sleep.

When my head jolted up, an orange glow came from the bank ahead and reflected in the shallow water that sloshed the left side of the canoe. The man in front jumped out. The craft scraped bottom and quaked as the men dragged it onto the bank. I fell against the side. Several shadowy men wearing hunter-style hats emerged from an encampment.

The Indian behind me swooped me into the air and into the arms of one of the hunters.

"She's limp," the hunter shouted, then rushed me to the campfire and laid me on a bedroll.

I couldn't move or keep my eyes open, but as a warm heavy quilt was draped over me, I glimpsed a green-coated man wearing a tri-corner hat. He squatted before me in the firelight.

"Tarnation. Get her some warm broth. Why isn't she dressed warmer? Not even a neckerchief. Hang on, girl. We need you alive."

I moaned and opened my eyes as the man sat me up while someone else held me from behind. Warm, salty broth was spooned into my mouth, but some dribbled down the sides of my chin until I swallowed.

Shivering returned.

"There you go." He smiled. "You're warming up now. Swallow."

I complied and then leaned away from the body holding me up and forced a whisper, "Where am I?"

"Safe." The man in front dipped the spoon in a mug.

Memories of Jessop's conversation came. He had mentioned a man's name. I held my palm toward the raised spoon. "Are you Mr. Smith?"

His eyes widened. "No, miss. He's not here. We're waiting on word from him in the morning. You're safe here. We're loyal subjects of His Majesty King George.

Loyalists. "Who are you, sir?" I studied his oval face with light-colored eyes framed by a short ponytail.

He handed me the mug and lowered his eyes before standing. "Get some sleep now." He gave a nod to the person behind me. "Bring her another blanket." Then he walked toward one of the tents.

I lifted the mug to my lips and finished sipping while scanning the camp. Seemed to be at least a dozen men—most white but at least four Indians. Lean-to shelters and a few canvas tents dotted the area.

One of the other hunters brought over a gray-woolen blanket and wadded an old coat for a pillow.

"Who is that man?" I pointed to the tent.

"I call him Captain." He tipped his hat and walked away.

They don't want me to know. Must be a spy.

I stared at the unattended canoes on the bank, imagining myself paddling in a fury back down the creek. *How far would I get? I don't know how to maneuver a canoe. Wait. The Kentucky River is southeast through those woods.* Thoughts of swimming across the creek and crawling through thick marshy cane and brambles brought back memories. *I did that before and almost died. Now it's cold. I'd be dead by morning.* My eyes burned from hot tears escaping down my face. I glanced up at two men sitting on logs across the fire pit dressed in hunting shirts, trousers, and round brim hats, but wearing soldier-like coats and black boots. They stared, smirking as if knowing my thoughts.

I lay down and turned away, sniffling. *My family knows I'm missing by now. They're worried and crying. Papa's holding Momma, but planning my rescue in the morning.*

Panic sped my heartbeat. *But it's a trap, Papa. They're using me to snare you like a rabbit.* Determination to escape threw off fear. *I've done this before, and I didn't die.* I pushed to my feet and moved toward the bushes, pointing.

One of the men on the log stood, shouldered his rifle, and nodded. He followed, but stayed back.

I shoved through the branches and dropped to my hands and knees, moving my petticoat to the side as I crawled. My turtle pace across moldy, damp leaves made my nose tickle and threatened a sneeze. I squeezed my nostrils between finger and thumb a minute and then continued.

Cold, trembling, and weak from wandering across the forest floor without reason, I collapsed flat and still. Hope seeped from my eyes as tears.

I stood and turned toward the flickering glow of the camp's fire. *What good am I to my family dead?* The ground crunched and creaked under my feet as I returned near the bushes where I entered. *I'll spy and give a report of everything when I'm rescued.* I relieved myself and shoved back through the shrubs, stumbling on a tree root but not falling.

The guard jumped back with raised eyebrows, then he snarled. "I was about to come in there after you, gal. Get some sleep."

"What creek is this?" I sat on my bedroll staring at the man as he now stood alone, warming his hands at the fire.

"Elk—Tarnation. Hush before I whip you." He picked up a stick and shook it at me.

I smiled and wrapped up in the quilt before stretching out. *Elkhorn Creek is on Papa's map. One day back to my family.*

Chapter Eight

"Wake now." A gruff voice near my ear startled me.

"Where am I?" I squinted and then gasped at the man squatted beside my head staring at me with pecan-shell eyes. My heart pounded as I gripped my blanket tighter, wanting to scream, but couldn't.

He's not one of the Indians from last night. His lips were black, and his flared nostrils held a silver hoop. Three diagonal yellow lines streaked across his copper cheeks.

Dangling from his elongated earlobes were large circular silver earrings with an intricate star engraved in the center. A crown of black hair adorned with spikes of porcupine quills, coarse deer hair, and three long reddish-brown feathers topped his otherwise shaved head.

Bile rose in my throat as he lifted me to my feet. "Come eat. Long day."

I'm still at the loyalist camp. Day after the dance. November eighth. I need a way to remember dates.

I swallowed and scanned the camp for the captain. Frowned. My teeth chattered from the cold. I adjusted the blanket around my shoulders and squirmed. "I need to relieve myself."

"Go here." The man held on to my wrist and gave a nod to the ground.

Horrified by the notion, I glared into his blank eyes. "Standing? In front of everyone?"

He didn't respond.

I shook my head and folded my arms. "I can't go standing. I won't."

"Spread legs. Squat." He turned his head toward the group of white men, revealing a tattoo of a turtle on the back of his neck.

"I'm going to the bushes." I jerked my arm away from his grip and turned toward a crop of shrubs.

His long arm came toward me before I could flee. He clutched my wrist and pulled me toward the captain. The turtle man released me and took a plate of meat from the table.

"Miss Shirley." The captain's tone bellowed. "You won't have the luxury of privacy or cleanliness for the next several days. You are a rebel prisoner."

I held my belly as if he'd punched me. "Why are you being harsh?"

He narrowed his eyes and remained curt. "I suggest you learn to relieve yourself in whatever position you are in. You will lose all daintiness before your journey ends. These Shawnee men will take you to a British outpost on the Ohio River to await an exchange."

His words exploded like cannon fire in my head. I fell to my knees begging, "Why? Why can't I...please let me stay here?"

The captain lumbered backward, frowning. His tone calmed, but stayed firm. "Word is being sent to your traitorous father. He must surrender to Captain Hamilton at Fort Detroit by the end of December, or officials will sell you to the Shawnee. Nothing I can do about it. You have to leave with these men."

I stood, trembling and crying. *I must get away.* "Please, sir...allow me to relieve myself in the bushes one last time."

"Go stand over there." He pointed to an empty corner of the camp a few feet away. "Turn away from us and relieve yourself. Not going to coddle you any more than that."

I staggered to the corner and faced the shrubs, scanning for the best escape route, now that I could see. *I still have no idea.* I sighed. *And I'll be caught within seconds. Too many men.* I reached under my petticoat and untied my undergarment, then let it fall to my feet. I moved it out of the way with my foot before squatting. My face burned as urine streamed downhill beside me. I heard snickers from the men. *Humiliating.* I stared at my undergarment before putting it in my apron pocket. *Less trouble for later.*

I stood and straightened my back, ignoring the men's gawks while making my way back to the captain.

The guard from last night handed me a plate with fried bread made with coarse ground corn and a charred fish. "You'll be all right, gal. Don't fear these men. They're loyal allies." He helped me sit on a stump.

"Thank you." I wasn't hungry, but needed to stay strong. *Don't know when I'll get to eat again. Must survive and get back home.* I imagined myself around a table with my family as I ate the bread and fish. *Wish I could let them know I'm alive.* I blinked away tears.

"We go." The turtle man came beside me, took my plate, and waved to three other Indians before pulling me to my feet.

I huffed at his rudeness. "I still need water."

One of the white men brought me a mug of black coffee, which did little to quench my thirst.

The Indian men circled me, waiting. The younger one wore his long hair loose, with a large, black-tipped white feather attached to a red-and-yellow beaded headband. He had a black stripe across his nose and cheeks with red streaks going down. The whites of a solid-black painted man's eyes appeared more fierce when he glared at me. The other brave wore a red brimless cap adorned at the crown with hand-sized brown-and-white feathers.

They all wore fringed buckskin hunting shirts and pants with black breechcloths on the outside. Each breechcloth had a row of round silver brooches along the edge. Turtle man also wore a silver necklace with a large round medallion of a turtle with a circular shell. He seemed to be the one in charge.

When he gave me a shove toward the others, I glanced at each white man in the camp. "Please don't let them take me away. Keep me here. I won't try to flee. Please."

The captain shook his head and walked toward me with a gray woolen coat. "You'll be safer with these men, miss. Winter is coming soon, and the fort cabins are warm." He draped the musty smelling coat around my shoulders. "Wear this so you don't freeze to death before you get there."

I sniffled. "What's the fort called? How far away?" I shuddered and slid my arms into the oversized garment that hung past my knees. Its warmth reminded me of Papa's hugs. I closed my eyes, imagining him but needing it to be real. *Papa, come for me.*

"Never you mind the details, missy. Mind these men." The captain stepped away.

"Come, chattering squirrel." The turtle man's hand latched on to my sleeve. "Much walk." He pulled me toward a trail leading away from the creek.

My stomach knotted as I wiped my face. *Be strong.* "Why aren't we taking the canoe to the Ohio River?"

"No talk." He quickened the pace.

Anger rose. *How am I going to know how to get home if we don't go back to the Kentucky River?* I peered at the red-tinted clouds in the sky ahead of us and to the right. *Still northeast. Day after the dance.*

Turtle Man stayed behind me, prodding me forward if I slowed. With one of his shoves, I tripped over a tree root and tumbled to the ground. "Ouch." I rubbed my banged toe. "Stop pushing me." I sat up thankful for the extra cushion from the coat that protected my arms. He lifted me up and out of the way while he righted the overturned rocks and smoothed the ground debris.

In a rage, I ran to a shrub, stripped off a handful of leaves, and tossed them into the air. "Try putting those back in place." I scuffed the heel of my moccasin across the ground for good measure.

The black-painted man rushed toward me with a raised tomahawk. I screamed and cowered, holding my head.

Turtle Man shouted, *"Mah-tah."*

Painted Man shoved me onto my side with his foot and then stormed away. I panted and lay still, regretting my outburst and fearing my fate.

Turtle Man lifted me to my feet and then slapped my face.

"Augh," I fell to my knees, holding my jaw and sobbing as it popped back into place. "I'm sorry. I'm sorry." I bent forward, trembling from the shock and throbbing pain.

"Nee-pah-wee-loh." His voice growled. "Stand up. No more cry."

Heaving breaths, I eased to my feet, hiding my face with my forearms.

Turtle Man parted my hands, lifted my chin, and glared into my eyes. *"Mah-tah."* He shook his head. "No more stubborn. Storm is coming." He pointed to the blackening clouds overhead and turned me toward the others, who were well ahead. "Go." He pushed me forward.

I sniffled and concentrated on each step as wrenching pain in my head overtook my body. My legs trembled, and my tongue felt wrapped in a bandage. *I need water, willow bark tea, and rest.*

The sky crackled over the ridge ahead of us. We veered off the trail.

Storm? Not now, God. I can't take any more trials. I willed myself to move faster, sensing Turtle Man about to push me again.

Lightning exploded in the sky. Rain pelted my face as we sprinted toward a rocky ledge and into a small, hidden cave. I rushed to the back corner and sat, huddling my legs to my chest, still sniffling. I wanted to lie down and sleep forever. *I'm not strong. Can't do this.*

Papa's voice in my head whispered, *"Come home."* I pulled the coat tighter, imagining his hug. *How?*

"You. Chattering squirrel—come drink."

I raised my head, glaring. *Why does he keep calling me a chattering squirrel?*

Turtle Man motioned me to a cane trough stuck in the clay wall behind us. Water flowed into his large half-folded hickory leaf and into his mouth. The men were taking turns slurping. *A spring?*

I stood, steadied myself, and crept over. "Mary. My name is Mary."

Turtle Man shrugged and handed me a fresh leaf. I folded it and guzzled the cold water until someone bumped me out of the way. I rubbed my wet hands over my sore jaw and waited for another turn.

The men ambled back toward the opening. They removed jerky from their bags but didn't offer me any.

I sighed. *Now I have to relieve myself.*

I moved to the entrance and looked at Turtle Man, tilting my head toward the nearest tree. He squinted at me, nodded, and then turned back. The men continued to converse in their language, which sounded like the same syllables rapidly repeated but in different combinations. I couldn't distinguish individual words.

I eased away, squatted in the downpour, then stood there, weighing the risks of running. *If I make it back to the creek, how will I make it past the loyalists' camp?*

The men's laughter drew my attention. They were watching me.

Turtle Man patted his chest. "Hiding Turtle." He pointed to the blacken tomahawk man. "Dancing Panther." The younger man was Loud Hawk, and the last named was Red Sparrow.

"I'm Mary."

He laughed and then shook his head. "No white name. No more, Chattering Squirrel. Now you, Stands in Rain." He rattled off something in Shawnee, which made them all laugh again.

I moved back under the shelter, shaking my head. "If I can't be Mary, then call me Daughter of Cage."

Hiding Turtle's head jerked back, and his gaze turned serious.

Does he recognize Papa's spy name? Have I made matters worse?

I slunk to my corner and sat cross-legged, rocking myself. *Where's the rescue party? This storm is washing our footprints away. Now what?* My sight fell on a sharp rock protruding from the wall beside me. *I'll cut small pieces of cloth from my chemise and drop them along the path when they're not looking.*

Except for an occasional glance, the men ignored me fiddling with my hem. By the time the storm ended in an hour or so, my coat pocket bulged with shreds of white cloth.

A circle of bright-blue sky broke through parting clouds, and I gasped with a revelation. *Hope is knowing the sky is still a brilliant blue above the ugliest storm clouds. All I have to do is be patient and wait for it.* Momma's smiling face appeared in my mind as if she agreed. *Is that why you always say, "It all comes out in the wash"? Thank you, Momma. I'll try to trust God more.*

"Stands in Rain. Come." Hiding Turtle motioned with his hand.

Guess I'm stuck with that name. I smoothed my bulky pocket before standing and took a deep breath before resuming the grueling march. *Hopefully, we'll make it to the British outpost before dark.*

I made sure Hiding Turtle didn't have to push me anymore, but I wished he'd stop watching me so close. After a while, I built up the courage to wet my fingers, reach into my pocket, and roll a small piece of cloth into a wad. My hand sweated as I held on to the ball. A painful yawn renewed the fear of being slapped again.

When I saw a large body of water ahead of us, my heart raced. I paused and faced Hiding Turtle. "What is this river?"

He stared past me. "No talk."

I tossed the scrap of cloth behind his foot and then stared up at the blending shades of pale blue and gray in the sky. *I'm losing hope again, God.*

Hiding Turtle nudged me toward the river. I gasped at its turbulent current. *Surely, we're not getting in with that thrashing monster.* The biblical Leviathan came to mind. Large tree branches swirled past, and some flipped into the air.

Turtle tugged on my coat. We stopped shy of the men raising two gray, hatchet-scarred canoes from the river and onto the bank, where they drained the water. *Sneaky way to hide them.* The dugouts were the length of two men. The width stretched from my left elbow across my chest to my right elbow.

"Relieve self here." He pointed to the ground, but his gaze never left the scene ahead.

I sighed and squatted. The on-demand urination came easier. I dropped another piece of chemise and returned to his side, studying his face for any sign he'd changed our course.

"Come." He quickened the pace to the flooded bank.

Dancing Panther and Loud Hawk were waiting to shove off in one canoe, and Red Sparrow motioned for me to sit behind him in the other.

My body stiffened with fear, and sorrow crushed my chest. *I'm about to drift farther from my family; I might drown.* Tears fell. *They'll never know a wild river swallowed me whole.* I stepped into the long dugout, crossing my legs to sit in the middle, and gripped the sides. *Here I am, God. Can you take me now?*

Hiding Turtle pushed the craft from behind until we splashed into the boiling cauldron. My chest pounded as the canoe pitched from side to side and up and down. Hiding Turtle sat and paddled fast into the fray, maneuvering into the main current. Red Sparrow focused on the course ahead and only used his paddle to slow our speed or shove debris away. I supposed Hiding Turtle was steering somehow, but I squeezed my eyes closed and concentrated on balancing and breathing. It wasn't until sometime later that I realized our northerly course. *Maybe this river flows into the Ohio.*

Remaining seated and silent, hour after hour, in the damp rough-bottomed canoe would have caused madness if not for the calming effect of billowing white clouds. They were blowing across the blue backdrop, headed toward my family. I hoped a multitude of angels were in them and would give Papa my location.

I also watched trees along both sides of the river shed their brassy leaves in shades of copper and bronze. The river was murky with them, yet the men continued to maneuver around treacherous logs and rocks until the sky became streaked with dark shades of orange and red.

My stomach grumbled in protest from having had nothing to eat since breakfast. The rocking rhythm of the canoe made me dizzy. I rested my head on my knees. When the craft changed to a westerly direction, I raise my head. The men paddled the canoe into the fiery sunset. We had entered the largest river I'd ever seen. *Has to be the Ohio. But where is the Kentucky River from here?*

I sat up and scanned the south banks, watching for notable landmarks. On Papa's map the Ohio River was shown to make a southerly bend a few miles before the Kentucky joined. *The British outpost must be somewhere before that. Once there, I'll know which way home is.*

Red Sparrow bumped my arm and handed me a wooden canteen like the one Papa had. I swigged the dirt-tasting water until the man grunted and took the water back. He handed me a piece of jerky and went back to watching the current.

I continued observing the landscape as I bit down on the jerky. Sharp pain shot from my jaw to my head, and my eyes watered. I sucked on the meat instead and swallowed the tangy juice, not sure of the animal source, but it wasn't venison, beef, or bear.

When the river veered northerly, excitement fluttered in my belly. "Will we be at the outpost soon?" I choked on meat juice.

"No talk," Hiding Turtle said. "Be still."

I tilted my head back and huffed. *Your name should be No Talk.*

As darkness swallowed all but a thin sliver of golden horizon, the men maneuvered the craft onto the muddy north bank. Red Sparrow jumped out and pulled us ashore.

I stood, patting the numbness from my rear, and moved several steps. Then I noticed that the men weren't making a fire or shelters. Instead, they were catching and eating night crawling beetles that popped and crunched and turned my stomach. I covered my ears and moved away. *I'll forage in the morning. Maybe find a few acorns. If Jesus could go forty days without food and water, I can make it a few more*

I sighed and raked a pile of leaves with my foot to make a bed. In the pale glow of the rising moon, I saw a large white grub and smiled. *Better than beetles.* I brushed it off and worked up a mouthful of saliva before swallowing it whole. *Maybe we'll make it to the fort tomorrow. I prefer to be rescued, God. Help me stay strong.* I lay still on the ground, but my head continued sloshing as if in the canoe. I yawned as the forest sounds faded. *I want to go home.* I sniffled and tried to pretend I'd wake from this bad dream in the morning.

Chapter Nine

Something bumped my shoulder. I jerked awake, staring into the face of Hiding Turtle.

"*Hah-skwah-lay-way*? Hungry?" His deep voice startled me.

I sat up disoriented and shivering from the cold. A light dusting of snow covered my blanket.

He pointed to Loud Hawk and Red Sparrow, who were at the creek bank. Loud Hawk held an arrow with several skewered fish. Red Sparrow lay on the ground, dangling over the bank. He skimmed the water, then plunged his hands in and tossed a largemouth bass onto the ground. Loud Hawk rushed to stab it.

"Stands in Rain. *We-thin-ee-koh*. We eat." Hiding Turtle motioned for me to follow him. "*Nah-meh-thah*. Fish. *We-kah-no*. Good eat."

I stood and glanced around. "Where's the fire?"

"Mah-tah." He shook his head, then took a fish and slit it open with a hunting knife.

After removing the entrails, bones, and skin, he rinsed it in the river and bit off a hunk of raw white meat. Juice spilled from the side of his mouth. The other men were doing the same.

Hiding Turtle gutted another fish and handed it to me. My stomach grumbled as I held the bass. *Papa and George got sick from eating raw fish. That's why I had to deliver his dispatch. That's why I'm in this mess.* I shook my head and tried the word that seemed to mean no. *"Mah-tah."*

He forced my hand up toward my mouth. "Good eat. Trust."

I've never liked fasting. I sighed, then sank my teeth in the tender, moist meat that tasted like mud. Each bite renewed my strength and resolution. *I'll escape from the British outpost as soon as I can.*

"We go." Hiding Turtle handed me the canteen for a drink.

After handing it back, I moved away for privacy. Hiding Turtle watched me with one eye. I left a piece of cloth and slipped a small stick into the coat pocket before standing.

Once seated in the canoe, Hiding Turtle shoved away from the bank. I waited until the men focused on navigation before I eased the stick out and peeled off the bark. With the sharp rock, I cut three notches. *Captured the evening of November seventh, today is the tenth. Where is my rescue party? I left plenty of clues.*

The course was calmer, but still swift. I watched the scenery for unusual trees, rocky cliffs, and shallows on the banks. The men didn't slow down. I had to urinate in the canoe where I sat—thankfully, enough river water sloshed into the craft to dilute the yellow tint. As sunlight slipped over the treetops, I worried. *How much farther? There haven't been signs of settlement.*

I glanced ahead as the canoe with Black Panther and Loud Hawk veered left. They waved and continued down the south flow of the Ohio River. Hiding Turtle and Red Sparrow nodded and paddled fast up a north-flowing river. *They're not taking me to the outpost.*

I screamed, "Where are you taking me?" My heart beat like a war drum. I glared at Hiding Turtle. "Take me to the British. I insist."

Hiding Turtle's face was stoic and unyielding as he paddled faster.

That's it. I'm going. I didn't care what would happen. Desperation drove me. I slipped off the coat, sucked in a deep breath, and dove over the side. The cold water sucked away my breath. I surfaced, coughing and gasping. My arms flailed as the weight of my petticoat prevented kicking to swim. *I don't want to die.* I rolled to my back, squinting at the bluest sky as my body floated in peace back down this river toward the Ohio. *Nothing I can do now. Maybe my carcass will be found and given a proper burial. God save me.*

Hiding Turtle's face appeared over me, with his arm holding out the paddle. "Live." I grabbed it, relieved, and he pulled me back into the canoe. My teeth chattered as Red Sparrow wrapped the coat over my shoulders. I slipped my arms in and pulled it tight, shivering and crying.

Hiding Turtle glared, then reached toward my face. I sniffled and closed my eyes, bracing for a slap. He squeezed my chin and gruffed. "See me."

I peeked at his stern face.

"No good to die. Be still." He sat back, tossed me another blanket, and resumed paddling fast.

Another foolish choice. My family wants me alive. But I'm angry. Where are they taking me? I sniffled, then cried into the blanket, stifling most of the sound. I stayed wrapped up and contrite.

I shivered long into the afternoon when my clothes went from soggy to damp. The heat of the sun warmed my face. When it finally reached my bones, I removed the blankets so they could dry. Then I slipped out of the coat and pulled the sleeves through. I laid the outside of the coat on my lap so the inside could dry and not sour. The men had been silent all day. *Is it because they almost lost me, or are we in a dangerous location?* I turned to Hiding Turtle, whispering, "I'm sorry."

He raised his chin with a grunt.

Not long after his grunt, my captors paddled into thick river cane. Red Sparrow climbed out and pulled the canoe while Hiding Turtle leapt into the water and pushed from behind. I remained seated and held the sides as the craft screeched through the sharp-edged cane that slapped my face. I whimpered and raised my arms to absorb the blows and slashes. The canoe stopped, and Hiding Turtle spoke to Red Sparrow, who grabbed an armful of supplies and my coat from the craft before leading the way through the tangle.

Hiding Turtle pointed to the bank. "Out. Walk."

I trudged through thick vines and brambles, wiping blood from my scrapes. When we came to a cleared space, I stopped. Hiding Turtle shoved me forward. I huffed, but steadied myself. *Is he still mad about my swim?*

Thorns snagged and ripped my petticoat. As we came to a clearing, Hiding Turtle grabbed my arm and pulled me to a semi-flat spot away from where Red Sparrow placed the supplies.

"I need my coat." Fear and confusion knotted my stomach. I glanced at Hiding Turtle's stone face and gulped. *He's still mad.*

"Sit." He pointed to the ground and moved behind me, holding my shoulders as Red Sparrow arrived. He placed a large river stone, a foot-long stake, and a length of rope by my feet.

Oh no. "No. Please forgive me. I won't try to escape again."

Without expression, Red Sparrow grabbed my ankles and wound the rope around them.

I cried as Hiding Turtle pulled my shoulders backward, laying me flat. "Please don't stake me down like an animal. I'm cold."

He tied my hands over my head while Sparrow hammered the stake, holding my ankles, into the ground. The river stone flew over my head, followed by another stake.

Snot and tears drained into my ears as Hiding Turtle hammered. Pain pulsed from my low back, across my shoulders, and up my arms to my hands. I watched them stroll back toward the canoe, laughing and talking. They drank from the canteen and ate fish. I sobbed, lamenting the loss of freedom and my coat. The frigid ground soon sent my body into terrible shaking and excruciating pain. Red Sparrow covered me with a blanket from my neck to my feet, then Hiding Turtle topped my torso with the coat.

My teeth chattered. "Please. Let...me...up...now."

They walked away.

Throughout the long, cold night, I shivered and cried to God. "Save me. Send Papa to rescue me." I sniffled and watched the starry sky twinkle above creaky bare tree branches. I shuddered as unseen things crawled around and over me. All I could do was reflect on the swift, harsh consequences of my escape attempt. My focus changed from escaping to staying alive. *I want to see my family again.*

Chapter Ten

The sensation of falling woke me as my hands and feet were released. Faint yellow shades in the sky glowed in the predawn grays, but I couldn't move.

"We go now." Hiding Turtle lifted my stiff body and stood me on my feet. He offered the canteen. My hands and arms trembled as I drank and gave it back to him. My whispered, "Thank you," came out hoarse.

Red Sparrow draped the coat over my shoulders and gathered the blanket.

They strolled toward the canoe, and I followed on wobbly legs. I eased over the side of the craft and plopped down. Red Sparrow handed me a raw fish.

"Thank you. I'm starving." I gulped it down as the men shoved the canoe away from the cane break and climbed in. Before they started paddling, I licked my fingers and sighed. I stretched my arms downward, rolled my shoulders, and then rocked my hips to loosen my spine. *I'll be extra quiet and compliant today. Maybe they won't tie me down tonight.* I scratched a fourth notch on my stick and shoved it into the coat's pocket. *November eleventh.*

The rest of the morning, I watched birds and squirrels dart around on the banks while I noted anything that stood out as a marker. *Just in case I'm able to get away someday.*

Late that afternoon, we made an easterly turn up a narrower river with large overhanging sycamore and cottonwood branches. Wafts of oak-scented smoke hinted at a settlement. My heart sped. *The outpost?*

As we rounded a bend, dogs barked, and voices rang out in the same language of the men. I grasped my throat. *Not British. Indian. What am I going to do now?*

At least a hundred buckskin-clad men, women, and children gathered on a sandbank north of the river, staring with large black-slate eyes. I couldn't breathe. My skin pricked. *This is worse than being staked down. God, I'm scared. Help me.* My head pounded.

The canoe jarred, and two Indian men pulled us ashore. Angry shouts rang out behind a parting crowd, and a towering, broad-shouldered man stomped toward us, waving a feather fan in his left hand and a club in his right. I grabbed the sides of the canoe to keep from passing out. I thought my heart would burst. Tears streamed down my face.

Atop the man's loose black hair sat a capful of splaying red, brown, and gold shimmering turkey feathers that bounced as he walked. His stern face was ridged and dark bronze like sunbaked clay. His long, sharp nose flared under wild, glaring dark eyes as he screamed words at us.

I froze, but Hiding Turtle pulled my arm. "Up. We stay here."

"How long?" My feet wouldn't move. Hiding Turtle peered into my eyes. "Come."

He took my arm and lurched out of the canoe with me stumbling out behind him. He released me and spoke in a calm voice to the fuming man.

The turkey-feathered man turned to a gathering crowd, conveying something that caused them to rush forward and encircle me.

I jumped back, closing my eyes and raising my arms over my face as spittle hit me from all directions. I cried and wanted to run, but my legs wobbled. My breaths heaved as I feared they would kill me. *God, why allow me to live just to die in an Indian village?*

Hiding Turtle moved between me and the people. He raised his hands. *"Hah-kah-way-tah-wee-loh. Kol-lah-chee."*

Whatever he said made the spitting stop, but the people hissed as they backed away. A few women moved closer and stared at me, but most returned to cooking, tanning hides, salting fish, and tending to children. I wanted to sit but didn't dare move.

Hiding Turtle and Red Sparrow grabbed my arms and lifted me like a rag doll, then carried me farther north into the village. We passed many round huts made of branches and thatched roofs. It was like a bad dream in a strange world. *When am I going to wake up in Momma's soothing arms?*

We stopped in a central yard in front of a long east-to-west-facing log structure where many men rallied, shouting all at once like angry crows. The turkey man dashed into the middle, but now the upper half of his face was painted white and the lower half black. He turned toward me, snarling like something wild and evil. I leaned closer to Hiding Turtle, but he nudged me back into place.

When the turkey man rushed at me, I jerked my arms free and flailed, attempting to flee. Hiding Turtle and Red Sparrow subdued my rage and made me face the devil-like man as I panted. He stopped a few steps back and stomped his foot, flinging dirt into my face while chanting and shaking a gourd with dangling feathers. I scuffed my heel, kicking dirt back, and spat. He glared and circled toward a seated older man who was dressed like Hiding Turtle but with more black-and-white-striped feathers dangling from the cap atop his long, white-streaked hair.

Hiding Turtle whispered, "Be still now."

I had no intention of being still. I growled, "Let. Me. Go," and wiggled my shoulders.

"Stay quiet." His tone rose. "Piqua village. Good place."

A good place? I seethed and jerked my gaze to his dangling earring, wanting to rip it out with my teeth.

Murmuring and shuffling drew my eyes to the parting crowd as a white man dressed in buckskin and a round black hat hobbled from the circle. A two-inch-long scar marred his left cheek. He glared at me with familiar dark-brown eyes. My eyes fell to the wooden stake where his left leg should be.

Isaiah Brown! I gasped and clenched my fist as he limped closer. *Oh, God. This isn't good. Why is he here? William thought he'd gone to Fort Pitt.* My knees buckled, but Hiding Turtle and Red Sparrow held me up.

"Don't let him take me. Please." I spoke fast and raspy. "He'll hurt me. I'm the one who shot his knee. But I had to get away from him. Please."

The Indian men resumed shouting at one another from the lodge. Hiding Turtle held my arm tighter. "Chief will say."

My stomach churned as Isaiah shuffled in front of me, grinning with tobacco-stained teeth. "Remember me, girlie? I'm buyin' you. These Injuns ain't dumb. They know ol' Jessop was paid fifty pounds sterlin'. The loyalists want to trade you for your papa. They want to hang him right bad." He spit tobacco juice on the ground by my foot.

I moved a step forward, raising my fists again, but was restrained by Hiding Turtle and Red Sparrow.

"You cost me a leg and my livelihood. I'm tradin' rifles and barrels of gunpowder for you. I'll take my pleasures for a while, then sell you to loyalists for a hundred pounds sterlin'." He scanned my body and sneered.

I shot arrows into his eyes. "And I'll find a way to kill you."

He raised an open hand and lunged for my face, but Hiding Turtle bumped him backward. Isaiah stumbled, lost his leg, and bounced on his rear, cursing.

People laughed and pointed. I stood taller and forced breath through pursed lips as Isaiah retrieved his wooden leg. A few men helped him up.

I flinched when a woman's gritty voice boomed in Shawnee behind me. A crowd of people gathered in a circle. Her fringed leather skirt swished around her ankles as she passed me and stopped before the men. Her white-streaked black braids were wrapped at the ends with yellow strips of cloth. When she held up a large, black-tipped feather, the seated man stood straight and waved her forward. She moved two steps closer to the man, who must have been a chief, then stopped. She spoke fast and pointed a gnarled index finger at me. Then I recognized the creased face of Whispering Leaf, the half-Shawnee woman from Crab Orchard settlement. *She told me to call her Whisper.*

I wanted to run into her arms. *She was friendly at the fort. Maybe she can speak for me and prevent Isaiah from taking me.*

I lunged forward, but again Hiding Turtle yanked me back. "Be still."

Isaiah hobbled to the chief, spewing, "This woman has nothing to trade. I want the girl." He patted his chest and pointed toward the supply mules. "I have guns and powder."

The chiefly man shook his head and left Isaiah and Whisper to speak with the Indian men who encircled him.

"What's happening?" I peered at Hiding Turtle.

He held a finger to his lips.

One of the Indian boys jogged in front of Hiding Turtle, speaking in their language.

Hiding Turtle glared into my eyes. "You stay. Be still."

His serious tone implied obedience could determine the outcome of my future. He entered the chief's circle. I struggled to be still but needed to relieve myself and wanted to throw up.

The circle opened, and I held my breath. *Something has been decided.* I looked for a reassuring glance from Whisper, but she frowned and watched the stately mannered chief. He spoke to the turkey man, who immediately screeched and danced around, waving his gourd.

The hairs prickled on the back of my neck, and urine trickled down my leg. Bile rose, which I then spewed onto the ground.

As drums beat, women and children gathered into two lines, facing each other from south to north and cackling like hens. They shook spikey clubs, sticks, and strips of leather with jagged stones or bones attached. Whisper stood beside Isaiah, wiping her tears from her cheeks.

I turned to Hiding Turtle and shuddered as he came toward me with drooping eyes, clenching his jaw. He placed his hand on my shoulder. "Daughter of Cage. *Oui-shi-cat-to-oui.*"

I recognized the words of the Shawnee Chief Cornstalk from the story Papa told us. It meant be strong, like in the Bible story of Joshua. *Something bad is coming.* I held my belly, as he and Red Sparrow abandoned me and went back to the chief.

I glanced back at the canoes, seconds from bolting, seconds from death, but a group of women surged toward me. I gasped and turned from them, crouching. They rushed as one, grabbing, pulling, and shoving. I writhed and shoved their hands away. A woman clawed me as she removed my coat. Others tore off my beautiful raspberry blouse.

"No. Stop." Rage boiled over. I kicked, pushed, and slapped, but to no avail.

Someone bit my arm as my petticoat dropped to the ground, and someone pulled it away. I shivered from the cold as I stood in my see-through chemise. My face burned with shame as I crossed my arms to hide my breasts. Someone tossed my clothes in the fire pit but kept the coat.

Something sharp prodded my back, forcing me toward the south end of the angry-faced rows of people. A young woman with large brown eyes stopped and steadied me before spitting in my face. Then she joined the others.

The chief motioned for Whisper and nodded.

She stepped in front of me with glistening brown eyes like dew on the forest floor. Her gravelly voice spoke broken English. "You must run through people. If you fall...you go with man." She pointed to Isaiah. She took my hand in her warm, leathery one. "Run fast...make it through...you stay." She raised her free hand and patted her chest before stepping away.

I nodded, gulped, and prayed—understanding the full consequences if I failed. A shiver ran down my spine. *Don't fall.*

The chief stood near the log lodge at the north end of the line, raising a pole with feathers on the end. When he lowered his arm, a man struck one beat on a large drum. The people shouted and shook their weapons. My stomach churned.

Slow, steady drumbeats thumped as a shove sent me stumbling forward. Something large and hard struck the bone in my shoulder, knocking me off balance. I screamed. Searing pain threatened to send me to the ground. I cried out, "Stop. Please stop."

The whipping intensified with my screams as leather straps ripped flesh off my back.

If I don't run, I'll die. I gritted my teeth and dashed forward, but stings, cuts, and bone-crushing blows continued. I cried and held my arms up to guard my face. Blood dripped from my forearms. Another club struck my back and sent me stumbling. I screamed. A moccasined foot's timely shove righted me. I concentrated on my unsteady steps. Strength waned. I spun in a circle, dizzy. My mind seemed out of my body. I saw my family in front of me. George shouted, "Be strong." Momma held out her arms, whispering, "Run to me."

When I passed the last person, the drumbeats stopped. I gasped and wiped my face. My legs tottered. I bent forward, holding my knees to keep from falling, but my body sank to the ground, shaking from my sobs.

Hiding Turtle lifted me into the air and carried me away from the people. He stopped in front of a small hut and lowered me to my feet in front of Whisper.

I shivered and saw Momma's face before me. Then Whisper came into focus. She held my face and grinned into my eyes with missing teeth and foul breath. "You are safe now. Come inside. I take care of you."

My throat burned as I spoke, and the world swayed. "I didn't fall? I'm alive?"

She hunched through a short doorway and helped me bend to enter. I stumbled forward and landed on my face, trembling and bawling.

Whisper rolled me to a pallet on the ground. "Lie here. You won Kokumthena's blessing. She will protect you here."

I continued to cry and didn't understand what she said. I wanted Momma.

Whisper held a peeled willow stick in front of my mouth. "Bite this for pain."

My teeth clamped down with groans as she cut and peeled my chemise along with flesh from the wounds on my back. I squeezed my eyes closed as she dabbed on a warm salve that soothed the pain. The sage aroma reminded me of Letitia. Whisper removed the stick from my mouth, and my teeth started chattering.

She covered my legs and rear with a scratchy wool blanket. "You made pretty blouse with Bedstraw roots. You help make dye."

I sniffled, remembering my beautiful raspberry blouse being ripped from my body.

Whisper went to a small fire pit in the center of the hut and added a log. Heat from the fire soothed my trembling but not the trauma replaying in my mind. I couldn't stop sniveling. *How am I alive?*

Whisper sat cross-legged beside me, stroking my temples. "Rest now. You're safe with me. No more harm. The forked-tongued Isaiah man must leave village. Our Grandmother Spirit, Kokumthena, will bring healing to your wounds."

I closed my eyes but couldn't sleep. Images of the beating repeated with angry faces and excruciating pain. I kicked and rolled from one side to the other, moaning.

In a few minutes, I heard the soft shaking of a gourd and Shawnee words being chanted. Something soft stroked my back and made me shiver. I opened my eyes to see the turkey man squatted beside my face with a bundle of smoking weeds and a kinder manner as he waved his feather fan over me.

"No. Go away." I gasped and then held my breath and turned away from him. "What's he doing to me?"

Whisper stroked my temples. "No harm. Rest."

I know this scent—hemp. The smoke made me dizzy, then sleepy and calm. "Please take me home."

Chapter Eleven

Sweet dreams of my family scurrying around the cabin in noisy chatter were interrupted by a throbbing headache and the reality of my situation. I needed to hear Momma say, "Everything will come out in the wash." *But how can it? I'm trapped in a nightmare, abandoned by God, bruised and terrified of my captors, except for Whisper.*

I groaned and pushed up, thankful I could sit on my buffalo fur without having gooey salve smeared on my back and forearms. *I've been here six days now.* I wiped my eyes, then glanced around the small dimly lighted hut for Whisper. But I was alone. I hadn't been out of the hut while recovering from my wounds. Having lost the stick I'd notched when stripped of my clothes, I found a scrap of discarded deerskin in Whisper's hut. I pulled the soft skin out from under the straw-mat that protected my furry pallet and scratched an eleventh mark with my fingernail. *November seventeenth. Eleven days since the night of my capture. Did my clues blow away?*

Wind gusts made the bent sapling walls and roof screech and creak, but the structure was tightly weaved and tied together with vines and river cane. The hut maintained its cozy warmth despite a small opening in the roof, where smoke from a small fire pit swirled upward and out. Sweet spicy aromas of garlic, onions, flowers, and a variety of dried roots and plants hung along the stick-framed walls and calmed my spirit.

I pulled a gray wool blanket around my shoulders, then lifted a clay mug to my lips and sipped on willow bark tea. Whisper had been leaving the soothing drink each morning before going out.

Bright light flashed as a flap covering the short doorway lifted. Whisper hunched inside and then stood, peering at me with sagging dark-brown eyes and a smile that lacked a few teeth. "Do you feel good?"

"Nee-wee-see-lah-seh-mom-moh." I spoke the "I'm feeling well" Shawnee greeting she'd taught me followed by "How are you?"

"I'm feeling well," she responded in English, then placed a bundle of deerskins on a small tree-trunk table near the fire.

I couldn't tell if she was as old as she appeared or haggard from a hard life. I remembered her prostitute status at the Crab Orchard settlement. She had been sold as a girl to a white man by her white father.

"How old are you?" I asked, hoping she wouldn't be angry. I wanted to know more about her life.

She stared at the fire pit and shrugged. "When my first moon days ended. Your age. I had to marry a white trapper. I had baby son. Five summers later, father and husband left with Shawnee men to fight with the French." She sighed and looked at a bundle of wild garlic a moment. "A season later, much sickness came. Young son and my mother moved to spirit world together."

My jaw fell open, and my eyes watered. "I'm sorry you lost your mother and child.

Whisper frowned and shook her head. "They are happy there."

I didn't understand. I'd heard of a place called heaven but thought everyone was sleeping for now. She glanced at me. "Sickness took many lives then, but spirit world is better than here."

Before I could ask about the spirit world, she continued, "Nine summers passed. Husband returned from war sick from wounds. Angry that son died. He beat me. Sold me to no good British. Thirty-five winters in white men camps."

"I hope your husband died from his wounds and wasn't allowed in the spirit world."

Whisper chuckled. "Life good now."

If she was thirteen when forced to marry, I estimated her age as sixty something.

Whisper squatted beside me. She rubbed her good left hand over my wounds while watching my face. Her right index finger was gnarled and seemed to hurt more on cold mornings.

When I didn't flinch, she stood.

"Come." Whisper stretched out her hand and helped me to the table. "Do you bleed?" She pointed to my crotch. "You have moon days?"

My face burned. "No." I shook my head, understanding her reference to menses. A twinge of panic caused my eyes to water. *I hope I'm back with Momma before it happens. God, please don't be so cruel as to let it happen among these people. I'm going to want Momma.*

She nodded and brought a plain deerskin skirt to my feet. "Chief Lone Duck says come out among us." Whisper peered into my eyes. "You will be safe. No more fear of Shawnee."

My heart sped. "Am I to stay here until I'm ransomed?"

"Not for me to say." She wrapped the skirt around my waist and poked the cylinder bone button through the slit in the back. Next, she secured a strip of leather across my chest and slipped a loose-fitting fringed blouse over my head.

I pulled the front out to admire the white, green, and yellow flower designs made using an unfamiliar substance sown onto the bodice. They weren't beads, but something hard and glossy.

"Sit." She smiled and patted a straw mat near the fire. "Now, hair."

I closed my eyes, imagining Momma unbraiding my hair. Whisper hummed as she brushed out the tangles. *Am I like a daughter she never had?* I needed to know. "Did you have other children?"

She paused and sighed. "Son has three sisters walking with him in the spirit world."

My chest ached for her pain. *How sad to lose them all. Did her broken mother's heart spur her to rescue me from Isaiah Brown and take me in? What if I hadn't met her before? Interesting coincidence or something God did?* I shrugged. "How did you get here? How did you get away from the fort at Crabapple Orchard?"

A grin spread across her face. "Four hunters paid for me with silver coins. While camped near the Scioto River, I slit their throats as they slept."

I gasped. Her tone sounded as if she had simply slit the throat of a squirrel or rabbit. *Could I kill a person like that?* I stared in wonder as she stood, opened a clay jar, and continued her tale.

"Took horses and supplies to Cornstalk's village. Hiding Turtle brought me here." She scooped out a dab of white grease with her finger, rubbed it in her hands, and smoothed my hair.

I recognized the sweet, slightly pungent aroma of wild geranium. She platted my hair in two braids and wound them with yellow cloth like hers.

Whisper backed up, grinning. "Put on moccasins and come. Chief Lone Duck is waiting."

I pulled on the shoes and stood.

She draped a wool blanket around my shoulders and took my hand. As we neared the door, I yanked my hand back and panted. My stomach soured. I felt naked and cold. I wanted to run as fast as my chest was pounding. "I can't go out there. Let me stay hidden."

Whisper hunched partway through the opening and extended her hand as if presenting an object. "Come see."

I gazed at the deep tan lines in her palm, bent forward, and shuffled outside.

She faced the yard, swooping her hand waist-high in a half circle. "Look among your new people and village. See. They are no longer angry. You are safe here. Forked Tongue Isaiah has gone."

I sucked in a deep breath, then trembled as the central yard where I was beaten drew my eyes west. Whisper turned my body in a slow circle. "Do you see homes?"

Scattered throughout the wooded area around the yard were more than a hundred round huts made from tree branches and hides. I gulped. *Larger and better protected settlement than any I've ever seen.* Each small yard had wooden frames holding stretched hides of various animals. The same type of cast-iron pots used by my family hung above small cooking fires. Young children giggled and squealed as they ran in a game of chase.

My breath caught. For a moment, I imagined Nancy and Charlie playing with them. Women carried babies on their backs while chatting and laughing with each other as they worked. No different than the women at the Boonesborough settlement. They no longer looked like the violent monsters from yesterday. *No! I won't care about these people.*

Coyote-looking dogs sniffed the air and stared at me before lying down. In a clearing east of the central yard, a dozen young braves took turns throwing hatchets at pumpkins attached to wooden poles. I shuddered, remembering Papa's account of a hatchet flying past his head into a tree during the skirmish at Point Pleasant. A dozen men shot arrows from their bows with terrifying speed and accuracy. I gulped. *Much faster than loading a long rifle.*

Whisper nudged me forward with her elbow and smiled. "Come. Chief Lone Duck wishes to welcome you."

I didn't move. "Why?" Sweat beaded on my forehead despite the biting wind. I covered my head with the blanket for comfort more than warmth, wishing to hide.

Whisper's warm hand grasped mine. "You will learn. Keep eyes down until I say. I will explain his words."

As she tugged, I walked and prayed. *God, I'm scared.*

Dark-eyed children darted close, giggling, and rushing backward when I flinched. My heart thumped as women who once stripped and struck me now smiled and followed us to the oblong meeting lodge in the center of the yard.

A large crowd of fierce-faced men appeared as if in a nightmare. But when the turkey man approached scowling, I thought of running. I froze as he circled me with a smoking bundle of sage and cedar, waving a large feather fan. Then he bolted to the chief's side with a chin raise.

The chief came toward me with several men that included Hiding Turtle and Red Sparrow.

Breathe. The smoke relaxed my nerves but made me cough. I lowered my eyes. My chest thumped, and my legs shook. Whisper moved behind me and leaned to my ear. "You may look at Chief Lone Duck now."

I raised my eyes as the chief faced the people. He held out a wide white-and-purple-beaded belt the width of my hand and the length of my arm. The center design of the belt featured two stick figures appearing to be holding hands. His guttural Shawnee words ended as a question, and the people responded in unison with one word.

The chief turned to me, offering the belt and motioning for Whisper. She moved to his side. After they spoke, she came before me and placed her hand on my arm.

"Chief Lone Duck is pleased. Our Great Spirit, Kokumthena chose you to be here, and the Supreme Being, Moneto is allowing her will. Accept this wampum belt of adoption."

I gulped and didn't move. *Adoption?*

The chief stepped beside Whisper and spoke in a soft voice. She smiled at me. "Chief Lone Duck wants you to take his hand. Feel the peace he has in his heart for you."

He held out his wrinkled, dark-skinned right hand.

I swallowed and extended my trembling right arm. Our fingers clasped each other's palms. Warmth radiated from him and stilled my jitters.

Whisper raised the wampum toward me. *I have no choice.* I released the chief's hand and held up my palms. The cold belt draped over my hands—accepted. *I'm betraying my parents.* Tears welled in my eyes, but I blinked them away. *Must be strong. God, grant that I may reunite with my family again someday.*

Chief Lone Duck smiled and held up a sinew with a black-tipped eagle feather dangling from it with two white beads. The turkey man waved his smoke and fan over it. Whisper took the chief's feather and tied it into my right braid and moved back.

I sucked in deep breaths as the windblown feather flitted against my cheek like a bird.

The chief motioned for Whisper to bring two wooden bowls. He dipped his left index finger in one and pulled out yellow paint. When he approached my cheek, I flinched and gasped. I stood still as his finger made a horizontal line across my face from one ear to the other. Then he placed three red dots on each cheek. The chief laid his right hand on my head and spoke words that made the people laugh.

Whisper translated. "You are now Shawnee. Yellow paint on cheeks honors courage. Red paint and feather honors warrior who spilled blood of Forked Tongue Isaiah."

My jaw dropped. *They know I shot him. I was desperate and terrified. Not brave.*

She continued. "Chief Lone Duck names you, Shoots in Knee." She grinned, but I gasped. *I should be Cowers Under Blanket.*

Drums beat behind the people, and a man started chanting. The people turned and gathered in a large circle around the fire pit, moving slowly in a counterclockwise direction. Whisper draped the wampum belt over my arm and motioned for me to follow. She demonstrated the foot shuffle as we joined the circle. We moved side by side as one. A shaking sound came from a woman wearing what looked like turtle shells around her ankles. The people added their voices to the chanting. I felt connected—and strangely safe. No longer afraid.

Dancing and feasting continued until late afternoon. That's when I noticed Hiding Turtle and Red Sparrow were gone. I asked Whisper about them.

"They are of Cornstalk's clan. Hiding Turtle married a woman from there. She was Red Sparrow's sister."

"Was?"

Whisper nodded. "Hiding Turtle was with Cornstalk's war party on the Ohio twelve moons ago. Wife and baby went to the spirit world. We must help put away food now. Come."

The story pierced my heart. Tears dribbled down my cheeks. *How horrible for Hiding Turtle to return from battle to such news. Twelve moons? That would be a year ago? Was he at the skirmish at Point Pleasant?* I sat stunned. *Is that where he heard the name Cage?* I wiped my face and caught up with Whisper.

I glanced around at the people in the village. A few days ago, they almost beat me to death as an enemy. Today they accepted me as one of them. *My people wouldn't be so accepting, and they wouldn't adopt an Indian.* Tears pooled again as I remembered how my mixed-Cherokee friend Eliza was shunned at Moore's Fort. I sighed.

For the first time in eleven days, my shoulders relaxed. Even though I didn't understand the reason for being here, I could be grateful. *Thank you, God, for bringing me to a merciful people.*

Chapter Twelve

Whisper added a log to the crackling fire inside our warm hut. A few sparks drifted toward the hole in the roof and then out. Melting snow dripped from a tree branch above and drummed on the hides. A few drips fell into our kettle of rabbit stew. While she wasn't watching, I scratched January eighteenth on a third strip of leather that represented my third full month of captivity. My heart broke. *Today's George's ninth birthday. He'll be grown by the time I see him again. Will my siblings remember me?*

I thought of my family every day and grieved, knowing they would be thinking about me too. I had mourned through Christmas Day, longing to hear Papa's voice reading the Bethlehem story in German. As the new year arrived with heavy snow, I knew there'd be no rescue until spring. My eyes watered, and my nose ran.

Whisper caught me holding the deerskin with one hand while drying my face. She knelt beside me with a muddy-green turtle shell. "Time to learn our moon days." She placed the hand-sized shell in my palm and pointed to the left of where the head used to be. "Start with this block, called Severe Moon." Whisper named each jagged square from the head section down to the tail, then explained how the seasons worked. "We are in the time of Pe-poon-ki, the North Person who blows cold air from the ice mountain."

I hadn't paid attention to the block designs on a turtle's back before. "Are all turtle shells the same?"

She shook her head. "Some don't have blocks. Snake lines are evil spirits sent by the Great Horned Spirit—never use. See small spaces on edge? Count from head and go this way." Her finger traced the outer shell in a counterclockwise direction, and I counted twenty-eight squares.

"These are the days in each moon. Sometimes more." She touched the second moon block. "Today—thirteenth day of Severe Moon. Crow Moon in fifteen days. Names are what happens in each moon time."

I nodded. "Like when it's time to pick berries or harvest corn?"

"Yes. When you have first moon day of blood, paint a red dot on shell. Then count twenty-eight days to know the next. Understand?"

"Yes." I sighed. *Hope I'm back with Momma before my time comes.* I couldn't keep my eyes from watering.

She took my hand and peered at my face, speaking Shawnee. "Why are you sad today? Answer in Shawnee."

Do I know enough words? I said the Shawnee words in my head and then spoke them. "I miss my family."

She raised her chin and stood. "Sorrow will pass someday." Her dismissive tone hurt. "Time to go outside and help make bear grease."

Sorrow will never pass. I want to go home. But how? They don't allow me to be alone.

Three mornings later, I marked the twenty-first day of January on my leather strip and stood. Wetness trickled down my left thighs. I lifted my skirt and bent to see blood dribble. I stared. My throat tightened. *It's happening.* I let the skirt drop. I couldn't blink away tears fast enough. I dipped my finger in the red paint and applied a dot to the turtle shell. *The sixteenth day of Severe Moon.* I counted ahead twenty-eight days, like Whisper had shown me to be prepared for the next month. I gulped, unable to think in Shawnee. I gazed at Whisper. "I need rags. My moon days have started."

She peered up from sewing a new dress. "Let it flow and come." She smiled and handed me the dress she was making. "Carry this."

Let it flow? I hated the dribbles that slipped into my knee-high moccasins that had taken hours to stitch as I followed her outside. I crunched through four inches of wet snow and left a mortifying trail of red dots.

Whisper held my right hand and yelled in Shawnee, "Shoots in Knee is a woman."

The people shouted, "May Kokumthena bless you with many children."

"Why are you telling everyone?" I ducked my head behind my left arm, venting in English.

She stuck to Shawnee. "You are honored as a Shawnee woman. No more a girl." Whisper led me toward a secluded, round hut.

No more a girl? I gulped as if I'd been thrown down a deep cistern. *I might as well be dead. A girl needs her momma at a time like this.* Tears slid down my face. "I need old rags to sit on."

Whisper shook her head. "Blood is sacred and full of life power. We let it soak into the ground to honor Kokumthena, giver of life."

On the ground? How horrible. I hate this. I want rags.

Whisper stopped at the entrance. "A new woman is coming in."

Women's voices responded in unison, "We will be her teachers."

Whisper moved back. "Remove the skirt inside. You will learn more Shawnee and the way of women while sewing quills on this dress." She pointed to the colorful designs on hers. "From this day on, I will speak only Shawnee to you, and you must learn. Stay in women's lodge for four days."

"Why only four days?" English flowed once last time.

Whisper lifted a stick and drew a circle on the ground, then quartered it. "Four is sacred for life." She tapped the top of the circle, traced it counterclockwise, and stopped back at the top. "Birth to death. Day to night. Dark moon to full. Winter to summer, four directions." She peered at me and shrugged. "You will learn." She grinned and then rushed away.

I gulped and eased inside the pungent, dimly lit hut. My timid greetings jumbled as I slipped off my boots and skirt. I stood exposed with a racing heart and burning face.

Three skirtless women sat on the bare ground around the warm central fire pit. They greeted me before rattling off names I didn't understand. One tossed a handful of dried sage into the fire, which had a soothing effect and countered the rank odor of stale blood.

The younger, black-skinned woman beamed and patted the ground beside her. She pointed to the pile of porcupine quills and then to four bowls of colored water before stitching a green quill onto a baby-sized garment.

Can't be pregnant if she's in here. I shrugged.

As she chatted and laughed with the others, I picked up a quill and moved my hand toward the green water.

The woman grabbed my arm, shaking her head. *"Mah-tah."*

The others chuckled and stared.

The young woman took the quill and clipped off the sharp black tip. She laid it on a board and rubbed a round stone across to flatten it before nodding to me to take over. While I went to work flattening, she removed the quills already in the bowls to a mat and spread them out to dry. Then she took six from my pile, dropped them in the green dye, and pointed to the other bowls. I nodded.

As we worked, the women gave me words and phrases to say. If I said something wrong, they laughed and made me start over, emphasizing the correct syllables and tone. By late afternoon, I could speak and understand the names of objects in the hut, including the women's names. I also learned enough phrases to piece together a little about each of my hut mates.

Raven Feather wanted to be pregnant by the next full moon and hoped that by making a garment, Kokumthena would grant her desire. Hole in the Storm Clouds had five children and was grateful not to be expecting. Dancing Rabbit's husband had gone to the spirit world a few years ago, before they could make a baby. She hoped to marry a man from the Panther clan if her brother-in-law, Chief Lone Duck, would allow.

I also learned the technique of sewing and folding one quill on leather with thin sinew. I stared in wonder—the single quill looked as if several glass beads had been attached.

Women from young to old came and went during my four days. I enjoyed learning more about their lives and beliefs. Hearing the married women speak freely of intimacy made my face burn with shock at first. But their lack of shame and lighthearted banter eased me into understanding the wisdom of learning from older women how to love your husband. I giggled at the knowledge gained. By the time I left the hut, I had shed my childhood with my first moon days. I felt like one of their daughters. They had become my friends.

A pang of guilt surfaced for enjoying the company of my captors. *I want to go home someday, but I don't want to be miserable all winter.*

Chapter Thirteen

A bitter cold settled into my bones as I lay awake in the darkness on the fourteenth of Crow Moon. Grief deepened the longer I lingered and thought of my family. *They won't be celebrating my fourteenth birthday today. Momma's most likely awake, praying for me and crying.* My chest felt as if a boulder had fallen through the roof and crushed me like a bug. In my home, February seventeenth was my special day. In this place, no one cared. I sniffled, but needed to bawl and wanted to be alone. My belly hurt from holding in the anguish. But I wasn't allowed to wander far from Whisper or one of the other women. I was given a stern warning to stay away from the horses and the riverbank.

Whisper hunched toward me in the firelight and placed a small cloth pouch in my hand. "Breathe."

I wiped my cheeks with my forearm and then raised the bag to my nose, sniffing the tingly scents of sage and cedar, which brought instant comfort. "Will I be allowed to leave someday?" I drew in another whiff of the herbs. "I miss my family...I want my momma."

Whisper frowned and sat cross-legged in front of me, shaking her head. She pointed to the wampum belt hanging on the wall behind my head. "You are Shawnee." Her tone stayed soft, but her eyes seemed to glisten. "New family. New ways. New momma." Whisper's mouth turned down as she patted her chest.

"You don't understand." I tilted my head back, blinking at the birch frame that held up the roof.

Her warm hand lifted mine to my nose and let go. "Breathe more."

I closed my eyes and inhaled the medicine pouch.

"Wampum holds the sacred promise you accepted."

Her curt tone raised mine. "I care about you and appreciate your care for me, but I miss my family and want to go home. What if I give the belt back?"

Her head flinched as if I'd slapped her face. Firm brown eyes warmed and glistened. "Wampum would be thrown on the ground and the Shawnee would be your enemy—forever." Whisper looked away from me, wiping her eyes.

I gulped down the lump in my throat. *She's hurt, but I can't stay.*

Whisper sighed and turned her head back to me, but stared at the ground. "If you are stolen by the whites—your promise isn't broken. Shawnee will remain your family. No more talk now. Come work." She stood and rushed outside.

I cupped the bag in my hands and held it to my face, sniffing deeply, then lowered it to my lap as anguish exploded into sobs.

In a moment, I stared up at the cross-poles. *Nothing I can do. Papa will have to come steal me.* "God, give him keen senses and a large rescue party in the spring."

I huffed and stood, slipping a buffalo-wool cape around my shoulders. I covered my head with a soft deerskin hood I'd stitched a few days after my adoption. The woman who stole my wool coat never indicated an inclination to return it. When I mentioned this to Whisper, she explained that the woman took the coat while I was an enemy of the Shawnee. Demanding it back would be rude. I would need to trade something valuable with her. Aside from keeping me warm, the coat wasn't worth bartering for.

I hunched through the doorway and gasped as the frigid wind struck my face. It whipped my fringed skirt against my ankles as I sloshed through melting snow to the fire pit where Stole My Coat, whose real name was Moon Flower, stirred a large kettle of bones.

The Shawnee women preserved all the various meats brought in by the hunters. Nothing was wasted. Once the bones were cooked, cooled, and busted open, the white marrow was eaten so the animal's essence and strength would dwell in the person.

I eased up to the fire pit. The wretched stench of boiling bones made me gag.

Moon Flower stopped stirring and moved away from the fire pit before squinting from under her rabbit-fur hood.

I forced a smile and spoke the hello greeting with its required question of "Do you feel good?"

"Hah-tee-toh," Moon Flower said. Then she answered the greeting with the polite response and asked me the same question.

Not in the mood to do this. I frowned and peered into her eyes. *"Mah-tah."* Then I mumbled in English, "I'm homesick and cold."

She leaned to my ear and whispered in English, "Feel better soon."

My jaw dropped. *She speaks English.*

Moon Flower headed toward the other women, and my heartbeat sped. *Will I be in trouble for being rude?* I lifted the long paddle and stirred. *Maybe she'll speak English to me again. I miss hearing it.*

When no one came to reprimand me, I turned my head to see the women going about their normal activity. Moon Flower carved venison into thin strips while others hung them to dry on racks over a low fire. Another group ground already crispy meat with grease and sweet peppery spices.

While I stirred the bones in a rocking motion, Momma hummed her German lullaby in my mind. My chest ached. Tears wet my cheeks. *I miss you, Momma.*

I calmed, but a numb mood settled in my spirit.

Moon Flower came beside me with another paddle and lifted a steaming bone to a flat cooling rack. She checked the bones for softness by hitting them with a stone.

I cleared my throat and spoke an apology in Shawnee with the proper greetings.

She smiled and finished her task, then took the stirring paddle from me and leaned it against the side before peering at me with glistening light-green eyes.

I gasped and stared at a strand of white-streaked auburn hair. *She's not—*

"My white family was killed." Moon Flower spoke in choppy English. "In a raid...on the Monongahela River. I was your age. My name...Sarah McCeary. Piqua good to me. I married bear clan man. Our son...Loud Hawk. Husband died...one year ago."

I cocked my head and frowned. "You never tried to escape?"

She shook her head. "No reason. No more white family." She rubbed her hands over the wool coat. "Coat is like...Father's. I will keep. Now. No more white words."

I blinked back tears and lunged forward, giving her a quick hug. I spoke in Shawnee. "Thank you for telling me your story." I gulped. "I'm happy for you to have the coat."

She nodded and pointed to a long rough-planed log where a group of women were crushing bones. "Take these there."

I sighed as she walked away. *I still have family and a reason to escape.*

As I lowered my armload of bones to the log table, dogs barked and one of the young braves shouted, "White men are entering the camp."

Papa? My breath caught. I rushed forward to get a better view, but hope vanished.

Ten Shawnee warriors stood at the northern trail with raised tomahawks as five white men dressed in red British waistcoats and white breeches stopped before them. Chief Lone Duck nodded, and the men led pack horses to the meeting lodge. Following these, two casually dressed white men wearing black tri-corner hats and green waistcoats entered with a bald Indian from another tribe. One of the green-dressed men presented a wampum belt to the chief. The bald man acted as an interpreter.

I scanned the men but didn't recognize anyone's face. *Are these men from the outpost? Are they going to take me to Fort Detroit?*

I hurried over to the gathered crowd and worked my way into a position of hearing without being seen by them. But the chief led the men into the lodge.

Whisper took my arm and led me to our wigwam. "Stay inside. Not good men." Her voice was firm.

I hunched through the doorway but considered making a run toward the men. *What if she's lying to keep me here?*

She nudged me inside and followed, but sat in front of the opening, peering out.

"How do you know they're not good?" I stared at the back of her head.

No answer. I sighed. "How long will we stay hidden?"

"Someone will come tell us." She continued to watch.

I sighed and picked up my sewing project—a leather pouch I had been quilling with green ivy leaves and gold vines.

The shadow of the sun moved two places before Moon Flower entered. She sat with her legs tucked sideways. "McKay man spoke this: 'Dragging Canoe wishes to meet with Chief Lone Duck after the spring Bread Dance. Detroit Hamilton wants Shawnee and Cherokee clans to become one against the rebel forts across the Ohio River. But he wants the clans to wait until guns and powder arrive.'" She shook her head. "This will be a bad time for all. McKay man also said two boys from Boone's fort were killed. Now the rebel whites are preparing to attack our clans in the spring."

Boone's Fort? My stomach knotted and my heart sped. *Please, God. Not George...or anyone I know.*

Moon Flower looked at me. "These men know you are here. They want Chief Lone Duck to name his price for you, so they can trade you to the Detroit fort. They promise payment when they come back during the Blackberry Moon."

She nodded to Whisper and crawled back out.

I stood on wobbly legs. "Wouldn't it be better for me to be back among the whites and be sold back to my family?"

Whisper's eyes narrowed. "No. These men are evil serpents. Some I remember." She frowned. "They will beat you." Her voice cracked. "Pass you around and steal your beauty."

She's frightened for me. I stared at Whisper and trembled inside. The ground spun under me. "Will the chief sell me to these men? What about the wampum promise?"

She shook her head. "I do not think Chief Lone Duck will do this."

Panic turned to rage. "He will be my enemy forever if he does. I will find a way to escape."

She sighed. "I will plead for you again if this thing happens. We need to keep still now."

I sat on my mat, laying the pouch aside, and pulled my legs to my chest. *The Blackberry Moon.* I examined the turtle shell and calculated five months. *July. I can't wait* to be rescued. I must get back and give warning of the coming raids. I'll have to start watching the guards and learn about the rivers and trails.

Chapter Fourteen

Throughout the month of March, I watched men come and go in canoes on the river and trek in and out of the thick, forested trails guarded by dogs and diligent young boys. Discouragement threatened to end my resolve. Taking a canoe alone without experience was out of the question, and their trails would only lead to other Indian villages.

The first morning of Half Moon fell on April fifth. The sun peeked over the eastern line of trees beyond the cleared field a few feet from the village. I peered at the golden haze of lingering fog and slogged through patchy melting snow with a hoe on my shoulder and followed Whisper. I watched for a rescue party to emerge from the woods. *Today would be good, God. If not, please bless and protect my family from raids.* I sighed as we stopped beside the other women and waited for instructions.

Chief Lone Duck's plump wife Tame Dove flipped her cloth-bound hair behind her back and faced the cornfield. She waved a large eagle feather, chanted a long prayer of thanksgiving, and asked Kokumthena to pour her essence into the soil to sustain us. Then we set out hoeing furrows, followed by young girls squatting every foot to dig holes.

My mind wandered to how similar some Shawnee beliefs were to the Bible stories I'd learned, though with a different twist. Their Moneto thought up the creation idea, but Kokumthena created everything and commissioned a turtle to carry the Shawnee to an island. The memory of Papa reading the story of Noah from his large German Bible prompted stinging eyes. *I want to hear your voice again, Papa. Are you coming?*

Moon Flower handed me a basket of smelly minnows. "Drop fish in the hole to nourish the ground."

I dropped the hoe and nodded, draped the basket over my shoulder, and went over to the first deep hole humming Papa's frog courting song to keep the sadness away.

Moon Flower came behind me, filling up each hole before poking a sacred corn kernel into the soil an inch before smoothing it over with dirt. She laughed. "I remember that song. Sing it."

As I sang, she bobbed her head and hummed along. Then whoops from the men rang out from the river behind us. Everyone stopped working to stare.

In a moment, a smiling young boy rushed among us. "Warriors have returned with many horses and the scalps of white men who were marking trees along the Kentucky River."

I clutched my throat as breaths caught. *Scalps? Surveyors? Papa!* Bile rose with the harsh reality of raids. I dropped my basket on the ground, held my hand over my mouth, and ran from the field. I lost my breakfast behind a shrub and sat on the ground, crying and praying. *I can't bear it if Papa is dead. If he's alive, God, please don't let him come. The danger is too great. Help me find a way out.*

When I could stand, I walked on wobbly legs to the riverbank. No one came after me. I squatted and washed off puke and sniffled. *Maybe I can steal one of the horses now that they aren't watching me. But which way would I go?* I turned my head toward the chopping sound up the bank. Two men chiseled out a new canoe while a group of men pulled a submerged one from the river storage and drained the water. I lingered as four of the men climbed into the craft and paddled away in the calm west-flowing current.

I looked to my right and left. *No one's watching me, not even the dogs.* My chest tightened. *How far can I swim underwater?* I swung my feet over the bank.

"Shoots in Knee." Dancing Rabbit stood with her hands on her hips. "Come away from there before the Great Horned Serpent pulls you into the spirit world. Time to help prepare food and grind old corn."

I scooted away from the river and stood, nodding as she waited. *The slave, Adam told Charlie about a river serpent that pulled children in. Must be the same one.* I couldn't suppress the smile in my heart. *A second more and I would have chanced it.*

As we passed the lodge where the chief and other men sat smoking pipes, I noticed Hiding Turtle among them. My throat tightened. *Was he one of the raiders? Has he come to take me to the British?* I focused on Dancing Rabbit's hair bun and quickened my pace to the beat of my racing heart.

"Shoots in Knee. Come."

I gasped at Hiding Turtle's voice, then turned to see dangling bloody tuffs of brown, black, red, and blond hair hanging from poles behind him. My belly churned.

Turkey man, whose name I learned was Turkey Claw, glared with venom. My feet froze in place or I would have rushed back to the river serpent. *Why is he angry at me?*

I gulped and forced steps, gazing at the ground until I stopped before Chief Lone Duck.

"You will stay here with us and not go to Detroit." His voice was pleasant.

Tears pooled as I glanced up at the chief and forced a trembling, "Thank you." *But maybe I should take my chances in Detroit.* My chest thumped as I contemplated asking.

"That's all, Daughter." He waved me away and drew puffs on his pipe.

I remained. *Breathe. Be strong.*

He blew out smoke and tilted his head. "You wish to speak?"

My eyes watered as I lowered to my knees. "I want to go to Detroit. Please. I want my white father to come for me there. I want to make sure his scalp isn't one of those." I pointed at the poles without looking.

Chief frowned but didn't speak. Instead, he took another puff.

Turkey Claw's eyebrows rose as his mouth lifted in a grin.

He wants me to go. I sucked in a deep breath.

Hiding Turtle spoke to the chief and then peered into my eyes. "Father's scalp is not here. No Detroit. Now go."

I gulped, stunned but relieved. *Papa's not dead. Thank you, God.*

Glaring eyes from Turkey Claw accompanied his clenched jaw. *I don't think he likes me.*

I lowered my eyes and backed away before stepping toward the grinding stones to help the women pound the corn kernels.

Whisper stopped working and leaned to my ear, speaking in Shawnee. "I heard Hiding Turtle's good news." She straightened. "He must know your father. Trust him. Detroit is a terrible place. I know. Come help me make rising powder for hoecakes."

"Not yet. I want to be alone." I hurried away, and she didn't follow. I ducked inside our hut and sat, hugging my legs, weeping and wanting to be wrapped in Papa's arms.

Being alone helped me sift the confusion from my thoughts. *These people aren't my friends. I can't become attached. I must find a way to escape.*

I needed to make friends with the guard dogs, learn more about the rivers without raising suspicion, and discover why Turkey Claw didn't like me.

I dried my eyes and hunched back outside. *I'll be compliant and continue to learn their language and customs, so they'll trust me.*

Whisper's face brightened with her smile as she led me to an empty lye barrel and handed me a scraping stone.

"Scrape the black residue from the barrel, then put it into the clay oven over there." She pointed to a knee-high beehive-shaped structure with a fire underneath, heating a hollow baking area. "When the flakes turn white, take them out to cool on a board. Later, scoop the flakes into pouches."

"What are they for?" I sat on a stump and tilted the barrel.

"Makes our hoecakes light." Whisper left me to the task. "I'm going to make turtle-shell rattles for our dance."

Maybe this is Letitia's secret ingredient. I couldn't help smiling.

The tedious chore took a few hours. After filling the last pouch, I waved for Whisper. She came with an oblong basket with handles on each side.

"Now we must hide the pouches. We don't use the powder in the sacred bread."

I cocked my head. "I don't understand why."

"We must use only what Kokumthena gives. Corn, water, and salt." She waved for me to follow.

Once filled, we carried the basket to the women's lodge and covered it with clean mats.

Whisper backed up and laughed. "Now, Kokumthena won't see."

I shook my head. "But didn't she allow the people to discover it in the first place? I still don't understand."

She grinned. "She allows for common use, but not for sacred. Tomorrow, we will make plain bread all day. Give her thanks for provision so she will grant abundance."

I nodded and followed Whisper outside. The people have a greater appreciation for the Shawnee's gratitude to their Grandmother for everything, but they also fear offending her. *Why isn't she offended by the killings?*

A crowd had gathered at the meeting lodge. We rushed to join them as Tame Dove held up her feather. Everyone stood quiet. Her round, smooth face scanned the people, and then she called out the names of twelve single young men. "These men will hunt four days." She called forward twelve single young women. "These are the sacred bread makers."

The people shouted, "It is good," and the chosen ones congratulated one another.

After supper, everyone separated into family groups except the chosen breechcloth-clad young men. They sang and painted their faces white with a green stripe under their eyes. After gathering bows, quivers full of arrows, and medicine pouches, they strolled into the darkening woods.

Jealous of the ease in which they left the village, I inched away from the fire and watched them become silhouettes. I moved a step forward and froze. *Just start walking.* Reason returned. *Can't walk to Kentucky from here. It will take too long, and I'll be tracked. I need to learn about the river.* I retired into the hut with Whisper, determined to prod her with questions.

"Why was Dancing Rabbit worried about a great horned serpent pulling me in when I soaked my feet?" I removed my feather and waited.

"Our river is called Mad. It's calm here, but men say the river serpent tries to overturn canoes in some places."

I slipped off my dress and sat on my pallet before removing my moccasins. "I don't remember Hiding Turtle and Red Sparrow having trouble on this river." I stared, hoping she would give me more information.

She grinned and rerolled her blanket pillow. "Perhaps they are known by the river serpent. They have made many journeys. Spirits allow safe passage to the strong and brave."

I dared one more. "Two days from where I was taken, they had a little trouble at a river northeast of the Kentucky. I thought it was going to swallow us. Do you know it?"

Whisper yawned. "Maybe the one they call the Licking because animals like the salt. Now go to sleep."

I lay down, wishing I had Papa's map and wondering how to draw one on a section of deerskin.

Chapter Fifteen

The chosen hunters shouted their return before dawn on April ninth. I dressed in the dark and slipped outside with Whisper.

A bright almost-half moon still sparkled behind the breeze-kissed tree branches in the south. *Still good light on the river.* I smiled and continued to the central yard, where yellow sparks burst from new logs in the ceremonial fire pit.

Turkey Claw moved before the hunters and waved his feather fan over the abundance of venison and elk. Then the men carried the meat around the circle, singing their thank-you songs to the animal spirits until daybreak.

"Shoots in Knee."

I startled to Tame Dove's touch on my shoulder. "Help skewer the venison on spits. Baste them with bear grease mixed with crushed wild onions and salt."

After a nod, I made my way to the pungent bundle of onion bulbs already laid out on a board. I peeled, crushed, and chopped with stinging juice burning my eyes. Into my blurry vision came the chief's daughter, Corn Flower. She was shorter than me, but carried herself tall and confident. I guessed her to be a year or two older. Her hair was black and slicked with grease, but the length had been wrapped in yellow strips of cloth and wound in a tight spiral circle secured to the back of her head. She placed a wooden bowl of bear grease on the board and gazed at my watery eyes.

"Thank you." I squeezed out tears, sniffled and then stirred the onions into the bowl.

"I'll bring you a wet cloth for your eyes." Corn Flower grinned and retrieved a small square cloth from a steaming kettle and returned.

"I'm glad you are learning to speak well." She beamed. "I've been wanting to be your friend."

I gaped, unsure of how to respond, but her gesture softened my heart a little. I stopped working and grinned. "I'm pleased to be your friend." *At least until I leave.*

Corn Flower drew close to my face and dabbed my eyes. "They are pretty and shiny, like fresh fallen brown leaves after a rain. Each are circled with a bold black line. This must be why you are so strong and connected to the earth."

Her deep stare and smothering closeness frazzled my nerves. I backed up, shrugging and holding my cheeks.

"I don't know, but others in my family are the same." Remembering them clouded my vision again.

Corn Flower giggled. "I've been told mine are dark like my father's. Hiding Turtle says they are like dark rum that makes him drunk."

After a shocked gasp, I grinned. "You're sweet on Hiding Turtle?"

Her whole body seemed to burst with excitement. "Don't tell anyone, but I'm going to choose him at the Bread Dance. I think he will accept. I know Father and Mother will approve if he agrees."

I frowned my confusion. "Choose him for dancing? I don't know your custom."

"During this dance, a woman can choose a man for a husband. If Hiding Turtle accepts me, we will go into the hut I have made over there." She pointed to a new hut southwest of the village and sighed. "I have to go back to work. I am one of the sacred bread makers. I'll share more later."

I stood a moment in shock, letting the full meaning latch itself to my mind. *So, no wedding? Just choose someone and....*

I shook my head and carried my mixture to the skinned venison, waiting to be skewered and basted. My heart beat fast. I couldn't stop thinking about what being with a man would be like. I'd heard details while in the women's hut each month, and each time my body tingled.

A cool breeze blew across my path, but it didn't relieve the powerful stirrings. I sighed. *Momma has been robbed of telling me about marriage.* The pain of missing her rose. *If I make it home someday, I'll pretend I don't know.*

In a few hours, I inhaled the sweet aroma of fried corn from the hundreds of hoecakes cooling on large grass mats in the shade under blankets. Thousands of flies swarmed and buzzed around the tables. My own roasting venison dripped juices sizzling into the fire, mixing the tantalizing smoke with that of the others cooking meat.

Four hours later, the venison had browned. I cut off a slice and savored a bite before the young men lifted the spits and carried them to a log table for carving.

While no one watched, I eased toward the lead guard dog, who stayed mostly near the river. The coyote-looking male had short reddish-blond fur, a white neck, cute floppy ears, and a long, black-tipped muzzle. He remained quiet and still as I squatted with the remainder of my slice of meat. I held it out on my palm as a friendship offering. He sniffed the air but stayed back. I tossed it to him and stood. "We'll work on being friends." I walked to the lodge to change. *Maybe he'll accept me.*

I changed into the new dress I had worked so hard quilling. I had designed a flower pattern on the bodice in green, tan, gold, and outlined it in red. I didn't mind feeling proud and wanting to show it off. I ran my hand across my quillwork. *A little wavy in places, but not bad.*

Whisper entered and smiled. "You did well." She came closer, checking my work. "Kokumthena will be pleased."

So would my momma. I blinked away pooling tears. Memories of the harvest dance came. *This is like the moment we went out to show Papa our new dresses.*

"Thank you." I smoothed the wrinkles from my hips, wanting to think about something else. "What does this dance mean?"

"We honor Kokumthena as the creator of life. She gives food and babies. But don't fear the forest protector, Misignwa. He smells his animals on our fires and comes to check our reverence. Our men sing his songs and he accepts our thanks. We take turns dancing all night and making life rhythms with the shell rattles on our ankles while the drums beat."

I raised my palms and shrugged. "Life rhythms? I don't understand."

"Feel your chest beating? Thump-thump, thump-thump? Life revolves around this beat. Sometimes fast because of joy, but sometimes a bad spirit makes the earth wobble." She wiggled her hand in the air. "Our dances bring balance back. Drums remind our hearts of the proper rhythm, and shakers keep the blood flowing on the correct path."

I nodded as if understanding but didn't yet. After Whisper changed into her beautiful new dress and tidied her hair, we joined the long line of women gathering on the perimeter of the ceremony area.

The last fiery swirls of the sunset sank behind the forest, then Turkey Claw shrieked. The memory of a Cherokee lunging at me from the bushes flashed across my eyes. I hunched down, holding my knees. The hairs on my neck prickled. I stayed down as men rubbed elk bones across long grooved sticks, which made a growling sound.

The designated hunters and bread makers converged into the center of the yard. Women moved sideways in the counterclockwise direction, keeping rhythm with their shakers while men sang and chanted.

I shuddered as a black bear lumbered out of the woods under the flickering moonlight. Memories of my encounter with an angry bear a year ago sped up my heart. When the bear straightened into a man wearing the full skin and head of a bear, my jitters calmed.

The bear man pulled a cane pole from the ground as he shook a turtle-shell rattle. He replicated the mannerisms of a bear as he danced among the selected men and women, which included Corn Flower.

After this, we feasted until miserable. I held my stomach and walked the perimeter of the village to help ease the bloat and test my boundaries.

Whisper came to me with turtle shakers. "Tie these on your ankles and come make the life rhythms."

I shook my head. "Can I just watch?"

She squatted and tied them on for me, then pulled me back to the circle. The shells were heavy and awkward. I stumbled and wanted to hide, but Whisper wouldn't let me leave. As I concentrated, the beats became part of me and fun.

Moments later, the married and older women dropped out of the circle. The remaining dancers each sauntered toward a selected man. I felt lost and moved away to watch.

Corn Flower danced toward Hiding Turtle, swaying her hips and rotating her shoulders and arms in an alluring manner. The other women were doing the same with the braves who had gathered closer with wild gawking eyes. Corn Flower led Hiding Turtle to the hut she had built. The men rubbed their hands over the dancers' bodies. I had never witnessed such a seductive display. Passions burned in me.

I fled toward the riverbank, peering into the starry sky, wishing I could fly away. I jumped as a silent dog stood in front of me with glowing yellow-green eyes. I whispered, "I'm not going anywhere." The creature eased closer, sniffing my hand. "Oh, you're the dog I shared a morsel of meat with." I showed him my palm as I sat on the damp ground. "Sorry, I don't have anything."

His tongue swiped a wet path across my hand, and then he laid beside me. I wanted to reach around him in a hug, the way I used to with my dog Drummer. Tears slid from my eyes, remembering him. I sniffled. A warm muzzle rested on my thigh. I laid my hand on the dog's neck, then wiggled my fingers into the soft fur under his ears and sighed. "Thank you, boy. I'm not going to name you or get attached, though. I'm not staying, and I can't take you with me."

No Name rolled to his back for a tummy rub. I lay on the ground beside him and complied.

When the shakers stopped, I opened my eyes. *It's dawn?* I looked to my side. No Name had left me there alone. I stood and brushed off dirt, then rushed back to the gathering. Corn Flower and Hiding Turtle were holding hands. I focused my attention on Tame Dove, who entered the center of the circle. Everyone stood still and silent.

Chief Lone Duck entered the middle of the circle and raised his feather. "Chief Cornstalk calls for all warriors to come to his village in one moon with war wampum."

The people cheered.

My blood ran cold as my mind interpreted his Shawnee.

"If we join our Cherokee brothers, the whites can be defeated. Only then will Misignwa allow his animals to roam the sacred hunting places once more. Our friend,

Detroit Hamilton, says this is a good thing. He will send the promised gifts in two moons. Blue Jacket will lead us south. Now, we will have the joining ceremony."

Loud whoops from the people rang in my ears. I stood in a daze, but anger rose with panic. *Blue Jacket? My family is in danger.*

I ran to Hiding Turtle. He flinched as I faced him, speaking English. "Please warn my father so my family can leave Kentucky."

He frowned and shoved me backward, then joined Corn Flower, who was waiting next to Chief Lone Duck.

I seethed, wanting to shove back. Instead, I stood there wobbling. *Maybe it's not the best time, but at least he heard me.*

Whisper and Moon Flower took my arms and led me to the lodge.

Whisper helped me sit. "You became like white ashes. Stay inside and rest now. Try not to worry about your white family."

Moon Flower rested her hand on my shoulder. "I will pray that your family will leave the fort before the wars." She kissed my cheek and left with Whisper.

I pulled my knees to my chest, bawling and rocking as the drums beat and shakers rattled. The people sang happy songs while images of burning cabins and the fearful faces of my family made me tremble. I couldn't stop crying, I couldn't breathe. *God, do something.*

Chapter Sixteen

On the morning of April eleventh, I found Whisper under a cloudless blue sky, setting up a wooden frame with a fresh deer hide. She greeted me and then place a knife in my hand. "Scrape off the leftover flesh."

I stood in front of the stretched-out hide and inhaled the refreshing scent of honeysuckle swirling in the cool breeze. No Name lumbered over, plopped at my feet, and curled up for a nap as I scraped putrid meat off the bone-colored skin.

Hiding Turtle glanced my way as he and Corn Flower passed. I shot arrows with my eyes. The couple stopped in front of his horse, where other men were mounted and waiting. He kissed Corn Flower's cheek and rode off down the eastern trail. Corn Flower wiped her eyes and then smiled at my accidental stare and bounced toward me. I sighed. *Why did I keep watching? I don't want to talk to her, least of all hear about her night.*

No Name raised his head as she approached.

I spoke the mandatory greetings but didn't smile.

Corn Flower greeted back and then pressed her cheek against mine in a family manner. "Hiding Turtle is my husband. Mother and Father are pleased with our union. He is kind and gentle."

I wanted to gag and blame it on the rotted flesh but took charge of the conversation. "Why is he leaving?"

"They have to meet with Cornstalk and then find out what the whites are doing. He will be back in two weeks. I better go help Mother now. I'll visit again later."

She hurried away while I reeled. *What the whites are doing? Hiding Turtle is a spy for the British?* My stomach churned. *I hope he gets caught.* I crouched and scratched No Name's neck, which soothed my angry mood.

Then he stood sniffing and turning his ears toward the northeast woods before barking once. He trotted to the three other village dogs alerted by four bare-chested men on horseback. Chief Lone Duck greeted them. *What now?*

They wore breechcloths, leggings, and leather headbands. Seated behind a fat older man was a blond teenage white girl with a brown-smudged face, matted long hair, and terrified eyes.

A captive! My heart pounded. I took one step toward the girl, wanting to comfort her and ease her fears, but Whisper grabbed my hand and pulled me forward.

"Come see. These men have come from the eastern waters. Not Shawnee, but traders in sacred shells Kokumthena created for wampum beads."

I gazed back at the girl, conflicted and concerned, as she followed the stern-faced man without raising her head. Her appearance and manner indicated ill treatment. Anger stirred in my belly. *What can I do?*

The man carried a fist-sized white-and-purple shell to Chief Lone Duck, who raised it over his head. The people cheered and then went to unload the horses.

I continued to watch the girl, desiring to coax her away from her captor and encourage her somehow.

"Carry these." Whisper placed a crunchy bag of shells into my hands. I followed her and the other women to a clean patch of grass, where we slowly poured them onto the ground. Tame Dove delegated a few women to sort them by quality and shooed the rest of us back to our chores.

I returned to scraping flesh from a deer hide. An elderly man sat nearby telling a group of children about the good days, when bear and buffalo were abundant. Then the topic changed.

"The white father's words were forked, like the Great Horned Spirit's. He said his children would not come to live on the western waters beyond the great warrior path. But they did come. And now they multiply like rabbits.

We will make war against his rebellious children so the land can heal."

I cringed. *His words are true, but my family didn't break the treaties.* All I knew was my family and friends were in danger. My throat tightened and tears welled. *I can't contribute to the war wampum.*

An hour later, all the women were called to an area with many stone slabs. Tame Dove quieted us.

"You will take turns cutting a white shell into a round bead. Only the most skilled will make the wampum beads."

I won't be among them.

When my turn came, I sat on the ground, took the chisel and stone hammer in hand, then gave the shell a hard whack. It burst into shards, and I glanced up at Tame Dove without remorse.

Her fierce black eyes glared into my soul as she shook her head. "Go to Moon Flower and learn to make holes in the white beads."

"May I help prepare food for supper instead?" I stood, wiping my dusty hands on my deerskin skirt.

"No." She shook her head and turned away.

Moon Flower whispered, "Sit here." As I did, she placed an iron awl on the pebble-sized bead. "Hold the bead tight and hit in the center. Like this." She tapped a perfect hole, then gave me a few to practice with.

I shook my head. "No, I want to speak with the captive girl. She seems afraid to leave the man who has her."

Moon Flower rested her hand on my forearm. "You must not interfere. Bad for you and worse for her. Not all Shawnee are kind." She pointed to the bead. "Make holes and pray for the girl."

I took a deep breath, closed my eyes, and purposely shattered each bead without fear of the consequences.

Moon Flower's mouth dropped open.

Whisper squatted beside me and examined the smashed shells. She grabbed my hand and pulled me to my feet. "Come away from here. You are defying Kokumthena."

We stomped away, neither of us flinching, then Whisper stopped. Her narrowed eyes met the anger boiling from mine. She huffed and pointed to a group of little giggling girls soaking corn in lye. "Go help them."

I turned from Whisper's scowling face and veered toward the captive girl. She sat alone under a large shady oak whipstitching, a man-sized moccasin. Her fright-filled eyes glanced up, then back at the shoe.

"Hello," I said in English.

Her eyes darted as if looking for someone before shaking her head. She lifted the bottom of her plain deerskin tunic, revealing a rope around her bruised waist that was tied to the tree behind her.

I gasped and sat in front of her. "Why are you tied?"

She frowned. "*Deutsh. Kein* English."

German. She doesn't speak English. My heart fluttered. *"Ich spreche Deutsch."*

She smiled, then tears dripped from her green eyes like raindrops from spring leaves. I held my pounding chest as we spoke German together.

"What is your name? Why does he treat you like this?"

She stared at the ground. "Adelheid Schulz." Her voice trembled. "He is evil. He beats me...forces himself inside of me many times a day." She covered her face, sobbing. I scooted beside her and stroked her arm. Adelheid took my hand and spoke in a raspy whisper. "He keeps me tied so I won't run away. He won't give me food until I do what he wants."

I huffed and rolled to my knees, cradling her head. "I hate him. How did he acquire you?"

She pulled away, and I sat back, wiping my eyes.

"Stole me from my family in Pennsylvania. We were clearing land, and I went to gather flower bulbs. He grabbed me before I could scream."

My throat tightened, remembering Mr. Jessop's stench when he grabbed me.

She sniffled. "I've lost track of the days, but I've missed at least four monthlies. I might be pregnant." She wept and cupped her hands over her face again.

Bile rose in my throat as my head pounded and my ears burned. "I'm sorry." I wanted to gather enough food and supplies for the two of us, untie her, and flee together.

But how and which way would we go? Maybe she can stay here.

"My name is Mary Shirley. I was stolen too—from the Boonesborough settlement in Kentucky territory, but I was adopted by these people. Maybe I can ask the chief's daughter to speak to her father about buying you from this man?"

Adelheid placed the moccasin on the ground and wiped her eyes. "I would like that. I'm glad you have a good place here. Thank you for coming. I feel stronger."

I stood, already planning what to say to Corn Flower.

"Mary." Adelheid's eyes were wide and hollow. "If they say no." Her voice slowed and deepened. "Please bring me a large knife so I can cut the rope." The darkness of her tone scared me. "I'll take my chances escaping. I can't keep living like an animal."

I blinked away tears and bent down, kissing her cheek. "I'll be back soon. Don't lose hope." I hurried to find Corn Flower. *They have to say yes.*

Whisper and Moon Flower were among the few women chosen by Tame Dove to cut the darker shells into wampum beads. Corn Flower sat with the other women cutting the light-purple shells.

I spoke the greeting and sat beside Corn Flower, whispering my request.

She frowned and faced me, shaking her head. "I will not ask this." Her tone was soft but firm. "Father will not offend a guest who has come a long distance to trade the sacred beads. Our clan doesn't have anything left to trade for that captive girl. Why do you trouble yourself in matters not for you?"

I glared and shoved to my feet. "How can you be so calloused? War beads are not more important than Adelheid's life."

My heart raced as I rushed to my hut with a firm resolve. *I'm going to free her. We'll sneak away together. Whatever happens.*

I placed a knife and extra food in my shoulder pouch, rolled and tied two blankets together for easy carrying, and bolted back outside. *Need your help, God, otherwise Adelheid and I will be seeing your face today.*

I hurried toward the tree with my chest thumping, then gasped and stopped. Adelheid was being led to the man's horse, with her hands tied behind her back. *No. I'm too late.* My throat tightened. All I could do was stand helpless and cry.

Adelheid glanced at me with wild, pleading eyes, and I wept unrestrained. She jerked away from the man and bolted toward the river.

"*Nien,*" I shouted and ran behind the men chasing her.

A splash sent numbness to my legs. When I reached the bank, I searched the slow-moving water for her body or bobbing head. The men stood watching, then shrugged and moved back toward their horses.

I shouted, "Get a canoe. Find her. Please."

Whisper grasped my arm and turned me. Her face was drawn in fear as she peered into my eyes. "She is gone. Come away. The girl is happier in the spirit world. No more pain."

I fled past the staring people, reeling, bawling, and ready to scream. As I ducked inside the hut, Adelheid's eyes searching mine for a reason to live haunted me. Her desperation to be free one way or the other became my own, but a voice in my head said, *Not yet.*

When Whisper entered late in the night, I sat up with a sore throat. "Please help me avoid preparing for the war."

She sat in front of me and took my cold hand in her warm, dry one. "I will, but you must be wise. Some noticed your broken shells, and many saw you speaking to the captive girl before she flew into the river to die. Turkey Claw is telling the people Kokumthena is allowing a bad spirit in the village because you are here. This is not good. I cannot protect you."

"Why does he think I bring evil?" I scowled. "What have I done?"

She sighed. "I don't know his mind. But don't give him a reason."

Memories of going through the gauntlet stirred fear. *I can't risk being beaten. Can't bring shame to Whisper. She saved my life and still protects me. My escape must be better planned, my rebellion more discreet.* "I'm sorry."

My voice quavered. "I couldn't bear the way Adelheid was treated. I wanted her to be saved from that man."

Whisper nodded and stroked my arm. "You have a good heart, but you must let her go. Sleep now. Long day tomorrow."

I laid down, crying. *Why didn't anyone help? Adelheid didn't even try to surface for a breath. Not even a struggle. I don't want to die like that. I'll fight to live and someday be free.*

Chapter Seventeen

I didn't want to leave the hut in the morning. I didn't want to pretend everything was back to normal. I wanted to wallow in anger and never forgive these otherwise merciful people. If only it had been a disturbing dream. But it happened.

Whisper stood near the flap on the doorway, staring at me.

I sighed and slipped on my shoes. "I'm coming."

The eastern sky glowed from deep-red swirls and gold-rimmed clouds. I remembered Papa's rhyme. "Red sky in the morning means a storm is coming." I sighed. *Fits my mood.*

An awkward silence greeted me as the people stared. I smiled even though my heart had hardened. I needed them to believe all was well. Eyes turned away and normal village activity and noise resumed.

No Name trotted to me, and I rubbed his muzzle before strolling toward the cornfield in the eastern meadow. I glimpsed Turkey Claw scooping what looked like round brown-topped mushrooms from the edge of the western woods to my left. I turned my head as he glanced up. *Hope he didn't see me watching.*

Whisper and I joined the women, going to the field to hoe and plant more squash and beans. I worked my space without joining the argument about waiting for the storm to pass.

Moon Flower moved to my right side. "Time to learn a Shawnee story for language practice."

"I'd rather not today." I continued cutting into the soil with my hoe.

"This one is about why the bobcat has a white chest. I will teach you, and then you tell it back to me. See how well you do." She hoed a furrow as she talked.

As I worked, the silly story lighted my sour mood. It reminded me of one of the Aesop stories I'd grown up hearing and reading from Momma's big book. I heard a moral for it in my head—that of showing compassion for captives like Adelheid or else rouse Kokumthena's displeasure. I repeated Moon Flower's story to her until I could do so perfectly.

Early in the afternoon, we returned to the central yard for a time of rest before beginning supper. I wiped sweat from my forehead and glanced at the gathering slate-colored clouds moving in. Dancing Rabbit gathered a group of young children and called me forward.

"Shoots in Knee has learned one of our stories. She will tell you about the bobcat's white chest."

I gulped with fright. *Tell it aloud to the children?* The story vanished from my memory.

The children gathered and sat on the ground, wiggly and wide-eyed.

A little girl, Sally's age, smiled up at me, saying, "Many moons ago."

"Yes." I swallowed to wet my dry throat—nervous but determined to add the moral.

I began. "A bobcat wanted rabbit for supper. He saw a nice fat rabbit sneaking past him and gave chase. But the clever rabbit escaped into the hole of a hickory tree. 'You're too slow,' the rabbit teased.

"The bobcat answered, 'Well, you're trapped. I'll eat you when you come out.'"

As the children leaned forward, grinning and nodding, confidence surged. "The rabbit devised a clever plan. He peeked from the hole just enough to speak. 'I'll come out if you build a small hot fire in front of this tree. When the coals glow red, I'll let you skewer and roast me, so I'll be tender and juicy.'"

I waited while the children laughed and clapped their hands. Corn Flower neared, holding baskets and smiling.

She'll know I'm chiding. My heart raced faster, but I concentrated on the children.

"The bobcat laughed and agreed. After building the fire, he sat licking his paws and waiting. When the embers glowed, he mastered a sweet tone and called out, 'My coals are ready, Rabbit. Come out as promised.'"

I paused. *Are you sure you want to say this?* I scanned the children. *Yes.*

"The rabbit grinned and leaped feet first, kicking searing coals onto the face and chest of the bobcat. When the rabbit returned to his clan, he boasted of his freedom and triumph over his cruel enemy. The bobcat returned home in shame for his pride and lack of compassion for the captive."

I glanced around at the listening adults and stared at Corn Flower, who frowned. I sighed, but continued. "Kokumthena will allow humiliating shame to come to those like the bobcat. His chest and face fur grew back white, making him easier to spot by prey and predator. His children wear the same marks of shame today."

The children clapped and cheered. "Tell another story."

Corn Flower moved beside me. "No, children. Time to gather ripened squash for our supper." She handed out the baskets and then peered at me with moist eyes. "Your meaning was clear and true. We are feeling the shame of the girl's death while she was in our village. Pray that

Kokumthena will show us more mercy than you have today."

My rawhide heart softened, but I wasn't sorry.

She sighed. "Even the bobcat wants to hunt in his own territory to provide for his family. The girl's death was unfortunate. I'm sorry you are angry." She took my hand. "Do you hate it here with us enough to die trying to leave?"

I flinched and stared at the ground. *Had my desire to escape reached a willingness to die?* I swallowed and faced her. "No."

"Good." She smiled and grabbed my hand. "Come help me dig ginseng roots before it rains. Father isn't feeling well and wants to restore strength."

I frowned. "What's wrong?"

"We don't know. Turkey Claw believes a trickster spirit entered Father's head two days ago and is stealing his energy and troubling his belly." She pulled my hand and led me west, away from the village, down a narrow musty leaf-packed trail.

Whisper's warning about Turkey Claw accusing me of bringing evil into the village slithered across my mind and prickled the hairs on my neck. "Does Turkey Claw blame me for this?"

Corn Flower stopped, then turned with a frowning gaze. "It's not your fault. He is the one troubling Father's mind with constant prodding." She handed me a curved-handled knife and knelt on the forest floor, stabbing the moist earth with her knife.

"He doesn't seem to like me, though." I moved a few feet over, squatted, and dug roots from the soft ground.

"He wants Father to strengthen our alliance with Detroit Hamilton by trading you for guns, powder, and the strong rum that makes the braves fearless. Father has forbidden him from speaking anymore about this. Don't worry about his silly notions. Father will be better soon."

So, that's why the man is so annoyed. I'm a valuable trade item. I wiggled the knife to loosen a root and worried.

Corn Flower lifted the roots into her basket and continued to dig. "These roots will keep him strong while Turkey Claw's medicine works to draw out whatever is making him ill."

The mushrooms? A terrible thought gripped my gut. I sat on the ground. "What kind of medicine? Does he use mushrooms?"

"I don't know. The healing knowledge comes from Kokumthena to him."

Is Turkey Claw poisoning him? Does he want to get rid of the chief and then me? Surely, he wouldn't be that evil. I blew out a deep breath and wiped sweat from my forehead. "I will pray for your father. How can I appease Turkey Claw?" I stopped digging and waited.

"Take him the roots you dig as a gift and let him know you do not wish to displease him or Kokumthena. Tell him you are happy to be Piqua Shawnee."

I pondered her suggestion as I dug a pile of roots. After practicing in my head several times what to say and do, I concluded the humility required wouldn't be sincere; it would be cowardice. *I haven't done anything wrong. You'll have to protect me, God, or get me out of here.*

Our baskets were full in a few minutes and just in time. The sky rumbled as darker clouds drooped. We sprinted back into the village as a gust of wind shook wigwams and sent people rushing about, retrieving items that were tumbling away.

"Shoots in Knee," Whisper called to me. "Come help." She was lifting a heavy buffalo hide. I helped hoist it over our round roof and stake it down. A moment later, the trees overhead swayed, whipped, and then bent in one direction. Whisper pulled me inside the hut, which then seemed to explode, sending branches twirling back down on us. I covered my head with my arms, feeling the sting of scratches and ripped skin. Then a deluge of rain made covering myself a waste of time. I heard moaning and crackling sounds all around the village for a few minutes. Then the wind eased, but rain continued to pound.

I shoved a pile of sticks away, sat, and yelled, "Whisper? Are you all right?"

Her voice strained over the swooshing sound of water pouring from the sky like a river. "A branch hit my head, but I'm still here." Shuffling movements followed from under a thatched portion of our roof. Her voice warbled. "Are you hurt?"

"My arms have cuts, but I don't think they're deep." I squinted as she shuffled out from under the debris and stood. "Feel around for the larger sticks. We can twist them into a frame to hold this part of our roof back up. We'll get out of the rain and rest a moment before helping others."

I remembered the storm that hit my family as we crossed the Cumberland Gap. *Did this storm hit them at the Boonesborough settlement?*

When the rain slowed, the sky lightened, and we emerged, assessing the damage and checking on everyone. No one died, but a few were harmed and some of the food storage was lost. Men and older boys dispersed in all directions to hunt and fish.

Whisper helped tend to wounds, and I helped women and children bend and retie saplings into huts. We shook off hides and attach them to the structures, then hung blankets on a clothesline so the steady rainfall could rinse off mud and twigs. I stood back, amazed at how quickly the huts were repaired and livable by late afternoon. The rose-colored sky deepened to blood red as evening came. We gathered around the smoldering central fire pit eating soggy jerky. Tame Dove sang a song of thanksgiving to Kokumthena for sparing our lives and for giving rains to help the corn, beans, and squash grow faster. A moment later, Whisper and I went to our hut and lay on the damp ground. *The rivers will be flooded now. Impossible to escape tonight. But I'm still alive. Thank you, God. Bless my family.*

Chapter Eighteen

Within two weeks, the village had recovered, and meats were salted and drying. Replanting the garden was hard work, but by April twenty-ninth the corn plants were growing straight again. As I stood dusting off my knees, Corn Flower stepped over her row and stood beside me.

"The wild strawberries are ripening. Would you like to go with me to gather some?"

Strawberries. I smiled. "Yes. Where?"

She leaned to my ear. "Come with me."

We walked down the western trail past her family's hut and turned down a narrow path to the riverbank.

"The river has calmed back down since the storm." Corn Flower parted a patch of river cane. "The best patch of sweet berries is a short distance downriver. Get in the canoe and we'll go."

I gaped at the short, wide, flat canoe. "Are you sure we won't get in trouble? I haven't been allowed near the river or canoes."

"Are you too afraid? It's safe. I take it out all the time. It's not like you're trying to escape. You'll be with me." She slid the craft into the river and held the stern. "Get in."

"I've never seen a small canoe before." I climbed in, wobbling a bit until sitting. My heart beat fast from the excitement and a sudden urge to toss her out and keep going. I gulped. *Learn how it works first.*

"My younger brother made it for fishing." She untied the rope at the bow from the tree branch and lifted a pole with a paddle on each end. A long three-pronged spear lay beside her feet. "Short and flat is better for balance. I take it out when no one sees. I like getting away to forage and daydream about Hiding Turtle." She chuckled and swayed from side to side, alternating the paddle ends to guide the craft in the center of the slow current. "I'm ready for him to come back." She turned, handing me the oar. "Here—you try."

I dug the paddle to the right and then the left, but the canoe veered too far south.

Corn Flower laughed. "Smooth and easy does it. Find the rhythm and stay in the center."

I concentrated on what the paddles were doing and felt the craft correct and glide as my strokes became like a dance. An image of Momma swaying with baby Sally filled my eyes with tears until I blinked them away. *Maybe I can leave Corn Flower here while she's picking strawberries.* My heart sped with the thought.

"Let me steer now. You're going too fast." Corn Flower grasped the oar and pried the water away until we slowed. She dug hard to the left and onto the south bank. "Here we are." She handed me one of the baskets.

I stood, looking west, longing for home. "How far is it to the larger river this one flows into?"

"I've heard men say it's a day's journey to the great river of the Miami clan. I'll pick on this side. You go pick those." She pointed a few steps away.

"I think it joins the one called Ohio in three days." I moved to the small red berries and bent, picking and chewing the sweet tangy seeds before adding some to the basket. *How long can I live on strawberries?*

I popped one in my mouth and saw Corn Flower studying my face.

She narrowed her eyes. "I hope you're not thinking about leaving me here."

I choked on berry juice and felt my face burning as I swallowed. "I...remember coming from that way. Just curious. I won't leave you." I frowned, feigning hurt feelings.

Her stare darkened. "Your manner grew distant, as if considering the foolish idea." She tilted her head toward the canoe. "I would have stabbed you with that fishing spear if you tried leaving me." She turned away. "Pick berries and remain my friend."

I pressed my lips and picked berries. *Corn Flower and her family have been good to me.* Guilt tried to prod an apology. *But they're sending warriors out with the Cherokee to kill my family. I won't be sorry.*

We picked in silence a few minutes, and I filled my basket. Corn Flower placed her full basket in the canoe and faced me as she lifted the spear.

My stomach tightened. *Is she going to kill me?* I gasped and stood without my berries, ready to run.

She grinned and pointed the sharp prongs toward the river. "I forgive you if you were thinking about leaving. I'd be wanting to get back to my family too if I had been captured by whites."

I sighed, lifted my berries, and eased forward, wiping tears that flooded my eyes. "Maybe someday our people won't be fighting over land, and we can live as one."

Corn Flower nodded and handed me the spear. "I'll show you how to fish. Come."

I eased behind her as she neared the edge of the river and peered in. *One shove. No. I can't be that cruel. Stop it.* I sucked in a deep breath and stood beside her.

"Watch for a large fish to swim close and thrust the prongs downward. There's a good one."

I missed. But as it came back around, I snagged it with one prong and tossed it ashore, proud of my new survival skill.

Corn Flower skewered the fish on a stick and then took the spear and caught a few more. "These will make a good supper. We better go back now. I'll paddle. Sometimes going back up stream is harder, depending on how much rain or snow."

I held on to the fish and watched the way Corn Flower worked the oar. She made it look easy, and I was no longer afraid of stealing a canoe. *This canoe.*

Dogs barked in warning, and Chief Lone Duck stormed toward us, scowling. My neck pulsed with my speeding heart. I stepped out of the craft with my basket and swallowed.

Corn Flower held up the stick of fish and stood silent as her father spoke. "You have not used wisdom. You did not get permission to leave in the canoe."

Tame Dove hurried toward us, frowning, but stopped a few steps away.

An angry-faced Turkey Claw came beside him, pointing his finger in my face.

"This one is to blame. She brings evil into our village. Chief's daughter is not safe with her. Kokumthena allowed the bad spirit winds to blow because of this one."

My legs teetered. I couldn't breathe.

"No." The chief's stern face glared at Turkey Claw. "My daughter is to blame, not Shoots in Knee." He winced and held his belly.

Tame Dove rushed beside him, but he held his hand up.

"I'm sorry, Father." Corn Flower lowered her eyes.

Chief Lone Duck shook his head. "Spend the rest of the day with your mother like a little girl. What will Hiding Turtle think about his wife being so foolish?"

Corn Flower's eyes brightened with her grin. "Have you heard from him? Is he back?"

"No one has heard from him or the men he left with." The chief touched Corn Flower's arm. "But we must have the War Dance now. Our warriors will leave in the morning."

"No." Corn Flower handed me the fish and ran to her family's hut.

I stood still, stunned and shaky.

Turkey Claw glared once more, then backed and turned toward the central yard.

I walked with Chief Lone Duck and Tame Dove.

Chief moaned, and Tame Dove took his arm. "Maybe you should lay down."

"No. It will be better in a moment. I need to go to the lodge. Turkey Claw has made stronger medicine so I can lead the War Dance."

Stronger medicine? I hated not knowing what was in Turkey Claw's brew. *What if he is using poisonous mushrooms? If I can find proof, I can tell Tame Dove. If I can save Chief's life, maybe he'll have braves take me home?*

I veered from the path through brambles that snagged my ankles and exposed arms, but I emerged near the place I had seen Turkey Claw foraging the day of the storm. *There they are.* I set the basket and fish down, then lifted a stick. I prodded a caramel-colored mushroom. The tip was hard. I applied force to bust open the top. I backed away, clutching my neck. The dark purple inside confirmed my fear. *It's deadly.* In a panic, I grabbed the basket and fish, then crashed back through the woods to the trail I came from. I didn't want Turkey Claw to know where I'd been. Doubts whirled like windstorms. *I can't prove he's using them to poison the chief. Wouldn't Chief Lone Duck be dead already? Maybe he's just sick? Giving a false accusation against Turkey Claw would end badly.*

I saw Whisper hanging red cloth to dry and went to the kettle to help. *I'll tell her my fear. She'll know if it's worth mentioning to Tame Dove.*

"There you are." Her tone was sharp as she glanced up, frowning. "I needed your help and tried to find you. Now I hear you and Corn Flower sneaked away."

I held up the basket. "Corn Flower wanted my help collecting strawberries. I didn't know she meant downriver. I'm sorry."

Whisper raised her chin. "Hang up these bandanas to dry. They are for the new warriors who are leaving."

I nodded and gulped before speaking English. "Forgive me, but I don't want anyone to know what I'm saying. I saw Turkey Claw picking the poisonous mushrooms near the cornfield a few days ago. Now Chief has been getting sicker. Could Turkey Claw be—"

Whisper put her fingers over my mouth. Her eyes widened. "You must not say. Bad to think. Why? No. He would not do." She shook her head and walked away from me.

I sighed and hung bandanas. Whisper stopped to talk to Moon Flower. Moon Flower's mouth dropped open as she glanced at me.

I felt relieved from worry. *If something happens, at least I've told what I know. I hope I'm wrong. God, heal Chief Lone Duck.*

Loud whoops echoed from a circle of young braves, shaking newly stringed bows. I turned to see one load an arrow, pull it taut, and launch it into a dead rabbit dangling man height from an elm tree. The speed and accuracy of their skill frightened me. I counted five arrows shot in the time it took to load one of my family's flintlock barrels. Panic fueled the churning in my belly. I hurried to the bushes and threw up. In a few minutes, I stumbled toward the hut, stopping as Moon Flower greeted me. "Are you sick?"

I held my stomach. "Yes. I can't watch the dance. I'm worried about my family."

"I will pray to your God to have your family leave before the raids."

"Thank you." I continued walking and went into the hut, still queasy. *What am I going to do?* I unbraided my hair and brushed out the tangles. *God, if there's a time for everything—it's time to lie. I can't join the celebration.*

Whisper entered and changed into her clean dress. She came to me and took the brush before plaiting my hair with some leftover white beads.

I looked up at the birch-bark ceiling, drew a deep breath, and frowned at Whisper while rubbing my chin—until I realized what I was doing and stopped.

"My moon time is early." I gathered my blanket, new mat, and sewing project. "See you in four days."

Whisper turned her head to me, but I avoided her eyes, ducked through the opening, and rushed to the women's lodge.

Dancing Rabbit and Hole in the Storm Cloud sat outside talking. We exchanged greetings.

"You are early?" Dancing Rabbit asked before I could escape inside.

"Yes." I nodded. "Are there others in the hut?"

Hole in the Storm Cloud held out her hand. "No. Come back out and dance with us."

"Maybe later. My head hurts." I squatted through the doorway into the dark breezy lodge and placed my mat, my pouch, and myself on the ground.

A high-pitched scream from outside made me jump. The women laughed, but I held my ears and struggled for air. Several more screams followed, and then the drums beat a *tom-tum* rhythm. I couldn't escape the meaning. Their shrieks became more exuberant and the drums louder until the inside of my head beat with them.

When the drumming stopped, my lodge mates entered and pulled me to my feet and then outside. They held my hands and sang. I cringed and stepped to the rhythm of turtle-shell rattles. Their songs championed the warriors who would fight the enemy and then return painted black, shaking many scalps.

My gut wrenched, and tears wet my face. I jerked away from them and rushed to a bush, falling to my knees before crumpling in a heap to my face.

More terrifying screams filled the air as cedar smoke swirled in the flickering firelight. Then, all at once, silence. I stood and moved closer, but stayed in the shadows and cried.

Chief Lone Duck left Turkey Claw's side and strode into the middle of the circle. "Whisper and Moon Flower. Come forward and join these."

I stood to see my friends join two other women. The chief waved his feather over their heads. "These are chosen to go with the warriors in the morning."

I gasped. *What? No!*

Heaving sobs, I dashed past Dancing Rabbit, ducking inside the hut as people cheered with the drums, rattles, and dancing. I plopped down. *What will I do without Whisper and Moon Flower? They have been my teachers and protectors.* I shuddered, remembering that Turkey Claw had just been speaking to the chief. *Is Turkey Claw behind this? Eliminating my protectors? I need to go with them.*

I rolled up the mat and lifted my bag before stepping back outside. The women glanced at me. I shrugged and waved, but hurried to my hut. I scooted inside and sat on my pallet. *If I'm allowed to leave the village with the war party, maybe I can sneak away and make it to the Kentucky River in time to warn the area forts.*

The plan sparked a surge of hope and excitement, but as the evening drew long, doubts rose with my impatience.

Finally, the drumbeats and shakers stopped. Whisper entered the dark hut and startled upon seeing me. "What are you doing here?"

"I lied about my moon days." A lump rose in my throat. "I couldn't join the war dance...against my family." I sniffled and dabbed my eyes. "I heard the chief call you and Moon Flower to go. I want to go too. Can you ask him?"

"No. You must stay here." The curt tone stabbed my heart. Her narrowed eyes fixed on mine as she continued. "War parties can't take young women or wives. Kokumthena would be angry and bring defeat. Only old women are chosen for cooking and treating wounds." She gathered various pouches for the trip while continuing. "The war parties are gathering at Cornstalk's village to wait for more warriors, guns, and powder. When all is ready, we will swarm south as one." She gasped and turned back to me, scowling. "You want to go so you can escape and give warning."

Her anger sent a chill down my spine. *Stay calm.* "Yes. I must. I don't belong here. My family is at Boonesborough, and they don't deserve to be attacked. Please help me and don't be angry."

Her nostrils remained flared, but her eyes and voice softened. "Nothing I can do. You can't go. Time to sleep now." She sighed and lay down without bothering to undress.

The anguish in my spirit troubled me all night. Sleep only brought nightmares of being chased by a large, snarling black wolf with glowing red eyes. Its teeth latched onto my arm, which woke me to Whisper crouching in front of me as she shook me awake.

"You must honor Chief Lone Duck's adoption. He cares for you as a daughter."

"It's morning?" I sat up, blinking the film from my eyes as her stern Shawnee words slowly formed meaning. She had skipped the pleasant morning greetings. "I'm afraid to be here without you." My eyes watered.

"You are one of the people. You belong here." She touched my hand, peering into my eyes with a depth I hadn't seen, almost as if she were frightened.

She frowned. "Stay away from Turkey Claw. I think you are correct about the mushrooms. He saw me speaking to Tame Dove last night." She sighed. "Later, she told him that she would make a new medicine for Chief Lone Duck. He narrowed his eyes at her and stormed to his hut. He might suspect us of knowing." Her eyes watered. "I think this is why Moon Flower and I are being sent away."

Whisper kissed my cheek and stood. "The Shawnee never say goodbye. We say, 'maybe somewhere I'll see you again' and you respond: 'until we meet again.'"

I stood and gulped down the lump in my throat. *"Sah-lah-no-key."* I reached around her in a hug, unable to stop crying. "You have been my most trusted friend. Please stay alive."

She nodded. "This is your hut now. Be strong." Her eyes watered as she stroked my cheek with a wrinkled hand. "I am proud of you, Daughter." She back away sniffling, lifted her bundle, and then rushed outside.

I held my squeezing chest, crying a moment before I could slip on my dress. I forced my feet to move outside on shaking legs. When I reached the line of women and girls facing the eastern forest, the last of the war party disappeared into the mist. *Will I ever see them again?* I fell to my knees, bawling with the others. *Protect my family, Whisper, and Moon Flower. Why are men greedy for land?*

Dancing Rabbit tapped my shoulder. "Come away now. Help me with salting fish."

Her words were like Momma's, "Staying busy is best." *But it isn't best. My mind and body are numb. My heart has been gouged out without a knife.*

I wiped my eyes and followed behind Dancing Rabbit. Sad-faced people returned to the usual rhythms of their lives. *I don't know how. I don't want to be here without those I love.*

My eyes caught Turkey Claw's gloating stare.

He's dangerous. I gulped and sprinted beside Dancing Rabbit, out of the evil man's sight.

Chapter Nineteen

I missed Whisper so much that I hung one of her dresses on two crossed sticks from the ceiling so that it dangled and twirled as if she were in it. I told the new Whisper good morning, and in the evenings, I asked questions. I spoke about important things, like Chief Lone Duck seemed to be better without Turkey Claw's medicine and that the corn was doing well. I also told her Corn Flower's secret. "She might be pregnant, but no one has heard from Hiding Turtle."

Throughout May and June, I had stayed out of Turkey Claw's sight as much as possible, but sometimes I'd get a crawling feeling up my spine that he was watching me.

I wiped my eyes and sighed. *I want to go home.* Each day, I hoped for and expected to see Papa lead a group of men here to make a trade. Then I decided to make a collection of jerky and other items I could pack in a hurry in case I ever gained enough courage to risk death and head off alone.

The morning of the twenty-eighth, I arrived in the cornfield to help harvest beans and the first cobs. My mouth watered anticipating biting into juicy kernels. I peered at Corn Flower, who set her basket near me. "Any word from your mother when we can celebrate?"

Corn Flower shook her head, frowning.

I knew why, but asked anyway. "Still no word from Hiding Turtle?"

"No." She sighed. "But maybe he's with our warriors. A runner arrived with the news yesterday that the war party made it south, to the Chickamauga village. Now, they are moving east to raid more settlements. I hope he isn't in the spirit world."

A buzzing sounded in my ears. I felt sick.

Corn Flower touched my arm. "I'm sorry. I shouldn't tell you about raids. I don't want your white family harmed."

I nodded and walked away with my basket of corn. She lifted hers and walked beside me, silent.

As we passed the men sitting at the main lodge, Chief Lone Duck winced at the cup in his hands.

Something's still wrong. What's in that cup?

Turkey Claw scowled at me and pointed. My stomach churned as his words blared.

"We should accept the ransom price for that one." He stared at the chief. "We can buy many rifles, lead, and gunpowder."

"No. She is not for sale. I have said before." Chief Lone Duck hunched over and held his belly.

I glanced at Corn Flower, who lowered her basket to the ground. When the chief saw us, he smiled and stood straighter. "Daughters, come help me home for supper."

I placed my basket beside hers, and we rushed to the chief and took his arms. His body radiated heat. People looked up, staring as we stumbled down the trail. When Corn Flower's two younger brothers saw us, they came and took over.

Tame Dove's eyes showed fear. "What has happened?" She felt Chief's head. "It's like fire." Her voice quavered.

I stood out of the way. Corn Flower held on to my arm and leaned to my ear. "I'm frightened. Father told Mother this morning that he is passing blood like something is eating his insides." She sniffled.

I blinked back tears. "I'm sorry he's in so much pain."

She dried her cheeks. "Thank you. I must honor him by staying strong."

He made his way to a circle of mats and squatted before plopping down on his rear, still holding his stomach while sucking in deep breaths.

I followed Corn Flower to the circle of eight scared-faced family members gathering and sitting on mats. I sat cross-legged next to Corn Flower. No one spoke but all stared at the silent husband, father, and chief.

He gazed at the ground, rocking and moaning.

When his skin paled to dingy copper, Corn Flower broke the silence. "Father, please stay with us."

The chief puffed, and then fell sideways to the ground, still and silent.

My hand went to my mouth. Tears burst from my eyes. *God, don't let Chief Lone Duck die.*

Corn Flower and her mother rushed to the chief's side. His youngest son ran toward the central yard. Tame Dove sighed and raised her head off her husband's chest and spoke to us through her tears. "He has gone from his body. Now we must help him make the journey to the spirit world in three days." She wiped her face. "Come, children."

Three days? I didn't understand if he had died or was still breathing.

The youngest four children knelt and kissed their father's cheek. Each said, "Until we see you again." Then they stepped back, sniffling.

Turkey Claw rushed up with several other men. When his angry eyes found me, he snarled, "Why is she here?" He pointed toward the village. "Go."

Stunned and gaping, I stood and backed away. *Why do I have to go?*

Turkey Claw shook a feather fan and turtle-shell rattle while chanting. I sobbed as Tame Dove and her children held one another and wept.

Soon, the whole village filled the yard and surged forward. Four men carried the chief's body inside his lodge. Corn Flower followed her mother and younger siblings into the hut, crying.

Is he dead? I sat on the ground, covering my face, weeping, confused, and growing afraid of the consequences if he were.

Dancing Rabbit coaxed me up. "We'll make special foods for the offering now. Come." She took my arm and led me up the trail with the rest of the people.

"I don't understand. Is Chief Lone Duck dead?"

"He is going to the spirit world to be with his ancestors, who are waiting for him to come."

My mind whirled. Then I remembered Whisper telling me about her children in the spirit world, but I still didn't know if the chief was dead yet.

"Come cook the green beans." Dancing Rabbit left me in front of a bowl of beans near the hanging kettle. I tossed them into the boiling water with a handful of salt. *If Chief Lone Duck is dead, I'm in a lot of danger. Who will prevent Turkey Claw from trading me to the British for trade goods?* I swallowed hard to keep the bile down. *Oh, God. What am I going to do?*

Turkey Claw summoned the men to the big lodge. I stirred the kettle and stayed out of the evil man's view. In a few minutes, four men carried shovels to the high hill northeast of the village as the rest of the men went inside the lodge.

In about an hour, Dancing Rabbit tasted the beans and nodded. "Bring these."

I lifted the handle with a leather pad and followed other women carrying platters and pans of meat, squash, and beans. *Why are we eating at the grave?*

Four hours later, the chief's sniffling family carried his deerskin-wrapped body to the bark-lined opening. Men lowered the body inside. One of his sons lowered a long cane pole and rested it upright on top of the chief's mouth.

What is that for?

The chief's family sat. Corn Flower hid her face on Tame Dove's shoulder, crying as the men laid branches across the grave. Young boys brought large pieces of birch bark and placed them on top. Men with shovels added a layer of dirt and backed away.

I sobbed and watched people scoop up handfuls of dirt and take turns sprinkling the soil on top. I wiped my cheeks and took a turn.

When a mound covered the bark, Turkey Claw removed the pole, leaving the opening. "Bring the offerings." He waved a feather overhead while the women placed the food at the head of the grave.

The chief's weeping family sat beside the mound, and the people sat in a circle around them. I slinked behind Dancing Rabbit to stay hidden from Turkey Claw.

As the quarter moon rose above the trees, people took turns singing joyful songs about the greatness of Chief Lone Duck. I cried and held my knees, rocking.

When the praises ended, a group of women wailed and led the chief's family away, leaving the eldest of the chief's young sons keeping watch.

I walked with Dancing Rabbit. "Please explain the hole and food left at the grave."

"Chief Lone Duck's spirit will linger with us for three days before joining the spirit world. We must supply provisions, so he won't become angry and evoke sickness upon us."

I pressed my lips, wanting to ask, *what if he was murdered?* "What will happen now?"

"During the next two days, we will take turns sitting with the family and provide the grave foods for the chief. Turkey Claw has been chosen as temporary leader until our warriors return from war."

Fear twisted my belly into a tight knot. *This is not good.*

By the second day, people avoided contact with me. Some even held up medicine bags and spoke chants as I walked by. Women shooed me away from mixing batter for hoecakes or handling any of the food.

I hurried to Dancing Rabbit. "What's happening?"

"Come." She took my hand and led me into my lodge. "Turkey Claw is saying that you poisoned the chief with mushrooms. He says Chief Lone Duck was wrong to allow you to stay here, and Moneto will bring sickness. The people are afraid of you now."

I huffed and spewed. "He's the one who gave the chief poisonous mushrooms. Tame Dove knows this. The chief got better when he stopped Turkey Claw's medicine. He must have sneaked the chief something in his drink." My eyes watered.

She frowned and spoke in a shaky tone. "If this is true...you are in danger."

I peered into her kind eyes. "Is there anything I can do to prove to the people I'm not guilty?"

Dancing Rabbit held my hands. "Stay in your lodge and keep sage and cedar smoke rising from your fire. I will ask the women to make dances and petitions to Kokumthena on your behalf. If you are to remain, Moneto will be suppressed." She kissed my cheek. "I will bring you food."

When she left, I gathered two bundles of sage grass and a handful of cedar chips. After placing them on gray coals, my lodge filled with smoke. I adjusted the opening at the top and lay on my mat, choking, crying, and praying to God. "Show these people Turkey Claw's evil against me isn't true. I believe in you, but I need to know you hear me."

I sobbed and prayed for my family to find safety from the raids. *They may think I'm dead by now. It's been almost eight months. Help them go on without me.* I imagined each one being a year older and taller. I sniffled. *Why didn't a rescue party come? How can I get away?*

Dancing Rabbit brought venison, corn, and green beans, but I couldn't eat. My stomach stayed in knots.

When light faded, I removed Whisper's dress from the hanger and cuddled it as I lay on my pallet and worried about my future.

Sometime in the middle of the night, a loud flapping near my ear jolted me awake. I grasped my knife and sat up, scanning the dark. "Who's here?"

Cicadas sang with the crickets, coyotes barked in the distance, and a hoot owl answered another, but only a warm breeze stirred in my hut.

When a burst of light flickered outside, I rolled to my knees and crawled to the opening. With my free hand, I pushed back the thatched covering and peeked out. Stars twinkled in the clear sky. *Not lightning.*

I shook my head, about to retreat, but jagged edges of a shimmering flame-colored garment rippled beside my lodge before whisking away.

My heart thumped. *What was that?* "Anyone there?" I gulped and stood with my knife ready.

No one scurried in the yard. I eased outside, walked around my dwelling, and rushed back inside. *What's going on?* Peace and warmth came with an image of being tucked under a giant wing. Then No Name nuzzled my hand. I scratched his neck until sleepiness compelled me inside. I lay on my mat with a strong sense of being protected by one of God's angels, like in the Bible stories. *Forgive me for doubting, but I'm losing hope.*

Chapter Twenty

Depression took hold of my mind. I had no reason to wake early, no chores, and no purpose other than to mark my deerskin with the date. *July eleventh.* For ten days, I'd kept a now sickening cedar-sage smoke slithering out of my hut. I sneaked out before dawn each morning to empty my chamber pot, breathe fresh air, and pet No Name. Then I'd come back inside and plop down.

"Shoots in Knee. May I enter?" Corn Flower's voice gave me a reason to sit up.

"Please enter." I stood with watering eyes and waited for her to speak.

She smiled and came closer. "Our grieving time is over. Are you well?"

"No." Anger spewed. "I've...been shunned and cooped up in my hut, all because Turkey Claw is accusing me of killing your father. Do you believe his lie, too?"

She shook her head and peered with soft eyes. "My family does not believe you are to blame." Her calm tone lowered my defenses. "Mother has confronted Turkey Claw for accusing you. She also questioned him about giving Father something in his drink that day. He denies harming Father, but has agreed to petition Kokumthena to send the lying Moneto out of our midst."

They don't believe him. I sniffled and blinked, but couldn't stop tears from falling.

Corn Flower reached for me, and I stepped into her hug, crying. "I'm sorry Chief Lone Duck has gone to the spirit world."

"Me too. At least he knows if Hiding Turtle is there or not." She pulled away, wiping her face, and then held my hand. "Come back among us."

I hesitated. "I don't want to."

She grinned and then pulled me up and outside. I squinted from the bright noon sun as Corn Flower drew me to the central yard. My gut churned with memories of the gauntlet. I puffed breaths to ease the panic.

Corn Flower removed a feather from her hair, waved it overhead, and shouted, "Listen to my words."

People stood watching, and Corn Flower continued. "Shoots in Knee is not guilty of evil. I claim her as my sister."

A few flat voices rang out. "We hear and accept." Some of the women smiled and nodded, others shrugged and turned back to their tasks. I didn't care.

Dancing Rabbit came to me with a plate of hoecakes and a bowl of stew. "You must eat now, then I will fix your hair."

Corn Flower laughed. "I'll be back in a few minutes." She went to the table and spooned stew into a bowl.

I sat on a log, then dipped the hoecake in my broth and savored the bite. *Hungrier than I thought.*

Corn Flower returned and sat beside me. "This is delicious. I haven't felt like eating much. I'm almost as skinny as you." She grinned. "Mother has decided that the Corn Dance ceremony will begin in two days.

Skinny? I looked at my stomach, arms, and legs, but didn't see a difference. I shook my head and devoured the stew, feeling life come back.

Dancing Rabbit approached with a horsehair brush. "You have been neglected, and the lack of sun has paled your skin more than normal. You will feel better again in a few days."

My new momma figure untangled and re-plaited my hair. Then she reattached the feather, which twirled in the hot breeze. My eyes watered as I remembered Chief Lone Duck's proud smile the day Whisper tied the feather in my hair.

When dogs barked at the northwest trail, I shuddered. *That's where men from Detroit entered.* I stood and scanned for No Name. His stance and bristled fur confirmed strangers. My chest pounded as village men positioned themselves with bows, guns, and spears as several white men, wearing green-woolen waistcoats, waited to be allowed entrance.

Turkey Claw and other men hurried toward them and spoke. One of the white men shook hands with Turkey Claw, who then turned to the village, shouting, "We will accept trade items from these men."

Fear knotted my stomach. *Am I part of the deal? That's been Turkey Claw's plan all along.* I gulped and stumbled backward into Dancing Rabbit. She caught and steadied me as Turkey Claw continued. "They come on behalf of Detroit Hamilton and their king."

Turkey Claw moved to the side and waved the white men in with twenty pack mules and many horses.

Dancing Rabbit joined the frenzy of cheering women who rushed forward. Noise and panic overwhelmed me. *I need to get out of here while they're not watching.* I slunk toward my hut as the women chortled and examined pots, skillets, and bolts of linen. White men carried rifles and barrels of gunpowder into the meeting lodge. Young Shawnee boys helped tether a large herd of horses. The older village men hooted and staggered up to a spouted barrel with tin cups, sampling its content.

Corn Flower hurried beside me, gaping and shaking her head. "These are the whites who promised my father payment from Detroit Hamilton. But he told them not to bring the rum drink. This is not good. Turkey Claw heard the chief's orders."

I slipped behind the stack of firewood and stayed in the shadow of the trees. "I'm going to hide here. Let me know when they're gone." *How can I slip away?*

She nodded and turned back to the fray.

"Shoots in Knee. Come here." Turkey Claw shouted my name.

I couldn't move. *If I don't go, he'll drag me out.* I swallowed bile and willed my moccasined feet forward. I searched for Corn Flower, Tame Dove, and Dancing Rabbit. *Where are they? Who will save me?* I forced steps and quaked. *I'm facing the Great Horned Spirit in the flesh.* The men standing with Turkey Claw gawked and grinned.

I stared at the ground, needing to throw up.

"Look at my face." His gruff tone sent a shiver down my spine.

I sucked in a deep breath, blew it out, and raised my eyes.

"This man highly favors you." Turkey Claw smirked and stepped aside.

The horrid Isaiah Brown lurched forward. Rage overtook my mind as I glared at Turkey Claw's narrowing serpent eyes. "If this man touches me—I'll kill him."

People gasped as Turkey Claw's slap found my head. Lights flashed in my eyes. I flew backward before landing hard on my rear. Throbbing pain shot up my spine and then my ears rang. I squinted and blinked at Turkey Claw's face as he lifted me to my feet. My legs wobbled like a rag doll.

"He has paid a large bride price for you. You will marry him tomorrow." His nostrils flared before he turned, snarling, and stomping away.

I spat on the ground. "No. I won't. You'll have to kill me." I bent forward, sobbing and holding my knees. *I'd rather die than marry Isaiah.*

Isaiah's wooden leg thudded down in front of me. I straightened my back, ready to claw out his eyes.

He beamed through tobacco-stained teeth. "You're mine."

I gagged from his rank breath. When I turned my head, everything went black.

I came to and sat up in the flickering firelight of my hut, confused, sweating, and trembling.

Corn Flower knelt beside me. Tears wet her cheeks as she wiped my forehead.

I grasped her hand. "How long have I been out?"

"The sun hides below the trees now." She frowned. "And night hawks are swooping up mosquitos."

Tame Dove stooped with pressed lips and handed me a cup. "Drink this to soothe your nerves."

"No." I pushed her hand away and sat up, crying. The cup landed on the ground, spilling and sending chamomile scent into the air.

She settled to her rear.

Anger boiled over. "I won't marry that man. I'll drown myself in the river like Adelheid."

Tame Dove's eyes darted. "We pleaded for Turkey Claw to refuse the bride price." She glanced at the roof and then back to me. "But he says refusing so many horses, guns, and bolts of cloth is unwise and will anger Kokumthena."

I eased to my feet despite the pain and raged. "You're willing to sell me to the devil man for trade goods? How does this please Kokumthena? Your husband wouldn't have approved. That's why Turkey Claw killed him. I trusted the chief's family to protect me."

Tame Dove flinched and then stood. She remained calm but stern. "We will consult Kokumthena, and the whole village must decide—but not tonight. Stay in your hut. The men are already full of rum, and soon they will beat wild drums." A callous smirk rose on her face. "News has come that our war parties have made successful raids in the south lands. Soon they will move up toward the Kentucky."

I sought Tame Dove's soul as I peered into her dark eyes. "Please allow braves to take me back to my people before this happens. My father will pay you more than anything this evil man offers. I promise we'll leave Kentucky. Please."

Her eyes narrowed. "Kokumthena does what is best for all of her children, not just for one." Her harsh tone ripped into my chest like a twisting butcher knife. She motioned for sniffling Corn Flower, who followed her outside without a glance back.

I sat on the hard-packed ground, shaking and sobbing. I reached for my paring knife and raised my wrist. *I won't be Isaiah Brown's woman.*

Heartbeat rhythms boomed on the drums as men chanted songs about bravery. I sighed and stared at the knife lying on my wrist and bawled. *I don't want to die. I want to go home.* I stabbed the knife into the dirt, praying, "If I die, let it be from the courage of trying."

A surge of peace and clarity came. I stood, then pranced in cadence with the turtle shakers over to the adoption wampum. I lifted it from its place on the wall and threw it on the ground.

I felt for the feather tied to my braid and tugged for tightness. I found the paint dye and stirred a dab of water into the yellow duck bile with my finger and streaked it across my cheeks, then dotted them with red paint. I chanted as a warrior, but this time in English, "I go to war against fear. My Creator Spirit gives me wings of strength and courage. I will trust the one who is watching over me. The enemy will flee before Mary Shirley, daughter of Cage." I sucked in a deep breath. *I'm going home. Either to my family or to heaven with you, God.*

Fraying nerves and crawling sensations on my skin threatened my resolve, but I pictured Papa's map with the flow of the rivers. *I can do this.* I placed my calendar in a beaver-skin pouch and then tucked it inside my already packed buffalo bag. It contained flint stones and packets of buffalo and venison jerky. I gathered the last of my hoecakes and stuffed them on top before tying the bag closed.

I rolled and tied my blanket for easy carrying, then slipped on my moccasins. After securing my leggings, I attached a sheathed butcher knife through a loop just above my knee but under my side-slit skirt. I tied one of Whisper's red bandannas around my forehead to identify me as Shawnee if seen on the river. Then I shouldered a beaver-skin water pouch and the buffalo bag before glancing around once more. *Nothing else I need.* I sniffled, thinking about Whisper. Life with the people had been tolerable until she had to leave. *She kept Isaiah from taking me and kept me safe. God, grant her a good life.*

Joy surged through me as I imagined the reunion with my family. *A few more days, and I'll be home.* I shrugged. *Or dead.* I shook my head and moved to the back of the hut. After parting the bark wall, I crawled into the dim light of a crescent moon. A few men staggered around, trying to dance to erratic drumbeats that matched the thumping in my chest. *I'll fight like a wild cat if I'm caught. I'll kill or be killed.*

I crouched and moved like a turtle through the dark, staying along the brushy fringe of the village. When I passed Corn Flower's hut, I veered left toward the river shrubs where the small canoe lay.

A twig snapped behind me. I turned my head. An arm grabbed me.

Isaiah's fowl inebriated voice slurred, "Where you goin'?" He reached around my waist with one arm and grabbed the back of my neck, pulling me against his body and toward his disgusting mouth before I jabbed my thumb in his eye. He released me, cursing God's name.

I side-kicked his wooden leg. He stumbled to the ground. "Damnation. Wildcat come 'ere. I'm goin' have you. Dead or 'live." He rose to one leg, trying to balance.

I whipped out my knife and fumed, "I'm going to have you—dead." I rushed toward him as a growling dog leapt from the darkness and knocked Isaiah to the ground before grabbing his neck.

Terrified, I squatted and held my breath as Isaiah's gurgling moans mixed with low growls. I cringed at the cracking, snapping sounds and felt sick. The groans ended. Isaiah Brown lay still and quiet. I gulped several times and stayed still, waiting to see if the dog would come for me. I couldn't stop trembling.

The dog pranced toward me, smacking and licking its glimmering nose. I whispered, "No Name? Is that you?"

He lay at my feet, panting. I sobbed and dug out a slice of buffalo jerky. My hand shook as I held out the offering. No Name took the meat, and I reached to pet him but gagged at the smell of wet dog and blood. I rubbed his paw instead. "Thank you for saving my life. You're a good boy. I want to take you with me." My heart broke. "But you're safer here. I'll never forget you." I stood, sniffling. "I have to go now. Stay."

I quaked as I backed toward the river, nauseated from what just happened. *Isaiah will be found by morning, and the loyalists will know I'm gone and come after me.*

I rushed to the small canoe, felt the paddle and spear on the bottom, then tossed in my supplies. I shoved the craft into the water as I climbed in, raised the paddle, and pried away from the bank. No Name jumped in behind me. His stench made breathing difficult.

I paddled with frantic strokes before remembering to find a calm, smooth rhythm. Once centered in the current, I glanced back at the dog. "What am I going to do with you? I can't throw you in the river, but you stink. I don't have extra food." I paddled and shook my head. "You're on your own. I told you to stay. You might regret claiming me. If you decide to go back, I won't blame you."

Soothing trickles of water brushing the nose of the canoe as it sliced through the gentle current helped calm my spirit. "Sometime tomorrow, the Piqua Shawnee and the Mad River will be behind us. The Great Miami will carry us downstream and into the Ohio."

I had been in shock when Turtle and Sparrow veered north from the Ohio River and paddled hard upstream. *Was it two or three days?* My mind was too muddled to think. *Downstream should be faster.*

Mosquitoes buzzed around my head and feasted on my face. As I swatted them, my eyes sought light. Occasional peeks of faint moonlight flickered through the tree branches, but not enough. I tried to listen for rippling sounds that could be tree branches or large rocks, but all I could hear were the shrill chirps of cicadas, frogs, and crickets.

Memories of being lost in the dark woods a year ago flooded back. Raspy breaths brought dizziness. *This is worse...I'm not in control.* "Maybe we should abandon the canoe somewhere and walk. No. We're in Indian territory."

The bow pitched forward, and the canoe jarred from side to side. My stomach churned. I held the paddle across the craft as water splashed in. No Name bumped the sides. The canoe bounced and scraped over rocks. *Rapids.* "Hang on, boy."

The turbulence lasted for several minutes and then returned to a calm rhythm. I closed my eyes and sucked in a deep breath of nasty dog, blended with wet wood, moss, and mud. I sighed and wept. *I'm at your mercy, God.*

I stared into the darkness for hours, listening to the calm trickles and ripples of the current. Then the rhythmic splashing of water against the sides of the canoe tried to lull my eyes closed. No Name yapped. My eyes widened at a hoot owl swooping across our path, screeching in protest to our presence. I almost wet myself.

A tree branch slapped my face, and the canoe jammed into a silhouetted snarl of fallen trees. It screeched to an abrupt stop and threw me onto my hands and knees. I heard splashing as the craft bounced in the torrent while I poked and shoved out of the snag with the paddle. "That was close." I sighed.

After guiding the canoe into the middle of the river, I glanced back. "You all right, boy?" He wasn't in the canoe. "No Name?" *Oh, no!* His head and paws bobbed in the water behind me. I didn't know how to retrieve him. *I can't risk trying.* Tears filled my eyes. "Go home, boy. Thank you for caring."

I faced forward and cried as the canoe sped through the current in the dark. I couldn't look back. *He'll swim to shore. He'll be all right. He's brave and smart.*

Chapter Twenty-One

After many sad hours, I forced a look back. The predawn sky blushed with swirls of plum, rose, and polished brass. *I've survived the night.* I knew No Name wouldn't be there but scanned and hoped.

I blinked away tears, then stared a moment longer, relieved no one followed. *They've found Isaiah by now, if the dogs left anything, and soon they'll discover I'm gone.*

I returned forward and rested the paddle across the bow to give my trembling arms and aching back relief. I dipped my hand in the cold water and splashed my face. *I'll be visible soon.* Fear grew as I searched the banks for Indian scouts.

My breath caught as a dog with reddish-blond fur, white neck, and floppy ears stood watching me from the southern bank, wagging his tail. Joy burst out of my belly. "No Name," I squealed.

Ignoring pain, I paddled to the bank as fast as I could. He jumped in, and I reached around his neck, weeping. "I'm happy to see you. Sorry you got tossed out, but at least you got a bath."

I scanned around and behind for reassurance. *No one following yet.* I smiled at No Name and the golden sliver of sunrise winking over the horizon, then paddled to correct our westward course. When the current slowed enough to rest again, I fumbled through the food bag, pulled out two slices of jerky, and gave one to No Name. "Your loyalty and bravery have earned you this reward." I sniffled and rubbed his neck. "You're going to have to learn English though, like stay, sit, and come." I chuckled, realizing how much I had to concentrate to get out that sentence. "I might have to relearn English. How can I be so mixed up with my own language?"

A variety of birds chirped on both sides of the river. I imagined them spreading the news about the captive girl who kicked hot coals on her captors and escaped with their best guard dog. Eight months of memories tangled my emotions and sparked fear of being recaptured. *This time, they'd probably kill me.*

I shook my head. *No time for that.* I went back to paddling and sped past large screeching birds that swooped into the river carrying off fish. After we rounded a bend, the distance between the banks widened, and a larger body of water lay ahead.

"We did it. This is the Great Miami River." I looked back as the Mad River spit us out of its mouth into a slower current. I shouted, "Ha-ha. We conquered you."

I resumed paddling, watching ahead and behind for other canoes. *I have to stay focused. Many Indian tribes use this river—not just Shawnee.*

I adjusted the red bandanna on my head, praying that I'd pass for a young Shawnee brave from the distance. *As long as they can't see my skirt from the shore. But if white hunters see me...God, don't let them shoot me.* I rose to my knees and paddled faster.

As the noon sun blazed, my mind screamed for sleep. *If I don't get some rest, I'll die.* My head pounded, and the miserable cramping in my belly meant my moon days had started.

When I saw a sandy bank, I drew the canoe into a shady alcove and hacked down briers and honeysuckle vines with the paddle. *I'll hide and sleep a little while.*

No Name leapt over the bow to the ground and sniffed before hiking his leg on a bush. He sniffed the air and went exploring. I watched for snakes and climbed over the side into knee-deep water. I tilted one side of the canoe over to collect a little water, then pulled the craft up the bank before turning it sideways to drain out the day's foulness.

After lying on the ground in the cool shade, I allowed my eyes to close. *An hour or two is all I need.*

Growling jerked me awake. *It's dawn?* I sat up, peering through a grayish-rose haze. No Name and a black bear stood opposite each other, exchanging intimidating growls. My heart raced as I tried to figure out what to do. I remained still but ready to shove the canoe and myself into the river if needed.

The bear sniffed toward the food pouches I'd forgotten to hang out of reach. He rocked his head and shoulders, grunted, then lumbered toward the golden glow behind the silhouetted trees. In his wake, birds flitted from tree to tree, and river frogs gulped and splashed into the water. No Name continued to watch and growl. Relief washed over me as I thought about what would have happened if No Name hadn't won the argument.

Throbbing pain shot through my arms and shoulders as I rose and listened to the forest awaken with chirping, croaking, and scurrying.

Tree branches shook and creaked in a warm southeasterly breeze as I pushed to my feet and gathered the supplies into the canoe. I gulped the last of the stale water from the pouch, then shouldered it and slipped my knife from the sheath. Creeping like a cat through the woods, I listened and watched for signs of human occupation nearby as I wandered in search of a spring.

My moccasins squished into a small ground spring near a hickory tree. I lowered the pouch opening into the water, careful not to let in sediment. Once plugged, I lay it aside and scooped out a handful of cool tar-colored mud. I smeared it on my skin to protect it from additional sunburn.

As I returned to the canoe, recent moccasin prints caught my eye. They led down a deer trail toward the riverbank.

Time to leave this place. My heart pounded as I shoved the canoe back into the sloshing river but held the bow, making a clicking sound to call No Name.

He came, then sat and stared at me, panting.

"Let's go, boy." I pointed inside the canoe, but he didn't budge.

He must be tired of being cooped up. My eyes watered. "Believe me, I understand. I'm tired too. I'll miss you." My heart ached like the day my dog Drummer lay dead after saving me. *Why did I get attached to this dog?* "Thanks for everything." I climbed in sniffling and pried away from the bank. "Until I...see you again."

No Name whimpered and leapt from the bank into his place behind me. Joy burst from my chest. I wanted to hug him, but had to paddle into the current. Once on course, I reached back and ruffled his fur. "I'm glad you changed your mind. I would have been so lonely without you, and...I feel safer with you here." I blinked away tears. "I'm afraid we stayed too long back there. Men from the village could emerge at any moment."

I scanned the river ahead and then glanced back several times. My nerves settled with a new thought. *Maybe they decided I'm not worth coming after since Isaiah's dead. They have the gunpowder and horses.* I shook my head. "No. The loyalists still want to take me to Detroit." I paddled faster.

To keep my mind from worrying, I told No Name about my family and why we came west. The memories seemed so long ago. Then I told him about my loyal dog Drummer and had to hush awhile and grieve.

No Name stood, whining as if wanting out. I paddled to shore, and we both found bushes to water. Then we drank. No Name lapped from the river while I guzzled from my pouch. I pulled buffalo jerky from the bag and lured him back into the canoe with a piece. I ate a slice and glanced up. *Late afternoon.* "We have to keep going. We're still in Indian territory, and I don't know the location of all the villages, but the Shawnee aren't the only tribes that live near this river. Papa's map didn't show any white settlements."

I rested my arms and watched the sky's blues splash with yellow, orange, and red as the sun rolled over a hill.

A moment later, the sound of churning water snapped me out of the stupor.

A large tree had fallen halfway across the river and formed a spillway. My heart pounded. *No way around.* I pulled No Name in front of me and between my legs, then held the paddle across the bow for balance. I sucked in a deep breath and squeezed my eyes closed as everything plunged forward.

The dip ended with a face full of icy-cold water. I gasped, coughed, and sputtered. The canoe bounced and wiggled, then righted and shimmied. No Name broke free of my legs and shook water from his fur. I sucked in a deep breath, grabbed the paddle, and steadied the craft. My supplies floated on the canoe's bottom in four inches of water. "At least we're still upright. Thank you, God. Now I need to find a place to camp and empty this water." I scratched No Name's neck. "I don't know about you, boy, but I've had enough. If I don't get out of this canoe, I'll scream."

When the river curved, I spied a low bank and drew the craft to the shallows. No Name jumped on shore and examined the area. My body ached and trembled. I lacked the strength to heave the canoe very far, but stepped behind it and shoved it into some shrubs. After listening for voices and sniffing the air for smoke, I slipped out my knife and cut a thin, long vine. I tied one end on the food and water pouches, then tossed the other end over a tree branch and hoisted everything out of animal reach.

No Name returned from the woods with a rodent of some kind and lay on the ground, enjoying it. I had to cover my ears for several minutes.

I lay down, stretching my arms back and resting my head on my palms, then stared into the deep plum sky holding up a thin, waning moon. "Thank you again, God, for sparing my life another day." I watched stars shimmer and one fell. *Surely, we'll enter the Ohio River tomorrow. I ache to be home.*

Restlessness filled my sleep, and when I woke before the gray glow of dawn, No Name nudged me as if to say, "Let's go." We shoved off, and I paddled with renewed hope. As a ray of light shone ahead, the river widened, and so did my smile. I paddled faster. "We're almost to the Ohio. I remember jumping out of Hiding Turtle's canoe somewhere near here."

Excitement burst out of my chest as a squeal when the canoe caressed the brassy-gold shimmer of the Ohio River. The gilt-swirled sky to my left meant the river was making the southern curve like on Papa's map. The current was fast but smooth, and soon the sky brightened into slate blue. I glanced back. *Still no one following. If they were seeking me, they would have found me by now. Colonial settlements lay on the south side. Boonesborough is southeast.* "We'll have to watch out for Indian hunters along the banks. I'll wave as if I'm a young Indian brave in too much hurry to stop." I stroked No Name's neck and faced forward. *Maybe they'll believe it.* "I'm glad this is a wide river. If we keep to center, they won't be able to make out details." I focused ahead, scanning. "Now, to find the Kentucky River. I have no idea how many days we'll be watching for it, but I hope it'll be recognizable, if not by revelation, then my best guess. But we're free! We're actually free."

Nothing had happened for two days, until this morning, July sixteenth. No Name sniffed the air behind us before I heard the sloshing water. Then out of the silver mist came a speeding canoe with two older braves. I gulped twice to keep from throwing up. *Stay calm. Can't outrun them.* I placed my paddle across the bow as they paused beside me, staring from wrinkled, tattooed faces. Their bare chests were also covered in tattoos of various shapes and swirls, and tall spiked mohawks. *Not Shawnee.* I raised my hand and shouted with a deep but cracking voice, "*Hah-tee-toh.*"

They nodded and resumed paddling ahead.

The ruse worked. My craft drifted for a moment while I cried from relief. Their elderly age reminded me that most of the young men were probably in war parties. I wiped tears from my mud-smudged cheeks. For the first time since I fled the Piqua village, I had real hope of making it home to my family.

I ate a few slices of jerky and continued to scan all around with mind-numbing boredom. Then the noon sun flickered on a south-facing flow of a wide river that entered the Ohio. I gasped. *Has to be the Kentucky.*

I grinned and aimed the bow toward the stream several feet ahead. My stomach knotted as I drew and pried the canoe up the Kentucky River, which seemed determined to force me back. *Maybe I should land and walk now. No, I'm not going to be defeated.* I paddled with deep, hard strokes, but the canoe pitched up and then tilted left. I leaned to the right, grabbing the sides to force the craft to balance, but my strength was gone. I pushed No Name out and screamed, "Swim", barely catching my breath before the canoe flipped on top of me, forcing me down the Ohio River.

Using the small pocket of air, I breathed once more, then lunged deeper underwater, and swam out from under the craft, only to be snagged on the surface by a jumble of tree roots and vines. I tugged and pulled free, then surfaced and caught my breath again before being wedged in branches. My arms were scratched and bleeding. *Must get out of this.*

A boisterous bark revealed No Name on the eastern bank of the Kentucky River a few yards away. My surge of joy turned to worry. *If he tries to come, the river will sweep him away.* I yelled, "Stay" in Shawnee so he'd understand.

When I spotted an opening in the tangle, I held onto the tree and lowered underwater again. I pulled free and climbed out. My feather still dangled from a strand of hair under the red bandanna. I reminded myself of its meaning and my worthiness of keeping it. *At least for now.* I reattached the feather and huddled my legs close, examining my arms.

At least I'm on the south bank, and I still have my knife. My whole body protested movement, but I gritted my teeth at the aches and stood on weak legs. I found a clump of plantain leaves and rubbed a crushed one on my scratches. After choosing a sturdy walking stick, I walked back toward the Kentucky River.

I shoved through vines and stumbled over tree branches for several minutes, watching for napping snakes. When I reached a low bank on my side of the Kentucky, No Name yapped from his bank, knelt, and wiggled his hind end as if wanting to play. I laughed and gained the resolve to force my exhausted body forward, reminding him to stay.

No Name remained on his side of the river but followed as I trekked along the riverbanks, watching for a way across. As sun-kissed shades of green and yellow filled the forest, the need to cross the river became a panic. *I can't be over here alone. I need No Name's protection.* I spotted a snag of tree roots a short distance downriver. *I can swim to those. Foolhardy or not, here I come.*

No Name whimpered and watched as I waded into the cold but refreshing river. I kicked hard and stroked fast, then crashed into the tangle. I caught a loose root with one hand and prayed for it to hold while grabbing a sturdier branch. Mustering my last bit of strength, I clawed up the bank and then sprawled onto my belly. No Name greeted me with zealous licks to my arms and face. When I could sit up, I cuddled and stroked him. My stomach growled, and No Name tilted his head.

"Well, boy. Time to forage before it gets any darker. All I have is my knife." I glanced at the amber sky. "We'll snuggle down here tonight."

I searched for a spring, but the only one I found was brackish. Blackberries and plant roots satisfied my thirst. I raked up a pile of roots with my foot before bedding down on my side. No Name approached, then stood near. I patted the ground in front of my stomach. He lowered, rolling to his back as I rubbed his belly. "You're a good boy. *I can't wait for you to meet my family.* My eyes watered. *Will I ever make it back?*

Chapter Twenty-Two

July seventeenth began with a rabbit carcass dropping beside my head. I sprang to my feet, clasping my throat, staring down at it and then at No Name. I sighed and shook my head before rubbing his neck. "Thank you, boy. I'll stick to grubs and such."

After foraging, I clicked my cheek for No Name to follow. "Let's go. We need to watch for Elkhorn creek and avoid loyalists somehow. But after we cross, the Boonesborough settlement should be a day or two away."

Midafternoon, we came upon a grove of mulberry trees near a clear spring. I squealed before eating its berries by the handfuls. At the spring, I drank and cleaned my scratched arm. When No Name stared back down our tramped southwest trail, he growled and bristled. I grabbed my knife and waited with a speeding heart and shallow breaths. *No time to hide.*

Leaves crackled and four breech-clothed warriors stopped in mid-stride and stared. I gagged from the skunk oil they used to cover their tracks. Three were bald and painted all over in black-and-white spots. The other man's face was painted white for war. His hair was long and loose, like a Shawnee man. A silver medallion with a bear symbol hung around his neck. Three eagle feathers dangled in the breeze from his red bandanna that reminded me of Whisper.

No Name sat in front of my feet, growling more fierce. A waterfall of fear tumbled over my body. "Shh. Stay," I whispered in Shawnee.

The men frowned at each other, then the Shawnee man came forward, tilting his head and spoke, *"Hah-tee-toh. Nay-hee-way Kee-tay-see-lah-wee?"*

He asked what I'm doing. I swallowed. *"Hah-tee-toh."* I continued to speak Shawnee. "This dog is protecting me. If I approach you as a friend, he might calm." I gulped.

The man nodded.

I eased forward, lying. "The white hunters stole me from the Piqua village. I escaped their canoe, and this dog followed."

No Name laid down but stayed alert while the man explained my words in another language. He turned back to me. "I am Gray Fox of the bear clan. These are Delaware people. We saw your trail through the woods."

He pointed back the way I came. "Foolish woman. Easy to track."

"Yes. I was afraid. Can you take me back to my people?" My throat tightened. *Please say no.*

Gray Fox peered at me. "What is your name?"

I gulped. *Can't tell him the real one.* "Stands in Rain."

He chuckled and told the others, who joined his laughter. Then his face tightened.

"We will rest here for darkness. Then we are going like panthers to the white man camp—down that deer trail." He pointed behind me.

I glanced back at the narrow winding path. My mind raced. *Loyalist or hunters? Doesn't matter.*

"We will kill them as they sleep and return here. Tomorrow you and dog will go with us to Chickamauga village and join Dragging Canoe's war." Gray Fox straightened the feather in my hair. "You have husband?"

I recoiled from his touch. "My man went with Cornstalk to meet with Blue Jacket." The pounding in my heart increased with my desperate story. "We joined during Bread Dance."

He frowned and grunted. "We will sleep now. Keep dog quiet. Are you hungry?"

He believes me. I sighed and nodded. "And parched."

"We have water and buffalo meat cakes." He pointed to the dangling bags the other men had hung on broken oak branches. "Don't make cooking fire."

He turned away, and I sucked in a relieved breath. "Thank you." I swallowed hard. "I will keep watch."

I went and sat cross-legged beside No Name, scratching behind his ear. I had no intention of going with them. *I won't remain a captive. If Whisper can kill men in their sleep, so can I. I must. I can't let them raid that camp, loyalist or not.*

When snores and heavy breathing began, I rose and scanned the men for movement. I slipped out my knife, crept forward, then froze, shaking my head. *No. I can't do it. I can't kill unprovoked.* I backed away and glanced around at what they had left unattended. One of the Delaware men had propped a rifle against a poplar tree next to his head. *Too risky.*

I crept to the oak tree and shouldered the canteen and one pouch of the meat cakes called *pem-me-kan*. I glanced at the men again and pressed my lips. On another tree hung a quiver of arrows with a bow. Holding my breath, I lifted it without rattling and then eased toward the trail.

No Name trotted ahead, sniffing the ground and bushes. I stayed quiet and quick, resisting the desire to run. Several yards away, I stopped and listened. *Are they coming?* No Name came to me but wasn't alarmed. After a deep breath, I resumed my fast but cautious pace.

When we came upon a creek, fear gripped my belly. I stood still, but dizzy. *Is this the Elkhorn?* No Name lapped water, then sat watching me peer upstream. *No voices. No camp sounds.* Birds flushed from a shrub as No Name pounced. My blood ran cold. I bent forward and held my knees a minute. When I could breathe, I chided. "Don't do that."

I scanned the path on the other side of the creek and held everything overhead, wading across through chest-deep water. No Name shook, then rolled in the leaves while I drank from the canteen. Squirrels and rabbits darted for cover as No Name resumed hunting. The sun lay atop the forest trees too soon. My nerves unraveled. *Should be at the camp by now. Am I lost?*

No Name bristled and sniffed the air. A dog barked a short distance away. I gasped. *Guard dog? Coyote?* No Name snarled, and I darted into the nearest bushes, crouching. I clicked my cheek for him to come, but he didn't. Leaves shuffled as something approached. No Name lunged toward it, out of sight. Horrible snarls and growls sickened me into sobs. I held my ears but heard the blast from a rifle, then a mournful yelp. *No Name? No!* I sniffled and held my breath as footfalls drew near.

A gruff man's voice bellowed in English, "Come out'a there."

My stomach fluttered. I stood, shouting, "Don't shoot."

I heard a snap, then a blast, as pain ripped through my left shoulder. I screamed and grabbed my wound, bawling and spinning before crumpling to my knees.

Blood covered my hand. Words poured out as I panicked. "I don't want to die! Please help me. I'm Mary Shirley. My family's at Boonesborough. Please take me there."

"What the—?" A scruffy-faced man wearing a black-brimmed hat rushed beside me and knelt. He removed his tan linen hunting shirt and pressed it against my shoulder as I cried out from the searing pain.

"I'm sorry, gal. I thought you were one of those Injuns we were tracking." He stared at my face. "Where'd you come from?"

Sobbing, I pointed my trembling finger back to the horse trail. "Four Indians...raiding...tonight."

"You escaped from them?" He frowned, shook his head, and wiped dried mud from my face.

I nodded and heaved breaths. "Not...your fault. I...should have spoken and waited to stand."

"Scared the—" He sighed. "Glad I didn't kill you. Save your breath. You're still bleeding heavy. I'm going to stand you up, miss. We have to walk to my horse."

When he lifted me to my feet, I wanted to bite off his ear. I shuddered, cried, and focused on breathing instead. "How far?"

The sweaty bare-chested man held me up as we shuffled through leaves. "Just a bit more to the clearing."

"I can make it." *Have to.* Imagining the reunion with my family boosted each wobbly step.

We walked into the clearing, and a black dog about No Name's size rushed forward, sniffing my leg. "Get back, Skeeter. Uncle Zeke come help. I just shot the girl William McGuire's planning to rescue from the dang Indians."

William? My breath caught. Unbearable pain kept me from speaking.

"Lordy be." A familiar-faced black man sprinted from the wood toward us. "That dog got away, Master Henry. But he's hit."

He got away. My heart leapt. "He's...my dog. Please...find him. Maybe..." I forced the words. "...he's not wounded too bad."

The man named Henry lowered me to my feet. "Hold her while I get my horse."

His slave, Zeke, held me. "Sorry, miss. Lost his trail. But ol' Uncle Zeke will go back and see 'bout 'um 'fore it gets too dark. You goin' be all right, miss. We got a man at camp can fix you up."

"You played the fiddle at Boonesborough." I peered into his deep-brown eyes.

He nodded. "That's the truth." He beamed. Then Master Henry Jones bought me from the Hendersons. My life's been a heap better. You the gal which came up missin'. Caused a terrible fright amongst the folks. They be mighty happy to see you—'cept for this bullet hole."

"I'll be all right." I sighed and sniffled. "I'm worried about my dog, No Name. I hope you find him alive." I swallowed hard. "But please, Mr. Zeke, don't search too far that you can't make it back to camp before dark. Those Indian men will raid as soon as night falls."

He nodded. "Don't you worry, miss. I'll be fine. But please call me Uncle Zeke. I'm not comfortable with mister."

"Well, all right, but you deserve a better name. If you were Shawnee, they might call you Midnight Panther."

He laughed, then pointed to Mr. Jones returning on a red horse.

"Help get her in front of me." Mr. Jones's droopy gray eyes peered into mine. "I'll get you to camp, miss. Mr. Brewster can doctor some."

Uncle Zeke stepped around me. "Hold the shirt tight to your wound. Camp's a little way. Now, lift your foot onto my hand so I can hoist." He held his large tan palm out, and I managed to comply without fainting from the renewed agony.

Mr. Jones scooted back as I sat sidesaddle, holding the shirt and my breath.

"William McGuire will sure be happy to see you, miss." Mr. Jones slid his left arm around my waist.

Suddenly, the pain dulled to a throb. I gulped. "William's...here?"

"He is. We were preparing a negotiating party to buy you back from those thieving savages."

I cringed at his judgmental tone. "They…weren't savage."

"Hang on, miss." He held the reins loose and rocked forward, and the horse lunged into a gallop, down a somewhat cleared path.

Oak and hickory smoke mingled in the breeze. I sat taller, ready to squeal. I drew in long, deep breaths of the aroma of roasting meat and coffee. Mr. Jones slowed the horse to a canter, and we entered a lantern-lit enclosure with fifty or so small canvas tents and one blockhouse-style log structure. My eyes watered as overwhelming joy, excitement, and relief threatened to render me unconscious. I blew out a breath and shook my head. *No. I want to see William.*

I blinked away tears. As the horse stood still, my body swayed and the pain in my shoulder throbbed.

Mr. Jones shouted, "Come get this girl. Tell McGuire to come."

Men gathered, and two stood on each side. I moaned as they lowered me to my feet. I scanned the crowd. *Where is he?*

The men parted. My heart sped. William strolled through, then stopped with a gasp.

"Mary? How in the—" He sprinted toward me, and I sprang forward, weeping and reaching for him.

As he neared, I fell against his chest, bursting with joy and tears at the same time. I snuggled deeper, breathing in the scents of a rain-fresh forest.

He moved back, looking at my shoulder, then swept me up and ran. "We gotta get that bullet out and pack your wound with salve."

We entered the oak scented blockhouse, and William laid me on top of a smooth rectangular table where a lighted lantern hung overhead. "I hardly recognized you at first. You're not a puny little girl anymore." I smiled into his deep brown eyes as he removed the bandana, smoothed stray hair from my forehead, and caressed tears from my temples. He winked and grinned. "I have a lot of questions for you later, but for now, who shot you?"

"I...well... Mr. Jones thought I was an Indian." Words jumbled in my head. "I had a dog." I sniffled, more lightheaded. "He killed Isaiah Brown. I stole a small canoe." Tears fell again. "Please take me home." I tried to rise.

William's forehead wrinkled as he pressed down. "Shh. You can tell me all that in English later. Mr. Brewster is here."

"I was speaking Shawnee?"

"Yes, with some English." He smiled down with dancing eyes, shaking his head. "But more Shawnee than I know, and I've been associated with them for years. I'm proud of you for being so brave and surviving among them." When he lifted the top of my hand to his damp lips, I forgot about my pain. *He's proud of me.* I squeezed my eyes to prevent watering.

William moved behind my head as an older man stood beside me with a wooden cup. "I'm Mr. Brewster, miss. I need you to drink this. It's a drip of laudanum in whiskey, but it will help with the pain."

William held up my head while Mr. Brewster tilted a wooden cup of bitter rust flavored whiskey into my mouth. I cringe from the burn, swallowed, then moaned while Mr. Brewster removed the blood-soaked shirt. I focused on his weathered face and clenched my jaw. He seemed about Papa's age and well-groomed. Then I noticed a long scar along his forehead and misshaped scalp where his hat sat a moment ago. He peered at my shoulder. "I need to cut and peel your garment off your wound." I grimaced and moaned with each pull and prod. Then he glanced up at William. "Come hold her down. This is going to hurt."

William leaned across my chest and held down my shoulder. His heart pounded against mine, but wrenching pain prevented the enjoyment.

Mr. Brewster poured moonshine into my wound and dug in with a knife. I writhed, bawled, and cursed. The table spun, and a bright light blinded me before all went dark.

Chapter Twenty-Three

I moaned and sobbed as the knife twisted deeper into my shoulder. "Stop. No more." My eyes shot open, then squinted from the lantern light. "William? Are you here?" A strong smell of moonshine permeated the cloth on my throbbing shoulder and burned my eyes. I removed it and attempted to rise, but stabbing pain shot throughout my stiff body. *No one is here.* Tears slid toward my ears as I lay still and stared at a flickering canvas roof. *I'm not in the blockhouse. How did I get on a bedroll in a tent?*

Then popping blasts from many distant guns prompted my excruciating side roll. *The Indian raid.* Sweat broke out on my forehead as I moaned and shoved up to sit. I shouted through cries, "Can anyone hear me?"

I stood and wobbled a minute before stumbling to the tent entrance. White flashes preceded more gunfire in the woods. My throat tightened. *Where's William?* A golden light caught my right vision and seemed to float toward me on its own. But soon a ghostly figure in a round-brimmed hat became a silvery-faced man carrying a lantern. He raised the flickering light higher as he neared. I squinted and shielded my eyes.

"Get back inside, miss. Don't want your wound to bleed. There's a pot in the corner behind a blanket for your relievin'. I'll fetch Mr. Brewster to check on you. Need help getting back inside?" He lowered the lantern.

I had to wait for his English words to make sense and then concentrate on answering in English. "No." My eyes focused on his gray-stubbled face. "Is the skirmish over? Where's Mr. McGuire?"

"Some of the men are still firing warnin' shots, but things be calmin' down. Thanks to your alert, we were prepared. The dogs growled an hour ago. The Injuns skedaddled back the way they came two minutes ago. I'll tell McGuire you're asking 'bout him." He raised the lantern again. "You hungry, gal? We got beans and hoecake simmerin'. No one ate while we readied for the raid. Best speak for a bite before it's all gone."

"I'm starving." My stomach growled as I nodded. "I'd love a hoecake and water, please. Thank you, Mr.—"

"Charlie Wayne, miss." He tipped his hat, nodded, and headed toward a central campfire before I could ask if Uncle Zeke had come in with a dog.

My eyes watered remembering No Name. *I need to know if he was found.* I held my throbbing shoulder and entered the tent, turning my thoughts to going home. *Wish I could fly back to my family. But I'll settle for a fast horse.*

After taking advantage of the chamber pot, I stepped around the blanket and sat on my bed, trembling from pain and weakness. My mind whirled with questions for William. The most pressing one was why a rescue hadn't been planned earlier.

Mr. Wayne's voice shouted, "Ya decent, miss?"

"Come in." I smiled when he entered, carrying a short-legged wooden table with a tin plate and a wooden cup. "Did the man called Uncle Zeke come in with a wounded dog before the skirmish?"

"Well, I don't know, miss. I've been a might busy. Mr. Brewster is tendin' a couple o' flesh wounds. He'll come in the mornin'. Says you're to be still so the wound won't bleed again and sip this tincture of laudanum for pain and sleep."

"Thank you. It's the worst substance I've ever had in my mouth."

He chuckled. "Yes, miss. Works fast though. Just can't take too much. You'll sleep like a baby." Mr. Wayne set the table on the ground without spilling a drop. He handed me the cup and then peered at me. "Mr. McGuire wants to enter. Want him to?"

My stomach fluttered as I nodded. My shoulder throbbed, but I didn't drink from the cup. I didn't want to be sleepy. For the first time in months, I cared about my appearance.

When Mr. Wayne left, I removed the feather from my braid. *I'll explain later. I need to know about my family.* My eyes watered. I spit in my hand, then rubbed and patted the loose strands of hair.

"Hello, Mary." William entered clean-shaven and hatless with damp-groomed black hair. His light-blue shirt drew me to his dark-brown eyes.

My, he's handsome. I sighed as he sat cross-legged in front of me. A hint of witch hazel tickled my nose and made me want to snuggle against his neck. My face burned as my heart responded to the turtle shaker rhythms in my head.

William grinned and set his plate on the table. "How's the shoulder?"

"Hurts. But Mr. Brewster sent something for pain." I blew out a breath.

My chest pounded as William's eyes glistened. When his lips parted to speak, I fired out questions. "How is my family? Did they move to a claim? How far from here? I want to go to them in the morning. Can you take me?"

He shook his head and clasped my hand. "Your family has had a rough time grieving for you. Thought you might be dead until your da learned you were being held for ransom. They're still at Boonesborough. Didn't want to move until you were brought back. When you're stronger, I'll take you home. It's a six-hour journey from here."

Shaking my head, I winced and stood, panting. "I'm...strong enough to leave...now. If you can't take me...I just need a horse."

William stood and touched my forearm. "Breathe, Mary." His gaze into my eyes drew me into a safe place. He lifted the cup from the table and placed it in my hands. "Take a sip. It will calm the pain overtaking you."

I sipped and sniffled.

"Are you ready to sit back down?" William waited to help.

Once seated, my heartbeat slowed, and pain eased into a dull throb.

William sighed and sat, clearing his throat. "Can you tell me how you got away?"

I shook my head. "Not yet. First, I need to know why no one came for me." I blinked tears and sniffled.

William frowned. "A party set out searching for you the next day. They found most of your signs until the storm. A month later, word came from one of our Indian sources that you were safe in a Shawnee town, but he wouldn't say which."

My mind relaxed. I wiped my eyes and took another sip of water.

He raised my face and peered with glistening eyes. "Your papa's been making inquiries since you were captured—learned you were on the Mad River west of Blue Jacket's town. He wanted to lead a campaign up there back in May, but I convinced him it wasn't best for you or your family." William sat back and sighed. "Do you understand?"

Tears flowed, but I sucked in a deep breath. "Yes. Thank you. Papa would have been killed." I grabbed William's hand and released the anguish from my heart, concentrating on English. "Hundreds of Ohio Indians from different clans left at that time to meet Cornstalk with war wampum. They're joining Dragging Canoe's war. That's all I can say for now."

William's hand remained in mine. "Your papa settled down when I told him I'd recruit a peaceful trading party and take supplies northward to negotiate your release."

I glanced at him and frowned, fearful of what might have happened.

"That's why we're at this camp. These men were willing to come with me." He turned to straighten out his legs. "The warriors you encountered may have been paid by loyalists who were tipped off. Unfortunately, they got away and will report on the girl who spoiled their plans."

"No." I gulped.

William's head cocked to one side.

"They're headed south to the Chickamauga village. One was bear clan Shawnee, and the other three were Delaware. Detroit Hamilton is encouraging the raids.

Hamilton is supplying the Piqua and other clans with gunpowder, rifles, and rum.”

Isaiah Brown's image tightened my throat and made me tremble. Without thinking, I withdrew my hand and drank a gulp of the bitter water to quench thirst. *Oh no.*

William clasped my arm. “I'm sorry. We don't have to talk about it anymore.”

I calmed and straightened. “I need to tell you everything before I get too sleepy.” My voice quavered. “I'll feel better getting it out.”

His jaw clenched as his eyes widened.

“Isaiah Brown was one of the men at Detroit. Twice he tried to gain possession of me.”

William's mouth fell open, and his face paled.

My chest pounded while I told him about the gauntlet and Whisper saving me. I paused with shuddering breaths, then confessed, “I...was adopted by Chief Lone Duck. He knew I shot Isaiah. That's why he named me Shoots in Knee.”

A slight grin relaxed William's worried face.

“The Piqua...became my family.” I withdrew my hand from his and held up my feather. “I've proudly worn my warrior feather given to me by Chief Lone Duck as a symbol of courage.” Remembering the chief made my eyes water. I drew another deep breath and stared up at the canvas a moment, blinking fresh tears. “The chief was killed a week ago by an evil man named Turkey Claw, who was greedy for Hamilton's gifts and Isaiah's bride price for me."

William's shoulders slumped, and his face lost color in the dim light.

I took his hand with a slight squeeze and peered into his moist eyes. "He didn't get to claim me."

William released a deep sigh as he sat back.

I let go of his hand to cover my yawn and wiped my burning eyes. "I escaped while the men were drunk with rum seven days ago. I sneaked to a small canoe. Isaiah saw me and followed." I stared at the ground, then peered at William.

"Do you need to stop?" He offered me the cup again.

I shook my head. "Bad image is all." I gulped. "Isaiah grabbed me, and I was seconds away from stabbing him, but my dog attacked...killed him." I bawled into my hands, remembering No Name jumping into the canoe with me.

William caressed my arm. "The same one Uncle Zeke is caring for?"

I squealed. "He found him...alive? Is he going to be okay?" My sobs were a mixture of joy and sorrow. "Can you take me to see him?"

"Uncle Zeke has turned in for the night. He said the dog will recover but limp. The bullet grazed his hind leg." William's eyebrows rose. "He'll have to stay here if we leave tomorrow. Uncle Zeke seems right attached to him, though."

My gut hurt with the thought. *But he's alive.* My shoulder had stopped hurting, but my vision blurred with dizziness and exhaustion. I sighed, finished the water, and stared at the cup. "This stuff works fast. I can't hold my eyes open anymore."

"Get some sleep, puny girl. I'll check on you in the morning." He winked and held my hand a moment before raising it again to his lips.

His teasing drew me back to our first meeting. I nodded with a slight smile. "Yesterday you said I wasn't a puny little girl anymore."

His face reddened as he lowered my hand and nodded. "That I did. But I'll be teasing you a bit longer."

I grinned and then sighed as he left. *I'm safe and almost home. Thank you for William being here, God. Can I have him?* I giggled for no reason and closed my eyes.

Chapter Twenty-Four

The clanking and banging noises that woke me before dawn came from Mr. Brewster as he set a metal washtub behind my privacy blanket. He'd already moved the chamber pot to the tent entrance.

I sat up in the dancing lantern light, still groggy. "Good morning, Mr. Brewster—or should I call you Doctor?"

"Morning, miss." He came into view. "It's just mister. I have experience in field dressing, is all." He approached, smiling. "Today is Thursday July eighteenth, in case you've lost track of our dates. I know the Indians have a different way of marking time."

I nodded and grinned. *I had my days correct.*

"I've taken the liberty of providing a tub." He pointed back. "I'll send in men with more hot water while I check on your wound."

Before I could ask about clean clothes, he held up a long deerskin shirt and men's tan trousers. "Mr. Wayne adjusted these. He thinks they'll fit you. Sorry, we've no women among us."

I beamed, still lightheaded. "Thank you. It will be glorious to wash off all this grime. I haven't had a proper bath in almost a year. Tell everyone thank you."

He chuckled and set the lantern on the short table beside me. "Some of these men have gone longer than that."

A few of those men entered, filling the washtub. I winced from the body odor as they tipped their round-brimmed hats. Most wore tattered hunting shirts in various colors and knee-high moccasins. *Do I smell as bad as they do?*

Mr. Brewster knelt on one knee and pulled back my rank-smelling bandage. I flinched from the pain and gagged.

"Looks good so far." He lifted a small but pungent leather pouch from his shoulder. "This is for you. There's wild garlic oil in a glass vial and clean bandages. Drip the oil into the wound after you wash and then before you sleep. Do this each morning and night and keep clean bandages on it until it closes with skin." He stood and stretched his back. "William McGuire asked when you can make the trip to Boonesborough. I recommend resting again today. Tomorrow at the earliest."

I don't want to rest another day. I sighed, but smiled. "Thank you."

I had to know about his former injury. "How did you get that scar and head wound?"

He came closer and crouched. "French Indian War, miss. If it hadn't been for your father, I'd be dead."

I gasped. "How?"

"He interrupted a young brave in the act of scalping me, then carried me to Doc Fleming." He grinned and stood. "Least I could do was volunteer to help retrieve you from the Shawnee when William asked. What a surprise you are. But then, knowing you're Cage Shirley's daughter—it's no wonder." He chuckled. "Enjoy your bath time. Come have breakfast with us when you're ready."

"Thank you." I beamed with pride at his respect for Papa, but scoffed at the implication of being like him. *Papa is genuinely brave—I'm rash and react from desperation.*

Mr. Brewster stopped the flow of men at the entrance. "That's enough. Let her be now. She'll come out when she's ready."

I stepped behind the blanket, undressed, and brushed dirt from my right foot before testing the bath temperature with my toe. *Warm but not scalding.* I teetered a bit while lowering to my rear and then sighed in the warm, soothing water as my exhausted muscles relaxed. *This is wonderful.* I found the sliver of lye soap, closed my eyes, and breathed the fragrance of home. I pictured Momma and my sisters hanging clean sheets; the younger children playing in the breeze, and Papa and George returning from a hunt, beaming. I squealed. "I'll be with them tonight."

As I washed layers of bear grease from my hair and grimy mud from my body, the water turned oily brown and slimy. "Oh my. I was atrocious. How embarrassing."

Once dried off, I dripped garlic oil into my wound, curtailing curses as I waved a breeze over the burn with my hand. Tears streamed down my face while I wrapped a bandage around my shoulder. *If I can do all this, I can make it home today.*

After sucking in a deep breath, I gathered my long black hair to the side of my head, braided then secured the end with my sinew. The baggy clothes draped my body, much like wearing a tent. I bent forward, laughing so hard my stomach hurt. But it felt good. *When was the last time I laughed?* "At least the men have nothing to gawk at."

I rolled up the trouser legs so I could walk, then folded my deerskin dress, fingering my green and gold quillwork, remembering every prick from the needle. *I'll reuse this for something.* I saw the red bandanna draped over the ceiling rod, already clean. I held a portion to my cheek. "Thank you for everything, Whisper. I'll never forget you." I kissed it and placed it with my dress. *Now to find No Name.* My eyes watered. *I need to pet him and say thank you and goodbye. Then I'll find William.* I sighed and stepped outside, among the snickering hat-tipping men.

One well-groomed young man with blue eyes and blond hair approached, grinning. "May I escort you to breakfast, Miss Shirley?"

I smiled. "Thank you, but I'm looking for Uncle Zeke's tent? I want to check on the dog he has."

He pointed. "Two tents to the right there."

I hurried toward the tent but saw Uncle Zeke eating a plate of salt pork and hoecakes. "Morning. How is No Name?"

He smiled and tipped his hat. "Mornin', miss. He's whimperin' some, but the wound looks clean. Go on in my tent and see him." He pointed to the small tent behind me.

"Thank you." I hesitated, fighting tears and then turned to Mr. Jones who sat beside Uncle Zeke. "I know this is selfish of me, but could you bring my dog to Cook's Fort on Indian Creek as soon as he can travel? I'm going to convince my family to leave Boonesborough soon. I'd really like him back."

"Well, least I can do. I'm sorry again for shooting you. When the dog is strong enough, Uncle Zeke and I will find you, Miss Shirley. Go on and see him now."

I wiped a stray tear. "Thank you, sir." I turned and hurried to Uncle Zeke's tent and went inside. No Name raised his head, sniffing and whimpering.

I sat beside him and rubbed him behind the ears. "Hi, boy. You must get well and stay with Uncle Zeke until he can bring you to me. I have to go on home. Wish I could take you, but it just wouldn't work. He'll take good care of you." I lowered my head to his ear and whispered, "I love you, boy. Somewhere I'll see you again." *I hope.* I kissed the top of his head, then stood and rushed out, crying.

I stood still and willed myself to stop sniveling so I could find William.

He was near the corral speaking with a man dressed in a linen shirt and blue pants. The man tilted his chin at me, chuckling as I neared. William turned.

My face burned from the shame of my attire drawing too much hilarity from the men.

William's eyes widened with his grin as he removed his hat. "Good mornin', Mary."

Nerves frayed.

"Ho-wee-see-wah-pah-nee. Hah-Koh-wee-see-lah-sah-mom-moh?" I spoke the greeting and tilted my head as his eyebrows kinked.

*"Nee-wee-see...*I'm a bit rusty with the Shawnee greeting. But how are you? You've a determined look."

I gaped and stepped back. "Horrified and embarrassed. I didn't mean to speak Shawnee. Guess I'm frazzled from everyone laughing at my ridiculous appearance."

The man with William grinned and tipped his hat. "Hello, miss. I'm Mr. Simmons." He didn't wait for my reply. "I need to eat a bite and get on to the next place."

As the man walked away, William smiled and offered his elbow. "Mr. Wayne can loan you his sewing kit."

I shook my head. "No time for sewing. I'm ready to head to Boonesborough. Ready to be in my family's arms despite Mr. Brewster's urging to stay another day. I know how to take care of my wound." I didn't give him time to protest. "I want to get my family back to Indian Creek before things get worse. As you well know, no one will be safe in Kentucky."

William's arm dropped to his side as he peered into my eyes with a wrinkled forehead and pressed lips. His reaction and silence sparked frustration.

I huffed and blinked away tears. "I've survived a gauntlet and fled from the Shawnee. I've fought the rivers...alone...in a canoe...to get back to my family." I sniffled. "I've been gone more than eight months. I didn't think I'd ever see them again." I wiped my wet face and glared. "I'm going with or without an escort. I just need a horse." I turned away to hide my watering eyes. *Am I out of my mind?*

"Mary. Wait. I'm sorry." He caught my hand, and his soothing tone returned my gaze. William peered so deeply into my eyes that I froze. A pulsing heat radiated below my belly when he came closer, shaking his head.

"You amaze me. You're like a fairy creature. Beautiful and powerful, but frightening at the same time."

My face burned. I stared at my feet, feeling my frown change to a shy grin.

"I know you're capable, but give me a minute to think things through. As you saw last night, there's major Indian activity in the area. Mr. Simmons arrived from Boonesborough yesterday morning. He said one of Boone's daughters and two of Callaways' were captured on Sunday—right from the east bank of the Kentucky in broad daylight."

I gasped and held my breaking heart as my thoughts whirled. "Who? Did he say?" I shuddered as I squeezed my eyes closed and shook away the intruding memories from my capture, but anger exploded from my mouth. "Why were they on the east bank? Is there still no security at Boonesborough?"

William grabbed my shoulders. "Mr. Simmons didn't know their names before he left, but heard they were rescued a day out. Near the Licking River."

I clasped my chest with relief. "I'm...glad they were rescued...so quickly." *That's the river I was taken up the day after I was captured.*

William stepped closer. My chest heaved as I faced his polished-oak eyes. He wrapped his arms around me and eased me toward his chest. My mind calmed as I nestled against him, ignoring the shoulder pain. I stopped crying. "I want to go home."

In a moment, he released me and moved back, taking my face in his hands. His eyes still glistened. "You're not going alone. But I'll drink a cup of coffee before I saddle horses. And we'll need a food pack." William raised his chin before stepping toward a group of men sipping from steamy cups.

I found Mr. Wayne at a makeshift table wrapping hoecakes in cloth. "Mornin', miss."

"Morning." I wiped my face. "William and I are leaving for Boonesborough. Can you spare hoecakes?"

"Yes, miss." He handed me the cloth. "I included extra venison jerky in here, too. I knew you'd be too rambunctious to sit still today."

I grinned. "Thank you for everything." I leaned toward him and kissed the salty stubble on his cheek.

He turned red and chuckled.

I hurried inside the tent and retrieved my garments, canteen, and the bow and arrows. With some pain, I tied the precious feather back into my braid. *Makes me feel braver than I am. And I earned it.*

When I went outside, William walked up with two horses and a pack mule. "You ready?"

"Soon." I went over to Mr. Brewster. "Thank you for saving my life."

He nodded. "Pace yourself, miss. Don't try to lift or pull with your shoulder, or you'll tear the wound open again. Let Mr. McGuire take care of you today."

I giggled. "Yes sir. I'll try. Been taking care of myself for a while, though."

Several men chuckled.

When I glanced at William, he was staring at the ground, shaking his head. He grinned and peered at my eyes while handing me the reins of a chestnut gelding. "He's a gentle two-year-old. Needs a name."

I smiled and went to the horse's head, letting him sniff my hand before I stroked his neck and smiled. "Liberty. I'm free, and he's taking me home."

William nodded. "Good strong name."

Ignoring pain, I stuffed food and clothes in the saddlebag, secured the bow and quiver of arrows onto the saddle along with the canteen, then traipsed over to William's bay stallion.

"What's his name?" The horse nudged my arm. I scratched him under the neck.

William's eyes danced as he smiled. "Babcock's Boy. I purchased him from Abe Babcock, one of my da's friends. Fastest quarter horse between here and Williamsburg."

I laughed. "That's a big boast, Mr. McGuire."

"Aye, and so it is. But he's been proved many times and saved my life more than once." He chuckled. "And he likes you. He usually bites. Shall we go?"

I stroked Babcock's Boy once more for good measure and then took Liberty's reins and walked away from the camp with William. I sighed and imagined the reunion with my family. *My siblings will have changed, grown taller, but I've changed too. If only I had enough arms to hold them all at once and for hours. I may never get enough hugs from my family.*

Chapter Twenty-Five

Making the dangerous journey with William lessened the fear, but not the caution. I followed his silent lead down a narrow trail, scanning the ground and bushes. Every few feet, we stopped and listened to the forest for anything out of place or disruptive. We sniffed the air for smoke and then resumed our snail's pace, serenaded by morning birds. I rubbed my throbbing shoulder when he wasn't watching.

About midmorning, William stopped and motioned for me to follow him to the riverbank. After checking for tracks and listening, he let Babcock's Boy and the mule drink. I led Liberty to join them.

"How are you doing?" He peeked around the neck of his horse.

I stopped rubbing and smiled. "A little sore, but doing well. My stomach flutters more with each step."

He grinned and pointed to a damp place a few feet away. "Good. Wait here. I'll fill the canteen at that spring."

I nodded and watched him without guarding my pitter-pattering heart. He strolled away and then knelt on one knee, splashing water on his face. Then Babcock's Boy blocked my view.

My skin prickled as William strode back, rugged, stubble-chinned, and smiling into my eyes as if knowing the depth of my desire. I whispered, "I need water."

He handed me the canteen and then stood in front of me.

I held it to my lips and guzzled until the fire in my belly went out. A droplet of water ran down my neck before I could dry it off with my hand.

William stared at my neck before his eyes met mine.

I gulped and stared back, wanting him to draw me into his arms.

He lowered his eyes and cleared his throat. "Time to get going. We'll cross to the south side of the river in about an hour. We're closer to some white settlements now, in case there's trouble."

"Good, I won't be so nervous." I stroked Liberty's neck.

William hurried back to his horse and the mule, tightening the saddles and supplies.

I breathed deep and slow, but the beating in my chest didn't stop. I plucked a large leaf from a hickory tree and fanned my face.

Several minutes later, William sighed. His eyes returned to mine as we walked. "I haven't had a chance to tell you that Hiding Turtle is one of my friendly sources."

My mouth dropped opened, not sure of what I heard.

"You need to know that announcing yourself as the daughter of Cage saved you from being taken to the loyalists. Hiding Turtle risked his life taking you to the Piqua village and keeping them from trading you to Fort Detroit. He's no longer trusted by the British. If he's captured, they'll hang him."

Tears filled my eyes as I sniffled. "Is this why he never returned to the village?" My heart ached for Corn Flower. "He has a pregnant wife there who fears he has gone to the spirit world."

William nodded. "I'll tell him this news when I see him next. He has heard of Chief Lone Duck's death. But he doesn't know it was intentional. You saw the chief killed?"

I nodded and sniffled. "His family believed Turkey Claw was treating the chief for a stomach ailment. This evil man picked poisonous mushrooms before the chief got sick. Chief didn't want to make an alliance with Detroit Hamilton, so Turkey Claw got rid of him, turned the people against me, and traded me to Isaiah Brown."

William nodded. "Makes sense." He clasped my arm. "Glad you got away."

"Me too." My body leaned toward him—desiring the comfort of his chest, the security of his arms, and something undefinable.

He grinned and moved away. "Let's make haste. Gotta get you home and relay this information to Hiding Turtle and other sources I can't tell you about."

I grabbed his arm, and we stood still. "Tell him to contact Corn Flower to let her know he's alive, and that I made it home to my people."

He nodded, and we continued at a quicker pace until we veered toward a low sandy bank. "We'll ride across the river, but your shoulder can't take the strain of crossing alone. I'll sit behind you on Liberty until we cross. Are you ready?"

Before I could answer, he placed his hands on my waist and helped me mount, then he climbed on behind me and took the reins. My heart sped as the horses and mule lumbered into the moderate current. As they swam across the deep river, I held on to the front rim of the saddle. William embraced me without squeezing my shoulder. I felt nestled and comfortable in a belonging sort of way.

As Liberty climbed up the bank, I didn't resist the force pushing me harder against William's pounding chest. Mine thumped and fluttered as his warm breaths caressed my neck. When we reached the top, the horse stood still, but we lingered in the embrace. My mind and emotions swirled like a whirlwind. *I don't want to let go.*

William ended the wonderful moment by dismounting and scanning the area. Then he mounted Babcock's Boy and whispered, "Let's go."

I ached for him near me.

About noon, we came out of the thick forest into a rippling grassy meadow dotted with wildflowers in shades of blue, pink, and yellow. I breathed in the sweet, tingly, warm breeze, and my eyes watered at the beauty.

"We'll dismount in the shade of that oak tree and let the horses graze a bit. We're in a more settled area now. A few blockhouses around if needed."

I smiled and sighed. "This is the kind of place I want someday." I swung my leg off Liberty's back, and William helped me down. I ignored the burning pain in my shoulder and sat under the tree, grinning at William.

He approached, shaking his head and chuckling. "Already one of Boone's claims, I think." William checked on the horses and mule and then sat beside me, stretching out his legs.

I gulped a swig of water.

William gazed at my eyes. "I hope your family will go back to Indian Creek—now that you're back."

"I'm going to make a strong case for leaving." I fanned my face again. "Will you stay at Boonesborough a few days?"

He shook his head. "I'll be headed out tomorrow to find Hiding Turtle. Then I need to give updates to the forts along the Holsten River on my way back to Cook's Fort. And hopefully, there's news from Williamsburg. Captain Clark and Mr. Jones took petitions to Governor Henry, requesting an end to Henderson's claim. Everyone wants to become part of the Virginia colony and put an end to the dangerous squabbles over land claims." He offered me his hand as he stood. "Ready to go?"

I accepted his help standing, but winced and rubbed my shoulder.

He frowned. "Can you stand the jarring if we ride again?"

"Yes. I can endure a full gallop." I mounted Liberty and rocked him into a canter for a minute before I felt a rip in my shoulder followed by an oozing. I slowed and applied pressure on the place.

William noticed and caught up beside me, frowning. "What's wrong?"

I peeked under the bandage. "A little tear. But not worth stopping for. Momma can patch me up again once we get there."

His brow furrowed, but we continued. He stayed beside me, glancing at me now and then.

The next moment, Babcock's Boy reared up, and William fell hard to the ground.

Like a terrible nightmare, screeching loincloth-clad Indians with red-and-black-painted bodies and Mohawked hair rushed to William with raised tomahawks.

I screamed and rode toward them, shouting in Shawnee, hoping at least one of them understood. "Get away from him."

The men frowned and stared at me. One placed his foot on William's chest, holding him down. Two came at me, pulling me off Liberty and onto my feet as I screamed in agonizing pain. Desperate to stop them, I yelled again in Shawnee. "May Kokumthena curse you if you harm me or my man." I held up my feather, heaving breaths and crying as blood from my shoulder trickled down my arm.

They glared and stood back, but looked confused and almost frightened. Out of the woods rushed a familiar-faced man. As he came closer, I recalled his name and spoke Shawnee. "Loud Hawk. I...know your mother, Moon Flower. I am Piqua Shawnee. Adopted by—*I can't mention the name of the dead*—the former chief who was murdered by Turkey Claw. I witnessed him do this. Turkey Claw does not deserve to be chief."

Loud Hawk frowned and stepped closer. "You know where my mother has gone?"

"She was sent with the war party to Cornstalk's village. She was my friend. I am Shoots in Knee."

He spoke another dialect to the men with him. They reluctantly allowed William to stand. He looked at me wide-eyed and didn't try to fight them.

Loud Hawk glared at William, then he spoke in broken English. "You. Friend of Hiding Turtle?"

William remained silent.

Loud Hawk glared and grunted. "Because woman is friend to mother, you may leave with one horse. Woman will choose. You. Tell all whites to leave this land. Before next Bread Dance. Or Shawnee and Cherokee will swarm like locusts. Much destroy, much death."

William nodded, then he glanced at me wide-eyed with clenched jaw as if concerned.

Loud Hawk turned to me and spoke in Shawnee. "Blue Jacket and Black Hoof will go to Piqua village and see if your words are true. Now take your man and leave this blood-soaked land." He leaned closer, peering into my eyes. "A curse on your firstborn son if you return."

I gulped and stumbled backward as if he had slapped my face. I coughed to free my throat from the squeezing grip of his threat. Loud Hawk turned to the horses and raised his chin. Trembling and unnerved, I went to Liberty. "Sorry, boy." I removed my belongings and moved to place them on Babcock's Boy. "This is our horse."

Loud Hawk motioned to the seething men and stormed back into the forest. One took Liberty and spit in

William's face as he stormed past and followed the others away with our mule and supplies.

I retrieved a wad of bandages from my pack and pressed them on my wound, moaning. Then my legs buckled. I collapsed on the ground, bawling and gagging. William limped over and sat, rubbing my back while I threw up and cried.

When he reached his arms around me, I laid my head on his shoulder, and my sobs changed to shuddered breaths. The rhythm of his heartbeat consoled me.

He pulled me away and sighed. "I owe you my life. Thank you...for Babcock's Boy. And thank God you knew that Shawnee man. When we're safe again, you can explain all that he was saying. I'm still in shock."

Me too. And I just told them you're my man. I reflected on the reality of what could have happened if I hadn't experienced life among the Shawnee. I shivered at the thought of William lying dead and me being kept as a captive. While a gust of warm air sent the canopy of trees whispering above my head, a deep gratitude filled my heart. *Thank you, God.* I sniffled and wiped my face.

I peered into William's eyes, sniffling and pouring out a desperate plea. "Please don't leave Boonesborough without me...and my family. I don't want to be there without you."

He scooted back a little and took my hands, peering into my eyes with his own glistening. "I'm a scout, Mary.

Leaving is what I do. Settlements and soldiers need me watching and listening for trouble. Information that can help end the war and the alliance between the British and the Ohio Indians. But I'll be coming around to see you when I can."

The pain of his words crushed my chest like a boulder that couldn't be moved or shoved away. He raised my hands to his lips and held them there for a moment. Despite my hurt feelings, his kiss sent a spark of life to my limp body.

"Our lives have been spared today." He cleared his throat. "And...my purpose..." He blew out a breath. "...is to help you complete the journey...back to your family who needs you. They're waiting for you an hour up this trail, and we need to go."

William released my hands. I saw his eyes water before he glanced away, flicking off what I knew was a tear from his cheek. He pushed to his feet, hobbled a bit, and then held out his hand.

My stomach fluttered as he lifted me to my feet and cleared his throat. "We need to ride. I sprained my foot in the fall, but it's usable." He held out his elbow. When I clasped his arm, he caressed the top of my hand and smiled. "We'll make it together."

William hobbled as we walked over to Babcock's Boy and examined him for injury.

"He seems all right. Now, to mount." He chuckled. "Aren't we a pair?"

I grinned. "I can get up by myself. There's a fallen tree you can stand on." I pointed to a large oak that must have been blown down by a storm.

"That's mighty handy." He nodded, and we led the horse to the tree.

After William mounted, I climbed on behind him and held his waist, grateful.

Chapter Twenty-Six

A faint waft of hickory smoke on the breeze sent my heart rejoicing as if I'd just arrived outside the gates of heaven itself. "Do you smell that? How much farther?"

William laughed. "A few more minutes."

When sounds of wood chopping and pots clanging reached my ears, I rocked forward, wanting to go faster, then I gulped with sudden panic. "No, stop. Please stop."

William slowed the horse before coming to a stop. "What's wrong?"

"I don't know, but I need to get off. It's too fast. Overwhelming."

I couldn't breathe.

William dismounted and groaned, then helped me off. He grimaced and held my hand.

I let go and moved back as if in a slow-moving dream. I panted and bent forward so I wouldn't pass out. *What's wrong with me?*

"Your family is just through that opening in the sycamore trees." His voice echoed.

I stood, blowing out breath. "It's panic—like I'm going to drown. I don't want to be seen and smothered by everyone in the settlement. Let me wait here while you whisper the news to Papa first. Let me sneak in somehow."

A growling, brown-bristled bulldog jogged onto our path and stopped. I grabbed William's arm and eased behind him with rapid breaths. I tilted my head around to see.

William shouted, "Hullo" and held his rifle ready.

"Come on in, Mr. McGuire." The voice sounded familiar.

I studied the sandy-haired man in the green hunting shirt and tan breeches as he emerged from behind a large oak tree. *Flanders Callaway?* He lowered his rifle, clicked his cheek, and the dog backed away and sat.

William shouldered his rifle and ambled forward. "We'll wait here while you fetch Mr. Shirley, please."

My heart sped with the mention of Papa. I stood beside William, but lowered my face from Flanders's stare.

"That you, Mary?"

My stomach fluttered as I gazed up and nodded.

"It's me. Flanders Callaway. Good to see ya. I'll go get your pa."

William grabbed his arm. "Be quiet about it. Don't want a ruckus. Just tell him I have news."

"Yes sir. Understand. Mima and my cousins were a might shook up from their ordeal, and they were only gone two days."

They must have been frantic. I'll want to check on Fanny.

Flanders's blue eyes stared at the feather in my hair. "At least they didn't turn Injun."

Turn Injun? I glared, but he turned away and started up the trail. Anger burned, and a knot formed in my throat. I sucked in slow breaths and turned to William. "Will people think I've become uncivilized?"

He frowned and shook his head. "Some might, but they don't know better. Do you want to sit down and wait?"

"No, I'm too excited." I moved a few steps down the trail where the view would reveal Papa coming without him seeing me until he reached the straight path.

"I'll move where your papa can only see me until you're ready."

I grinned and nodded. My already speeding heart did a flip when William jutted his chin and pressed his lips as if trying not to smile at the person coming. Then I saw him. My mouth dropped open at the sight of more gray hair than I remembered. He wasn't smiling. Tears welled until I couldn't stand his sorrowful face any longer. I stepped beside William.

Papa stood still, staring at me as if not quite knowing me. Then his smile shot an arrow into my heart as he sprinted toward us. "Mary, *my liebchen*. Oh, *mein Gott. Danke, danke.*"

Before I could move forward, William held on to my good arm. "He doesn't know about your shoulder."

"Oh, Papa! Yes, it's me. Is everyone safe?" I took a step toward him. "I've been so worried. I heard about raids near here."

William blocked our path. "Her shoulder is wounded, sir."

"We are all well." Papa wiped his weathered cheeks and frowned at my shoulder before easing his arms around me, cuddling my head against his chest. "What happened?"

I wasn't ready to relive the moment. Before I could answer, William cleared his throat. "She was mistaken for an Indian. Shot...by one of our guards." He sighed. "Mr. Brewster fixed her up, but we had a little trouble from a small party of Indians on the way."

I clutched my arm, remembering being jerked off Liberty.

William wiped his cheek. "Mary." He cleared his throat again. "Saved my life...she knew the Shawnee man."

His emotion made the event replay in my mind. It had happened so fast. I reacted without thinking. *But it's true. Those men would have scalped William in front of me.*

Papa reached for William's hand. "This is a joyful day." His voice cracked. "Thank you...for recovering my daughter...for bringing her back to us."

William shook his head. "She found *me*, sir—yesterday afternoon."

Papa's mouth fell open and his eyes widened as William continued. "And she would've come without me this morning, so I thought I'd better come along."

When William winked at me, my face burned. He grinned before glancing at Papa. "I'll go on ahead and cause a distraction, so Mary won't be mobbed."

He tipped his hat, and I pined as he led Babcock's Boy down the path.

When I turned my attention back to Papa, his eyes watered and blinked. He peered into my flooding eyes and held my face. "I thought I saw a ghost, but you are real." A tear escaped down his cheek. "God has returned my little polliwog." He slowly wrapped his arms around me.

My gut wrenched as I sobbed against his chest and breathed in the scents of my childhood—beechnut tobacco and the wildness of the forest. *I'm home and safe.*

Too soon, Papa moved back and shook his head. "And you're taller...almost grown."

My face burned. "I'm still your little girl." I fell back into his arms, sniffling. "I've missed you so much." My heart pounded as I peered at Papa's watery eyes. "But we must leave Kentucky. War wampum are being exchanged among the Shawnee and Cherokee. Loud Hawk said they will attack by spring, like locusts."

Papa nodded. "The kidnapping on Sunday was the final straw for many. You'll notice men working on stockade walls, but hundreds of families have already left. It's the greed and distrust among our own kind that I fear. We'll go back to Indian Creek. Now, I need to get you home to Momma. She has cried for you every day."

"I've needed her so much my chest aches." I drew a deep breath, then sighed. "Can you sneak me in? I don't want the whole settlement gawking at me yet. I'm already nervous about seeing my brothers and sisters all at once with their questions. Too much to tell."

He nodded and grinned. "I'll tell them to hold their questions, but they'll be dancing and shouting when you walk in. It still seems like a dream to me." Papa held out his elbow. "Let's hurry. William's arrival will have stirred curiosity, and that Flanders Callaway has leaked the news by now."

"Sounds like the Flanders I remember." I snuggled Papa's arm as we left the trail and maneuvered around the sycamore and elm trees. As we neared the privy, I gasped and tugged Papa's arm to stop. I gasped. "That's where Mr. Jessop grabbed me...dragged me to the river...tossed me into a canoe with two Cherokee."

"That dang Jessop." Papa's eyes narrowed as he raged. "Fanny Callaway alerted me when you didn't return from the privy."

She must have been frantic. I hope she doesn't blame herself.

"We found Jedidiah Hamilton next to the tree with his throat slit." Papa sighed and shook his head. My eyes watered at the memory of the guard tipping his hat in the moonlight.

"That was a terrible night for everyone." Papa urged me forward. "Let's go."

We passed the giant green elm tree where log benches had replaced the tree stumps used for meetings. A few younger children were jumping on and over them in a game of chase. I might have seen Charlie among them, but Papa and I continued our quick pace. I glanced at the men chopping sharp points on long logs. Other men were placing the picketed posts in a line along the riverbank. We leapt over the freshwater spring before rounding the southeast corner of our cabin.

Papa held out his hand to stop me as he peeked around, laughing. "Almost everyone is gathered around William. Some are watching the north trail. Let me go first."

Papa opened the cabin door, waving me inside and giggling. "The family must be among those watching the trail, expecting to see you coming. I'll fetch them."

I nodded, somewhat relieved to have a moment alone to reflect and remember. I closed the door and breathed in the scents of home. Squirrel stew simmering above the coals. Sage, wild garlic, and onions hung drying from the rafters. Tears welled as I glanced around at the rolled pallets lined against the walls, the long wooden table, chairs, and my old dresses hanging undisturbed on a rod along the wall. I chuckled. *They won't fit anymore.*

Then I saw my beautiful green neckerchief and sucked in a breath. I dropped my pack on the board floor where I used to sleep and pulled the neckerchief from the rod. I snuggled it around my shoulders, missing the girl I used to be. *No. She's still me. I'm just older, and I'm home.* I removed the feather from my hair and placed it with my other things in a keepsake box. *I'll tell my family the story of the feather someday. When I'm ready. It's safe with my other memories for now.*

The door whooshed opened to Momma's tear-streaked face with more worry lines than I remembered. She also seemed more weathered and pale.

"Momma," I squealed and rushed to her as every pent-up hurt, worry, and fear rose from my belly and poured out of my eyes.

"Mary, Mary...Oh, my sweet Mary. Thank you, God, for bringing my daughter home." She glanced at my shoulder and eased her arms around me, sobbing.

"Momma. Momma." I snuggled against her, bawling and inhaling her honeysuckle-scented auburn hair. She rocked and hummed a German lullaby as the rhythm of our hearts reunited and calmed.

We embraced and sniffled for several minutes before she eased back, holding my face, peering into my soul with her puffy green eyes. "My girl has become a beautiful woman." After drawing a deep breath, Momma wiped her eyes and sighed. "Now I'll care for that wound."

I wiggled out of the hunting shirt as she lifted it off. "Augh, it's trying to fester. Wrap up in this clean blanket. I'll give the brood a quick update and gather supplies." She kissed my cheek and peeked outside.

Nancy squeezed past her and bounded toward me, staring and grinning before embracing my waist. "Mary. I missed you so much." She sniffled. "Did you know I'm six now?"

I chuckled. "Yes. And taller." I wiped away a tear, held the blanket in place with my sore arm and hugged with the good one.

She beamed up at me as a bossy voice chimed in.

"Let me in here." Eight-year-old Susie threaded forward, frowning and crying as she peered. "Your skin is darker, but you still look like Mary, just tired. I'm glad you're not an Injun like George said." I flinched and gasped from the pain of the words as she wrapped her arms around me. "You're taller and grown, like Momma, though." She moved back, smiling, and then glanced at Nancy. "We need to fetch clean spring water so Momma can clean Mary's wound. "Sorry you're hurt."

They left wet kisses on my cheeks before racing back outside. George's relayed words still stung my soul as a mature-faced Lizzy moved in for a quick hug before staring at my face, sniffling. "I didn't think we'd ever see you again. Papa said you were living with the Shawnee, but they didn't hurt you. I'm sorry you were shot. I'm so happy you're home." She held me close, and we cried together.

"I can't believe you're almost eleven. How have you been?" I eased her back and peered.

Lizzy sighed. "Well, Papa said I can't talk long because you need to rest and heal. But I promise to update you on everything tomorrow. You do look exhausted. I have to let the others in to welcome you home." She kissed my cheek and opened the door to four-year-old Charlie.

"Charlie." I squealed and raised my arm, readying for his hug. But he stayed back, studying my face as if he didn't know me. I'd been his second momma since his birth, bonded by his antics and adventures. I sniffed back tears and smiled. "I'm Mary. Remember? I used to chase you all the time."

His head tilted with a grin, then he rushed forward and kissed my cheek. "You're it." He giggled and rushed back outside with my heart, leaving the door open. I chuckled and planned how I'd surprise him with a tag back later.

The love and acceptance I'd received from my siblings so far eased me back into my wonderfully boisterous Shirley clan. I stared outside, wondering who would come next.

A taller, frowning-faced George crossed the threshold, but instead of excitement he glared. "Glad you're not some savage's squaw." He smirked, but it wasn't his usual orneriness.

My heart broke into splinters. *He meant to condemn. What's happened to my nine-year-old brother?* Shocked and angry, I moved in front of him, wanting to slap the Horned Serpent out of him. "Never call them savages again."

George flinched with wide eyes.

I drew closer. "They're no more savage than we are. Savagery comes with war, and the British are paying them in rum and guns to raid."

George gulped and lowered his watering eyes. "I'm...sorry...Mary."

"I know you're repeating the ignorance of others, but I won't allow it. These people love their families and mean to protect them the same as us. Most of the Piqua Shawnee took good care of me and are the reason I'm still alive and sane. Don't hate what you don't understand." I sucked in a deep breath and moved back, wiping my face.

I gazed at the sad-faced boy in front of me, wishing I had stayed calm. "I'm sorry to vent. I love you, George. I've missed and worried about you." Crying resumed.

His arms reached around me. "I missed you so much. I was afraid you were dead. Men talk about girls being taken and forced into...well, you know. I was angry and worried. I'm sorry. I didn't mean to make you mad. It's like that time you nearly smacked me with a spoon for teasing you about almost shooting Papa."

I sniffled and squeezed him as much as I modestly could with one arm.

He moved back, rubbing his eyes, sniffled once, then peered at me with his proper smile. "I'm proud of you for staying strong, and I'm glad you didn't have to marry anyone." His ornery grin accompanied a wink. "I'm going to the stable now. I want to talk to Mr. McGuire."

I caught his sleeve. "Ask Mr. McGuire for the bow and quiver of arrows I tied to his saddle. I want you to have them."

His grin widened. "Really? Thank you." He kissed my cheek and hurried out the door.

Momma held two-year-old Sally's hand and came in front of me. "She's your sister, Mary. Remember?"

She studied my face but clung to Momma's skirt.

I knelt so she could see my eyes. "You've grown up. It's okay if you don't remember. I can't wait to have a tea party with you again."

Sally nodded and smiled. "Mary." Her arms wrapped around my neck and I squeezed her against my chest.

"Oh, Mary. It's wonderful to see you."

Katie's voice boomed behind me, and I stood, turning then gasping at how beautiful she was. *Had I never noticed before?*

Katie set a bundle of clothes on the table and came toward me with glistening eyes. We reached around each other's necks with opposite arms, sobbing. I squeezed her closer and kissed her cheek.

Her breaths shuddered. "I missed you so much. It's like part of me had died. And it's been frustrating being the eldest child. I'm glad you're back to take over."

"I missed you too." I stepped back. "You've changed the most. Prettier and more grown-up."

She wiped her face. "Thank you. Do you really think I'm pretty?"

"Yes. And your fern-colored blouse brightens your shiny green eyes." I stroked her soft blushing cheek and admired her for the first time. "I'm sorry for being mean to you in the past. I was jealous."

She giggled. "What? I've always been jealous of you. You're beautiful even now with tanned skin. But look what I have for you."

She stretched to the table and held up a violet blouse and a dark-sage petticoat. "Looks like they'll fit. Jemima wants you to borrow her clothes until you have new ones.

Flanders told us you were back but dressed in baggy men's clothes. Jemima cried and gathered these for you. I have a new apron you may keep."

My heart swelled at Jemima's generosity. "I'll thank her tomorrow. How is she? I heard about the kidnaping. Why were they on the eastern bank?"

"Well, it's not my story to tell, and I haven't wanted to pry. But they were out in a canoe before we all heard screams. When they were brought back Tuesday, Mrs. Callaway fainted and had to be carried inside. They all seem better now."

When Momma entered with a basket of fresh plantain leaves and a bucket of hot water, Katie went to the threshold. "Everyone, stay outside now. Momma and I have to tend to Mary's wound." She closed the door. "What do you need me to do?"

"Crush these plantain leaves with wild garlic." Momma scooted a chair from the table and waved for me to come. "Sit here."

I sucked in a deep breath and prepared for more pain.

After Momma cleaned, salved, and bandaged my wound, I walked to the corner fingering the blouse, chemise, and sage-green skirt, enjoying the lightness of the cloth and the fresh scent of lye soap in them. *No more buckskin dresses.*

The clothes fit, and I felt regal as I padded barefoot across a gray board floor. "When did we get boards?"

"In February." Momma came to me with a brush, and I sat in a chair at the table. "I'm glad I insisted on it before the spring rains came and flooded the river."

Her fingers loosened and untangled my braids. "Some of the lower-level cabins kept two inches of water for a month. This settlement was doomed from the beginning."

Momma's brushing brought sweet childhood memories. Peace settled in my spirit.

"We would have moved to Papa's claim if conditions had gotten worse. I think Papa sought to comfort me on your birthday."

I sniffled. "Missing you on my birthday was the worst. I started having my menses shortly after."

Momma pulled me to her chest. "My heart is broken that I missed my daughter becoming a woman. What do the Indian women do about their blood flow?"

"Nothing." I pulled back, giggling as her mouth dropped open.

She frowned. "What do you mean?"

While she re-braided my hair, I explained my experience and how the four days of rest from chores spurred more energy. I left out what I'd learned about lovemaking.

"When your next time comes, I'll give you a set of rags you must wash and dry for each time after that. But there'll be no sitting around for four days." She laughed. "Call everyone in to help carry supper to the table outside."

She turned away, still wiping her eyes.

I wiped my face, exhausted, still overwhelmed, and somewhat in shock, but bursting with joy and pride.

Chapter Twenty-Seven

Once the table was set, I beamed at my family gathering around the table in the shade of our oak tree. I sat on the log bench beside Katie as if I'd never been away, but it felt like a dream.

Papa's face was wet. "I'm too emotional to pray aloud." His voice cracked. He swiped his eyes with the palm of his hand and then dried them on his shirt. "Hold hands and silently give God thanks for bringing our Mary home, for quick healing, blessings, and that peace with the Indians will hold."

I took Papa's and Katie's hands and bowed my head, feeling the warmth of love radiating from their hands and hoped that mine flowed through them to each one. *Thank you, God.* I sobbed and sniffled in tune with my family.

Papa sighed and said, "Amen."

My breaths shuddered, but I smiled at my family. "It's wonderful to be home. I know you want to hear about my time with the Shawnee. But I can't talk about it yet." I sighed. "I'm too exhausted and emotional. I can share more tomorrow and as days go by."

Papa nodded. "You're still in shock. It'll take a few days to adjust. Share when you're able. Let's eat."

I sniffled and lifted a spoonful of the stew to my lips and sipped. I closed my eyes and held the savory broth in my mouth, remembering and enjoying the flavors of wild onion, garlic, turnips, beets, and squirrel that had been soaked in milk to make it mild. My family was too quiet. I opened my eyes to grins around the table.

I chuckled and peered at Momma. "Squirrel stew sure tastes better from your hearth, just like Papa says when he returns from a long survey trip."

Momma's face turned red. "Thank you, Daughter. Now eat."

In a few minutes, Papa sat back and folded his hands on the table. He looked at Momma and sighed. "I'm sorry to ruin our joy, but I need to share news." He folded his hands on the table. "One of the scouts brought the recent *Pennsylvania Gazette*. It contains a declaration from colony delegates, informing His Majesty King George III of the intent to separate from his authority and become an independent nation."

Momma's hand covered her mouth as Papa continued. "This means we are officially at war with Great Britain. Delegates from each colony have bravely signed the declaration, which means certain death if they're caught and we lose the war. Now that Mary is back with us, I think it best to go back to Indian Creek with the families, leaving in two days." Papa turned his gaze my way. "Will you feel up to the long trip?"

I chuckled. "Traveling with my family will be glorious." *If you only knew.*

"What's to become of the couple who are leasing our home?" Momma asked. "Where will they go at such abrupt notice?"

When Papa rubbed his chin, my heartbeat rushed, as it always did to his gesture. "I'd like to sell to them and settle near Cook's Fort. I think we'll have help enough to build a new larger cabin." Papa's gazed turned away from us as he stood and went to William McGuire, who was still limping.

I stood too fast and placed my hands on the table. *He's saying goodbye.*

Papa shook William's hand, then motioned for me to come. I gulped, but hot tears fell with my steps. William removed his hat and smiled. Papa seemed to be suppressing a grin as he took two steps back, folding his arms. "Mr. McGuire would like to speak with you."

I restrained the desire to throw my arms around his neck and beg him to stay.

William smiled as I stood before him. He didn't seem bothered by Papa's presence.

"I like the Shawnee custom of saying 'Somewhere, I'll see you again.'" He took my hand and kissed it in front of everyone.

Heat swirled in my belly, but instead of being embarrassed, I felt proud. My stomach fluttered and my eyes burned. "Thank you...for bringing me home. Be safe." My eyes watered. "Until I see you again." I moved forward, wrapping him against me like a blanket.

He blew out a breath and stepped back, smiling at Papa with a red face before nodding. "Mr. Shirley."

Papa grinned. "Take care, William. See you in a few days."

William mounted Babcock's Boy and tipped his hat at my family before urging the horse into a fast gait. My body ached with the longing to go with him. *Why can't we go now?* I sighed and wiped tears away.

Papa came beside me and slid his arm around my waist. "William asked if he could help us get settled." Papa chuckled. "I don't think he's interested in me so much."

I grinned, but didn't know what to say. My face flushed with wonder and panic at the same time.

"Two years. You're still my little polliwog for two more years. Shall we rejoin the family?" He offered his arm.

I peered into his eyes, suddenly feeling disconnected. *What's wrong with me?* "I'll

be back in a few minutes. I...need some time alone."

I sprinted to the freshwater spring, bawling and lowering to my knees before splashing water on my face. *Why do I feel this way? I was fine before William left. I don't belong here anymore. But that's nonsense. I'm home with my family. What's happening?*

I startled from footfalls behind me and leapt to my feet, squealing, "Fanny."

She held out her arms and hobbled toward me. "I've missed you so much."

We reached around each other, weeping. I moved back and kissed her cheeks. I didn't want to talk about my experience yet, but I wanted to hear about hers. "Can you tell me what happened on Sunday?"

She shook her head. "Not yet. It's too hard." Tears fell down her face. "I came...to beg your forgiveness...for not walking with you to the privy the night you—"

I held up my hand and shook my head. "It wasn't your fault. I never blamed you. It was that Mr. Jessop who lay in wait for an opportunity to grab me. He was paid by loyalists to do so."

"Where did they take you?" Her eyes widened.

Don't say too much. "I ended up in a Shawnee village where I was adopted. It was horrible and frightening at first, but they were good to me. It became too dangerous there after the chief died."

Fanny's face paled with glazed eyes. *No more.* "I'm sorry to frighten you. Somehow, God allowed me to get away and end up in William McGuire's arms...I meant camp." My face flushed.

She sniffled and shook her head. "Well, I've been tormented ever since we were taken. Mima convinced Betsy and me to go with her in a canoe to soak her sore foot. The current was strong, and we drifted too close to the east bank." She held her chest, and her breaths shallowed. "The Indians had been watching. They grabbed us, and we had to travel along the razor-sharp ridges and through thick cane."

Fanny pointed to her shoes. "That's why my feet are cut and bruised. They were going to take us to a village to be wives. We had a horrible time, but nothing compared to what you've endured."

She peered at me, smiling. "I'm so thankful to God you're back. I need to go home before my ma worries and has another fainting spell. Let's talk again tomorrow. I want to know about these feelings you have for William McGuire." She giggled, kissed my cheek, and limped backward. "You let it slip out, you know."

My cheeks burned as I cleared my throat. "There's a strong attraction, and Papa thinks William is interested in me." I sighed. "I think I want him, but two years is a long time for a man like him to wait." Reality intruded. "And he'll always be gone scouting. Who wants to feel like a widow all the time?" I cupped my hand over my mouth. "I'm sorry to rant. I just figured out why telling him goodbye earlier depressed me so." I growled and shook my body like a dog shook off water, then stood still and breathed. "Talking to you has helped me shake off feeling lost."

"Good." She giggled. "But that shaking thing was scary."

I grinned. "I'll walk you home, and then I want to go visit Letitia before settling in with my family." I held out my good elbow.

Fanny nodded and clasped my arm. Then we hobbled toward her cabin.

"Romances seem to be blooming for all of us." She laughed. "Sam and Betsy will marry on her birthday in three weeks. Jemima and Flanders won't be far behind." She stood still and peered at me, beaming. "And John Holder has asked to court me. Can you believe it?"

I chuckled. "I remember you wanted to watch him dance."

When we arrived near her home, I kissed her cheek. "See you tomorrow." My eyes watered. *I'll have to tell her we're leaving, but not yet.*

I hurried toward the Gatliffs' cabin, and Letitia rushed out, holding her belly. "Aye, Mary, I was about to come see about you."

We embraced, and then she stepped back, beaming.

"William was burstin' with the story of your escape, and here you are, even more strong and beautiful, just like he said. I think he's fancyin' you a bit." She chuckled and caressed her stomach.

I held my hot face, not quite sure what to say.

Letitia's brow furrowed. "You don't care for William?"

I sighed and faced her. "I do...but life is too uncertain."

"Aye, and you're a wise one—you are." Letitia smiled. "But I wouldn't be opposed to havin' you as my sister-in-law someday."

I shrugged my good shoulder. "Why would he want a puny little girl like me?"

She grinned. "His eyes dance when he talks about you. He was torn about leaving but needed to get on toward the Clinch River forts before returning home to Fort Cook."

My eyes watered. "Yes. He told me." I sighed, cleared my throat, and changed the subject. "Are you expecting a new baby?" I pointed to her belly as she rubbed it.

"Aye, sometime in the spring. And I'm prayin' for a lass this time. At least, we'll be safe at Cook's Fort by then."

I gasped. "When? We're leaving Saturday. Papa wants land near Cook's Fort this time."

"Yes, and William told us as much after he spoke with your da. I'm excited that our paths are mergin'. You'll be seeing William when we get there; so you will."

I laughed, reached around her waist in a hug, and then kissed her cheek. "I need to go settle in with my family before they think I've abandoned them. I look forward to visiting more." I moved back and grinned. "Oh, and I learned the secret of your fluffy hoecakes. It's the potash from the lye barrel."

She chuckled. "Well, now. I'll expect you to be keepin' that to yourself." She beamed and turned.

I chuckled and rushed past gawking onlookers. But I smiled and waved to Jemima and Betsy, who stood with Fanny on the Callaways' covered porch. Most likely extracting information about our visit.

My shoulder and head throbbed from doing too much. I stood still and stared at my family's cabin. Visiting my friends helped me reconnect to my life. *I'm all right now. This is where I'm supposed to be.* I sucked in a deep breath. *William might be my future, but my family needs me now.* I smiled, raised the latch, and went inside.

My family gathered around me in one hug. Our soft cries and sniffling almost sounded like turtle shakers. Peace entered my spirit. My body swayed with my family in a new sweet rhythm. *I'm finally home.*

Acknowledgments

This third book in the *Dangerous Loyalties* series would not have been possible without consent encouragement from family members, critique partners, writer friends, editors, motivational vloggers, and my awesome fans. THANK YOU!

Special Thanks to Certified Genealogist Patrick G. Meguire for confirming the McGuire sibling connection.

About Author

Phyllis A. Still is living her dream as an award-winning author in Texas. She is an eighth-generation descendant of DAR Patriot, Mary Shirley McGuire, the inspiration behind the *Dangerous Loyalties* series. Phyllis loves her family, pets, road trips, history, and playing games with her grandchildren. Her adventurous childhood through seven states created her vivid imagination and a love for stories about people who have overcome hardships.

I love hearing from my readers. Please consider leaving a review online at Barnes & Noble, Amazon, Goodreads, or your favorite book source. Join my Dangerous Loyalties Series fan group on Facebook. Learn more about me at phyllisastill.com

Ready to learn what happens next?

Palisades of the Heart

Dangerous Loyalties, Book Four

"A curse on your first-born son if you return."

Loud Hawk's warning weighs heavily on Mary's heart as she and her family arrive at Cooks Fort in Western Virginia in August 1776. She hopes for a fresh start and courtship with William McGuire.

William dreams of raising fast horses in Kentucky with Mary by his side—when she's ready to trust. Yet his love for her is boundless and only William's love can conquer the palisade of fear protecting Mary's heart.

When a vengeful shaman's lie endangers all she holds dear, her warrior spirit rises into action. She will no longer live in fear.

Inspired by Daughters of the American Revolution Patriot Mary Shirley-McGuire. *Palisades of the Heart* is the fourth and final book of the thrilling award-winning Dangerous Loyalties Series.

If you enjoy an emotion-packed romantic story packed with heart-racing and gritty scenes of life or death, this Young Adult Historical Romance is for you.

Buy *Palisades of Heart* and enjoy your dangerous adventure.

Let me know you survived. Please consider leaving me a review on Amazon.